Praise for *Lord Sebastian's Secret*

"Marvelously inventive."

—Booklist

"Delightful Regency romance…this is one I will reread again and again."

—Night Owl Reviews, 5 Stars, Top Pick

"Vivid characters and lively plots… The underlying message, that quirks and struggles should be no impediment to familial or romantic love, is conveyed with warmth and tenderness."

—Publishers Weekly

"A busy and steamy romance."

—Kirkus Reviews

"*Lord Sebastian's Secret* is delightful entertainment!"

—Long and Short Reviews

Praise for *What the Duke Doesn't Know*

"Ashford soars to new heights of literary excellence by creating a cleverly conceived story that takes all the traditional elements readers love in Regency romances and making everything seem refreshingly new. Throw in Ashford's gift for creating intriguingly different characters and her dry sense of humor, and you have a romance worth cherishing."

—*Booklist*

"A unique heroine...remarkably well-written...she is quickly becoming one of my favorite romance heroines. Every bit of *What the Duke Doesn't Know* is a joy to read, and I can't wait for the next book in this, so far, fabulous series."

—*Fresh Fiction*

"Enchanting...a charming romance."

—*RT Book Reviews*, 4 Stars

Praise for *Heir to the Duke*

Also by Jane Ashford

Nothing LIKE A Duke

JANE ASHFORD

sourcebooks
casablanca

Copyright © 2017 by Jane LeCompte
Cover and internal design © 2017 by Sourcebooks, Inc.
Cover art by Alan Ayers

Sourcebooks and the colophon are registered trademarks of
Sourcebooks, Inc.

Published by Sourcebooks Casablanca, an imprint of Sourcebooks,
Inc.
P.O. Box 4410, Naperville, Illinois 60567-4410
(630) 961-3900
Fax: (630) 961-2168
www.sourcebooks.com

Printed and bound in Canada.
MBP 10 9 8 7 6 5 4 3 2 1

One

THE FRONT AXLE OF THE POST CHAISE SNAPPED AS ONE wheel slammed into a deep rut, throwing Lord Robert Gresham against the side window hard enough to bruise. The loud crack, sudden sideways lurch, and bumping drag that followed spooked the team pulling the coach. The vehicle lurched and bounced as the two postilions struggled to get the four horses back under control.

Robert braced his legs and clung to a strap until they'd slowed enough for him to push his way out and help. He leaped to the head of the off-side leader and held on to wet leather. Mud from churning hooves filled the air, spattering his top boots, pantaloons, and greatcoat. A spray of the sticky stuff slapped his face as the horse tried to rear. "Be still. It's all right," Robert said, using the easy combination of reassurance and command he'd learned from his brother Sebastian.

It was a number of minutes before the horses were calm and the men could verify that the post chaise was irretrievably damaged.

"We didn't see that dratted hole, milord, what with all the mud," said the elder postilion.

As if on cue, the rain started up again, a slow but penetrating drizzle. A chilly drop slipped under Robert's coat collar and trickled down his back. "A bad stretch of—" He looked up and down the narrow, rutted track. "I suppose one must call it a road." He noticed that one of the horses had pulled up lame. The coach tilted forlornly in the middle of the lane, which curved around a small stand of trees just ahead. "We need to move the chaise." If another vehicle came barreling around that turn, the results would be disastrous. Not that traffic appeared likely.

"We'll drag her off to the side," the man replied. "And Davy'll ride back to that farm we passed and see about help."

He didn't sound optimistic, and Robert imagined he was right. The replacement would be whatever old thing the farmer kept in his barn. And it would take a couple of hours to procure. Robert looked around. There were no houses in sight, no buildings of any kind, actually, although they were no more than ten miles, he estimated, from his ultimate destination.

Robert sighed. It had been a long, hard journey into the North. If he hadn't promised friends that he'd visit…but he had. Turning up his collar, he made his way over to the trees. The foliage, still thick in early October, kept off most of the rain. And it felt better to be out in the fresh air. He watched the postilions coax the team into dragging the coach off to the side. The younger man then mounted one of the horses and rode back the way they'd come. The other unhitched the remaining animals and led them over to a patch of grass, running his hands over their legs and checking for other injuries. Robert pulled out his handkerchief and wiped his face. It came away muddy, and he suspected it hadn't removed all traces of dirt. He leaned against an oak and resigned himself to a stretch of boredom. So much for his early start today.

The rain dripped from the leaves overhead. A light wind rustled through them. The horses sampled the grass. The postilion settled himself under another tree. Robert thanked providence it wasn't colder. Time ticked past.

Gradually, Robert became aware of a sound beneath the murmur of water. It was a soft whining, as of some creature in distress, and intermittent. Just when he would decide he'd imagined it, it would start up again.

The next time this happened, Robert searched for the source. He had to wait through another period of silence before he found his way to a low bush. Raising one of its branches, he discovered a huddled bit of dark fur. When he bent to look closer, a small head lifted, and dark eyes met his.

It was a dog, quite young, he thought, soaking wet and shivering. As he eyed it, the whimpering began again. The sound seemed involuntary, because the tiny creature stared at him without demand, or hope. Even as Robert gazed, the puppy's head sank down again, too tired, or dejected, to resist whatever fate was about to descend on it. The brown eyes closed.

Robert straightened. He strode over to the chaise and pulled out one of the blankets provided to cover travelers' legs. Bringing it back, he draped it over the puppy and picked it up, wrapping the small shivering form in warm wool. Cradling it in one arm, he retraced his steps.

"What's that there?" the postilion asked as he passed. "A rat?"

"No, a dog. A puppy, really."

"What sort of dog?"

"A mixed sort, I believe." It hadn't looked like any breed Robert knew.

"What's it doing out here, then?"

"Lost, or abandoned. Perhaps something happened to its mother."

"You ain't going to put it in the chaise?" said the other man.

"I am," said Robert. And suiting action to word, he climbed into the leaning vehicle and set the bundled blanket on the slanting seat beside him.

The puppy stirred and looked up at him. It was still trembling.

Robert reached out. The little dog cowered away, and Robert felt a flash of anger. What blackguard had taught this young animal to expect a blow? Moving slowly and unthreateningly, Robert rubbed the water out of its fur. Overall, it was black, a trifle shaggy, with odd stripes of brown along its sides, like tiny lightning bolts. Its ears were rather large for its size. They were pointed, but flopped over at the tips.

The puppy's shivering abated when it was dry. It nestled into the blanket until only its nose and eyes were visible.

Robert reached into the pocket on the inside of the chaise's door and retrieved the remains of a sandwich packed for him at their last stop. The puppy flinched at the sudden movement, and trembled at the crackle of paper as Robert unwrapped it. "It's all right," he said. "Or, it may be, unless you need milk. God knows where I'd find that." He pulled a shred of beef from between the slices of bread and held it out. The puppy sniffed, but didn't move to take it.

Robert placed the meat on the blanket. The little animal hesitated as if it couldn't quite believe its luck, then lurched forward and snatched the beef. Teeth snapped and chewed. Perhaps the dog wasn't as young as he'd feared, Robert thought. Perhaps it was simply small.

They continued in this fashion until all the beef was gone, and most of the bread as well. The dog gained enough confidence to take the last bits from his hand. Robert completed the ruin of his handkerchief by using it to wipe off the mustard. "Better?" he said when the animal would take no more.

The dog tried to stand, as if concluding that it was time to move on now that it had eaten. All four legs shook under its tiny weight, and it fell back to the blanket, which had shifted enough for Robert to see that the little creature was a male. "No need to stir," he said. "It's a foul afternoon."

Indeed, the rain was beating harder on the roof of the chaise. Robert cracked the door and asked the postilion if he wanted to join him in the carriage.

"I'll stay with the horses," the man replied from his refuge under the trees. "I'm used to being out in all weathers."

"If you're sure?"

"Certain sure, milord. Could you be sure that animal don't befoul the coach?"

"I'll watch him." Robert cupped a hand in the rain, wetting his sleeve, and offered the dog a bit of water. He lapped it up, and Robert filled his hand with water twice more before closing the door and sitting back, feet braced against the sideways sag of the seat.

The rain pattered above. Otherwise all was silence. Waiting was tedious. Robert hadn't had anyone to talk to for hours, days. "What are you doing so far from a farm or village?" he asked the dog.

Wary brown eyes watched him.

"I expect it's a sad story, and you'd rather not think about it," Robert went on. "I don't suppose you know Salbridge Great Hall? I'm on my way to a house party there."

One of the dog's ears twitched.

"No, I hadn't heard of it either. But I understand that it's the showplace of its district."

The dog shifted in the blanket.

"Well, that's what Salbridge said. It's true we are speaking of Northumberland. The standards may be lower." Robert gazed out at the sodden landscape. "I've never been so far north. I begin to see Randolph's point."

His companion made an odd sound, something like a gargle.

"Randolph is my brother. One of my brothers. He lives up here. I thought that an added inducement when the Salbridges urged me to come. I can't think why just now."

A gust of wind rocked the carriage on its springs. The dog nestled deeper into the blanket.

"Precisely," said Robert. "But when friends beg for

support one must rally 'round. I'm to lend luster to their gathering."

The small dog cocked his head.

Robert smiled down at him. "I assure you that luster is one of my gifts. Hostesses count themselves lucky to have me. They, er, vie for my favor. Unlike— But I'm not thinking of her. I've given up thinking of her. I'm going back where I belong."

The small dog's gaze had become unnervingly steady. It held no threat that Robert could see. He would have said, rather, that it was speculative, philosophical. Would have, if the idea hadn't been ridiculous.

"I like helping people enjoy themselves," he added in the face of that unwavering regard. "I'm good at it." And if he didn't feel quite as convivial as usual, Robert thought, well, he would soon recover his high spirits.

The dog curled up and went to sleep. Robert made himself as comfortable as he could on the tilted seat. And together, they waited.

Just under two hours from the time of the accident, a vehicle came trundling up the road. Robert's dire predictions were fulfilled when he saw the second postilion at the reins of a rough farm cart, with two thick wheels digging into the mud and a tattered canvas cover over the back.

"I thought you'd rather get on, even in this heap, than wait for a new chaise to be fetched, milord," the man said when he pulled up. "Don't rightly know how long that would take."

Standing in the muddy road, Robert eyed the rustic equipage and the two large farm horses pulling it. No doubt the ride would rattle their bones.

The men moved his trunk from the chaise to the cart. He was going to have to perch upon it, Robert saw. There was no room for anyone but the driver on the seat. At least the rain had eased. Gathering blanket and puppy, he climbed up.

"You taking the animal?" asked the older postilion.

"You expect me to leave him here?"

"Well, I dunno. He ain't a toff's sort of dog, is he?"

"Would you like him?"

"Me? I got no use for a dog."

It was just as well he refused, because Robert realized that he had no intention of handing the animal over. There was something curiously engaging about the small creature.

Lord Robert Gresham's subsequent arrival at the Salbridges' estate was quite uncharacteristic for a gentleman recognized as a pink of the *ton*. He was wet and muddy, his fine clothes horridly creased. He was worn out from the jolting of his disreputable vehicle. He had no hat—it had blown off during the last part of his journey and gone tumbling down an escarpment—and he carried a mongrel dog under one arm. Indeed, the grooms in the Salbridge stables very nearly turned him away. Thankfully, one who'd seen him in London came forward to confirm his identity.

"Broken axle," said Robert.

"Ah." There were general nods at this piece of information.

"Can some of you help me with these lads?" the postilion asked, climbing down from the cart and going to the massive horses' heads. "They've done well, and I promised to have them back tomorrow."

The grooms moved forward to help, and to retrieve Robert's trunk. He followed the latter two as they carried his luggage through the stable yard to a back door. He didn't intend to knock at the front in his current state and track mud across an immaculate front hall and staircase. He'd use the back stairs to find his assigned bedchamber and clean up before he greeted his hosts.

His luck was out, however. The Countess of Salbridge was in the kitchen, conferring with the cook, so she was among the group that turned at his entry, blinked, and stared.

There was nothing for it. Robert smiled, swept off an imaginary hat, and gave her a jaunty bow. "Hullo, Anne."

"Robert?" she said, incredulous. "What are you— Whatever has happened?"

"Long story. Started with a broken axle on my post chaise. And, er, went on from there."

The dog chose this moment to pop his head out of the blanket and stare about the room, shifting his gaze slowly from one person to the next, and the next. A kitchen maid gestured. Robert thought it was a sign against the evil eye. The countess bit her lower lip.

"Go ahead and laugh," Robert told her. "I live to amuse."

She did. "Oh, Robert," she said after several moments of mirth. "Only you could carry off such a… memorable entrance."

He gave his audience another elegant bow.

Several hours later, bathed and changed and feeling renewed, Robert sat in a luxurious bedchamber reading a letter from his mother, the Duchess of Langford. The missive had followed him from Herefordshire, where his family had most lately gathered for his brother Sebastian's wedding, to Robert's rooms in London, and now here to Northumberland. Aware that he hadn't behaved quite like himself at the wedding, Robert wondered how he would answer his mother's inquiries about his well-being. The answer that came to him was…later.

Setting the page aside, he stared out at the sweep of gardens outside the window. Salbridge Great Hall might be at the ends of the earth from a Londoner's point of view, but it was a fine old stone pile. Parts of it looked to date from Tudor times, others from subsequent centuries. The interior had been refurbished with modern comforts.

The rain had lifted. Rays of afternoon sun illuminated turning leaves and late blooms, a manicured autumn vista. From this height, he could see the River Tyne in the distance. "I am very well indeed," he tried aloud.

From a cushion by the hearth, his newly acquired dog turned a steady gaze upon him. The pup's small stomach was rounded from the large bowl of scraps he'd ingested. Any other young dog would be dead asleep after such a feast, Robert thought, but this one was keeping a careful eye on his surroundings.

Meeting those brown eyes, and for some reason unable to look away, Robert had the oddest thought. He felt like a man who had always lived in a fine house, pleasing in every detail, and then one day discovered that a great cavern lay beneath it. In all his years, he'd never suspected the cave existed. When he explored this new subterranean realm, he found it a marvelous place, full of things he'd never dreamed of. The expansion excited and challenged him. But then, after a time, he encountered difficulties, bitter disappointments. And he began to wonder if the cavern was undermining the foundations of the house above, threatening general ruin.

Robert shifted uneasily in his chair. What the devil? That was not the sort of thought he would have had a year ago. It wasn't the sort of thought *anybody* had. "It's a relief to be back in my own, er, natural habitat among the *haut ton*," Robert told the dog. "I should never have ventured out into circles where my gifts aren't valued."

The dog stared. Not in a belligerent way, but as if he could see right through Robert to the very back of his head.

"I'm not thinking about her," Robert said. "That was simply a…glancing reference. To the past. I told you, I've given up thinking about her."

One of the little dog's ears moved, just slightly, as if he'd heard something off.

"This visit will be like relaxing in one's own comfortable rooms after a long journey," Robert added. "I am all anticipation."

The pup offered a soft response. Not a bark, or a whine, or a growl. Actually, it sounded uncannily like some ancient curmudgeon at the club clearing his throat. Robert waited, almost believing that some sort

of crabbed pronouncement would follow. Of course
it did not. He gazed at his new companion, who
returned the favor with solemn, unwavering regard.
"I shall call you Plato," Robert said. "You seem to
deserve the name."

He put the letter aside and rose.

"I trust you will behave yourself," he added, indicating the box of sand he'd shown the dog earlier. He
had no idea whether the pup—Plato—would use it,
should the need arise, but he hadn't wanted to leave
him in the stables. Who knew how the pack there
would receive him? Heading for the door, Robert
wondered whether he could enlist his valet in Plato's
care. Bailey would arrive tomorrow with some things
Robert had wanted from London. Doubtful. Unlike
his brother Sebastian, Robert had a strictly professional
relationship with his personal servant. Better to tip one
of the footmen to check on Plato now and then.

Robert left his bedchamber, strolling toward the
beautifully curved stairway that led to the lower
floor, catching a glimpse of himself in a mirror as
he descended. He did not, of course, stop to ogle
himself in the glass. He was well aware that his new
coat fit him to perfection. Weston was an artist with
the shears. Robert knew he had the shoulders to fill
the coat out, too, even if he wasn't as tall as some of
his brothers.

He showed a fine leg in his buff pantaloons, and the
careful tousle of his auburn hair flattered his handsome
face. The folds of his neckcloth would excite the envy
of the young men—and many of the older ones—
here. He looked, in fact, exactly like what he was, a

pink of the *ton*. And he did not care a whit why people called it *pink* or what that might mean. He'd given up thinking of such stuff.

There was a momentary hitch in Robert's step as he once again forced his mind away from the subject of a certain young lady. If she was incapable of appreciating his gifts, then she could just…go hang. He'd had much more fun back when he didn't think of her. Hadn't he? Yes, of course he had. And he was here to have it again.

Robert reached the bottom of the sweeping stair and walked along a lower corridor toward the buzz of conversation in the great drawing room. The tone was bright and excited, full of expectation. Gerald and Anne were known for their lavish hospitality, and for providing a perfect balance of planned activities and freedom at their house parties. Not here. They hadn't lived in this house before the old earl's death last year. But their established reputation as artists of diversion had lured guests all this way from town. Robert assumed there would be hunting, though he didn't know the country, as well as walks and riding and indoor games and music and more. Or, guests could choose to lounge about with a novel in front of the fire on a crisp October day, or write letters, or whatever they liked. It was a familiar, beguiling prospect.

Robert entered the drawing room, a large chamber that ran along the back of the house with a row of tall glass doors that gave onto a terrace above spreading lawns. Beautifully decorated in ivory and blue, the room was dotted with comfortable groupings of sofas and chairs that encouraged conversation.

Just now at midafternoon, however, most of its denizens were clumped together discussing plans for the rest of the day.

It was a promising gathering, Robert thought as he paused near the door. There were several young couples he counted as good friends and others closer in age to their hosts.

The largest group, though, clustered around Lady Victoria, the daughter of the house. She hadn't received a proposal during her first season, so her parents had invited a number of eligible young men to the house party, along with some of her female friends to balance the numbers. Robert ran an appreciative eye over the latter, noticing several very pretty faces that he'd seen about town. He thought he'd danced with one or two of these ladies. In a minute he'd recall their names.

Robert's closest friend among the Salbridges, the eldest son and heir, was not present. Laurence was off at his intended bride's house for the hunting, Robert remembered. Some suspected he'd offered for the Allingham chit chiefly because her family had a huge estate in Leicestershire, but Robert knew that to be only secondarily true. Laurence had been quite taken with Marie as well. He'd told Robert so. Of course her enthusiasm for sport was probably part of the attraction. Robert smiled at the thought.

Lady Victoria gave him a brilliant smile in return. He couldn't have asked for a warmer welcome. Robert started forward to join the group.

He'd hardly taken two steps when the sounds of an arrival behind him made him turn back to the door. Then, for a moment, he thought he was delirious. It couldn't be. But the figure standing in the opening was solid flesh, not a phantom. "What are you doing here?" he said.

"I've come for the house party," answered Flora Jennings.

She was as beautiful as ever. In a simple pale gown, her figure was a marvel of subtle curves. Her black hair was dressed in curls, wisps falling about the pale skin of her face, clear-cut as an antique cameo. She presented a serene picture—until you noticed the fire in those cornflower-blue eyes.

"I was invited," she added with a touch of familiar asperity.

"You can't have been." He hadn't expected to see her again, unless he sought her out. They moved in completely different circles of society. The sight of her here was like running into his mother at a bare-knuckles boxing bout.

"Do you imagine I would push in without an invitation?" she asked.

The snap of challenge in her voice brought back countless verbal jousts. She was inarguably, unmistakably, here. "I don't think you could," he replied. "I'm only surprised to see you among people you profess to despise. Don't you have cuneiform tablets to translate in London. Or something?"

She frowned at him. He was quite familiar with the expression.

A sturdy woman in her mid-forties emerged from behind Flora. She had sandy hair, regular features, and a gown that proclaimed fashionable good taste. "Hello, Lord Robert," she said.

Here was the explanation for Flora's presence. Harriet Runyon was related to a great swath of the nobility and received everywhere despite a marriage once thought beneath her. No doubt she'd managed the invitation. "Mrs. Runyon."

With her customary air of sharp intelligence, and of brooking no nonsense, she replied, "How pleasant to see you."

Robert's refined social instincts signaled a whiff of danger, like the rustle in the undergrowth just before something formidable bursts out to surprise you. Which was odd. "And you, ma'am," he said. He offered them an impeccable bow. "Welcome to Salbridge."

Robert resumed his walk over to the group of young ladies. Lady Victoria greeted him warmly as an old friend she'd known since her early teens. He set himself to entertain them, and soon elicited a chorus of silvery laughs. It wouldn't hurt a bit to let Flora Jennings see how charming most females found him.

Two

"DO SMILE," SAID HARRIET RUNYON.

Flora exposed her teeth. That would have to do for this crowd of lavishly dressed people who had all turned to stare at her when she came in, and then turned away again with cool disinterest. That was what they did, Mama would say. They turned their backs. Flora could almost hear her mother's voice, retelling the story of her ejection from society after she defied her aristocratic family and married a poor scholar, a tale of fears becoming real and pain masked with truculence. All her life, her mother had assured Flora that they could expect nothing but disregard or snubs from the *haut ton*. That history had made walking into this room rather like stepping into the lions' den. But Flora had been braced for it. She knew how to put up a brave front.

And she didn't care what they thought. She hadn't come to make a splash in society. She'd come… Her thoughts tripped up here and came to a stop over the fact that Lord Robert had not been glad to see her. Through all the months of their close acquaintance this year, he'd greeted her so warmly whenever they met, with a smile that was nearly irresistible. She'd grown accustomed to the welcome in his intense blue eyes, had begun to take it for granted. She hadn't known that until a moment ago, when she'd found it gone.

On the other side of the opulent room, he was surrounded by a circle of pretty girls in gowns that cost more than any three of hers. He looked so very handsome, and utterly at ease. He was making them laugh; clearly they found him charming. He didn't spare her a glance. Anger, and apprehension, flooded Flora. Now that they were in his exalted social circle rather than her much more humble one, he meant to snub her, just as Mama had foretold. Flora had thought she was mistaken about him, but what if she wasn't? She'd had years of rigorous mental training; she was not prone to mistakes of judgment.

And after all, who would believe that a darling of London society, and the son of a duke, was truly interested in the unfashionable daughter of a scholar? Of course she'd thought that his claim to be fascinated by her intellectual pursuits was some sort of jest. According to everything she'd been taught, men like Lord Robert Gresham were nothing *but* shallow posturing, through and through.

And here came the sardonic inner voice that Flora both dreaded and appreciated. Lord Robert had actually buckled down and studied her father's writings on Akkadian, it pointed out. He'd hung about her home in the dowdy precincts of Russell Square for weeks. He'd followed her from London to Oxford. He'd given her that melting smile whenever she encountered him. Until today. Until a minute ago.

Flora felt an unfamiliar sinking sensation. She looked longingly back at the hallway, wondering if she could still escape.

"Stop scowling," murmured Harriet at her side. "Really, Flora. You must do better than this. We should go and say hello to our hosts. Come and meet the Salbridges."

"I don't think so."

"Flora, this isn't like you. Compose yourself." Harriet moved to partly shield Flora from the other guests. "What *is* the matter?"

"I shouldn't have come," Flora murmured.

"Are we going to rehash all that again? Now? This is not really an appropriate time and place, my dear." When Flora said nothing, the older woman sighed and quietly began to tick off points with the air of a woman who had cited them before. Which she had. "You enjoyed your brief taste of society in Oxford."

"Parts of it," said Flora. It had seemed so pleasant, then, to wear prettier dresses and attend evening parties and…fritter away her time, Papa would have said. She'd met Lord Robert's mother and discovered that a duchess could be both sensible and cordial, not the least high-nosed. But she saw now that a few outings in a university town were nothing compared to a true conclave of the *haut ton*.

Harriet looked exasperated. "You decided you wished to increase your social experience."

She had wanted more from life than she'd accepted previously, Flora admitted silently. But for some reason, she hadn't pictured a host of strangers from the upper reaches of society giving her sidelong glances, wondering who in the world she could be. There seemed to be so many of them. Well, who did they think *they* were, these…natterers?

"And you were quite forlorn when Lord Robert left town with no plans to return," Harriet added.

"I was not!" She spoke far too loudly. Heads turned. Conversations faltered.

Harriet gave the crowd an impenetrable smile. They subsided.

"I was *not* 'forlorn,'" Flora hissed. What a limp, pathetic word! She'd never been forlorn in her life. It was the opposite of all she'd been trained to be— acute, observant, active, and intelligent. "I may have missed his…conversation. I took Lord Robert at his word, you see…that he wished to be…a friend. And now I arrive here and find that he is quite displeased to see me." Flora kept her voice rigidly steady. "He was not glad. At all."

"He probably wasn't," Harriet replied.

"What?" She'd expected a denial, or at least some sort of excuse.

"When one is running away from something," her older friend said, "one often doesn't like to be chased. At first."

"I am *not* chasing him!" Flora spoke more softly this time, but with utter revulsion.

"I didn't say he was running from *you*," Harriet pointed out.

Flora felt her cheeks redden. But curiosity overcame embarrassment. "What did you mean?"

"We really haven't time for a philosophical discussion." Harriet gave the gathering another bright, general smile. "So, are we to do this or not? It would cause a minor scandal to simply turn and leave. And I must say that you won't get another invitation as brilliant as this one, Flora."

What did she want? Across the room, one of the girls around Lord Robert gave a musical trill of laughter. He looked achingly handsome, and charming, and…inordinately pleased with himself. What was that slang phrase—a care-for-nobody? That seemed to apply. As far as she could see, that is, because he pointedly did *not* look in her direction. All the other times they'd been in a room together, he'd concentrated on her. It had been a heady, tantalizing experience. But the *ton* hadn't been watching then, she thought. The idea hurt, but Flora faced up to it. If she'd been wrong to change her mind about him, it was best that she find out, once and for all. Then she'd know what to do.

Flora put her shoulders back, her chin up. In any case, everything didn't have to be about—was *not* about—one maddening man. She gave Harriet a nod.

"Good girl. Come along. And, my dear?"

Flora looked at her chaperone.

"A smile is not a concession," Harriet added with a lift of her sandy eyebrows. "It is a…a tool, shall we say. A rather versatile one. It can pry things out or smooth things over. Substitute for things one doesn't wish to confide. Very useful."

The thought made Flora smile.

"Much better." Harriet led her over to a couple near the center of the large room and introduced her to Gerald and Anne Moreton, Earl and Countess of Salbridge. They were both about Harriet's age, and Flora knew they'd been friends for years. That connection had made her invitation possible. The countess was also a distant relation of Flora's mother. She strongly suspected that Harriet had reminded her of this when her hostess asked, "How is Agatha? I haven't seen her in an age."

"She's well," Flora replied, not quite truthfully. Back home in London, her mother was fretting, as agitated as Flora had ever seen her. She'd admitted that it could be helpful for Flora to extend her social horizons, while being terribly worried about what might happen to her when she did.

"You're also a cousin of Robert Gresham's, are you not?"

Flora suppressed a start. She doubted that Harriet had provided this information. It seemed the countess had made her own inquiries. "Very distant," Flora said, proud of the indifference in her voice. "Third or fourth, perhaps. We used to try to work it out when I visited at Langford as a child." There, let her noble hosts chew on the fact that she'd stayed at a duke's home. They needn't know that *all* the visits had been years ago. Flora felt her resolve returning. She'd decided to come here, and she'd been taught to trust her own thought processes, even when she didn't quite fathom them. She would not draw back, and she did *not* feel Lord Robert's presence at her back like a constant pulse of heat. That was irrational.

"You must meet our daughter," the countess said. At her signal, one of the young ladies left the circle clustered around Lord Robert and joined them. "Victoria, this is Miss Flora Jennings."

It was actually Lady Victoria, Flora thought, as they exchanged bobbing curtsies. The room was full of titled people, some of whom would certainly despise the daughter of an obscure scholar. Who'd been worth a dozen of any of these fribbles, she thought automatically. Flora caught herself. One did not draw conclusions before an experiment had really begun. She didn't have proof of their witlessness. However certain she might be, she mustn't overgeneralize. Papa had taught her more intellectual rigor than that.

"How do you do?" said Lady Victoria Moreton in a soft voice.

Everything about this daughter of the house seemed soft. She was a creature of rounded contours and wide brown eyes, several inches shorter than Flora, and garbed in a white muslin gown. Her brown hair was sculpted in gentle waves about her pretty face. There was something old-fashioned about her, Flora thought, though her dress was certainly the latest thing. She looked as if she'd never been denied anything in all her years.

"You must present Miss Jennings to the young people," the countess said. "I think we've gathered quite a lively group, Miss Jennings, even so far from town." And then, her duty done, the hostess turned to talk to Harriet.

Flora followed Lady Victoria back to the knot of guests that included Lord Robert. As they joined them, Flora was irresistibly reminded of a herd of horses, jostling and sidling when a new animal was introduced into their ranks. The idea made her smile. A medium-sized gentleman across the group smiled back.

Lady Victoria introduced her and recited a list of names, moving around the circle. Flora memorized them with the automatic precision of a trained mind. The task offered no difficulty to one who'd been drilled on cuneiform symbols from the age of seven. She was received with politeness as a minor novelty. She wasn't someone they knew, and people like this expected to know everyone important, Flora thought. There was a stir of silent speculation when Lord Robert mentioned that they were already acquainted. "Cousin of mine," he added.

With three words, he'd slotted her into a recognized category, Flora saw. She was a visitor from the far edges of a great family. Possibly a poor relation, considering her gown. She couldn't dispute such a verdict. It was perfectly true. And Lord Robert Gresham was perfectly free to point it out to his grand friends, if that was what he wished to do. Never mind his claims, this spring and summer, to value other measures of worth—intellect and education and industry. It was a very good thing she'd come here, Flora thought. If she hadn't, she might have kept on believing him.

Everyone returned to their previous conversations. It was actually a relief not to be the center of attention any longer. At first, Flora thought they were playing some kind of geography game, naming prominent places in London. Then she realized they were establishing where they'd last met—weeks ago, during the season—with bits of reminiscence about certain balls or evening parties. As she had attended none of them, she had nothing to contribute. Members of the *haut ton* were rather like butterflies, she thought. They hovered, vividly colorful, above the lower reaches of society. They flitted from one gorgeous locale to another, oblivious to the misfortunes that befell others not so very far away. They were stunningly decorative. After a few minutes, she caught Harriet's admonitory eye and remembered to smile.

Flora stood and listened. She was accustomed to being the center of lively discussions at home, but she didn't really mind being left out of this one. The topic was dull, and anyway she would be better occupied observing and analyzing the people who were to be her companions for the next month. Now that she had their names, she could put faces to the descriptions Harriet had provided on their long journey up to Northumberland.

The room was dotted with attractive young men. Wellborn, well-heeled, well-bred, Flora thought. Well-behaved, well-set-up. No, she was stretching now. But they were all those things. Harriet had told her that the young men were here for Lady Victoria. Or perhaps vice versa. Good matches, in any case, lured in by the hunting and hospitality toward a possible settlement of the girl's future. It was a common thing, Flora knew, and she couldn't summon quite the level of derision she might have expressed in earlier years. People had to meet, after all.

Her gaze lit on Lord Robert and skipped away before he could catch her looking. He was the handsomest of them all, in her opinion. Harriet had said he wasn't considered a likely suitor, though he'd be welcome if he decided to show interest in Lady Victoria, ten years his junior. Only three years separated the two of them, thought Flora. Harriet had warned her to avoid mentioning her age, as some would consider twenty-five to be nearly on the shelf. Lord Robert turned to smile at a young lady with copper-colored hair. He looked delighted with her. Lady Victoria joined them. Flora felt a pang in the region of her heart. With fierce discipline, she dismissed it.

The young female guests were Lady Victoria's age, her particular friends, Harriet had said. Flora noted that they hadn't been chosen to make the daughter of the house shine in comparison. Several had to be judged much prettier than Lady Victoria; she must be generous or confident, or perhaps both. Flora banished a sneaking wish that she'd been less magnanimous. All the girls looked so assured and graceful in their pale muslin dresses.

Flora realized that Lord Robert was coming toward her. Her pulse sped up as he stopped by her side.

"I've come to beg your pardon," he said. "I was rude. Please accept my apologies."

Flora could only nod. He hadn't spoken to her so curtly even when they'd been mired in one of their running debates last summer. He seemed different in other ways as well. His clothes looked more—she groped for a word—complicated than they had in Russell Square and Oxford. His neckcloth was more intricate, his waistcoat more opulent. More than that, though, he had a larger *presence*. If she'd thought of it at all, she would have predicted that he'd be less impressive surrounded by the cream of the *haut ton*. Outshone or overshadowed with other noblemen all around him. In fact, it was the opposite. He stood out—polished, assured, every inch a duke's son. And just, perhaps, the tiniest bit intimidating?

"I was startled to see you," he went on when she didn't speak. "Knowing how you hate the fashionable set."

"*Hate* is a strong word."

"We can dispute my word choice, but you cannot deny that you've expressed contempt for the *ton*. Emphatically and often."

"*Contempt* is—"

"Another strong word. Indeed." He smiled at her.

Abruptly, treacherously, Flora was ambushed by a memory. It had been late, at her home in Russell Square. A group of her father's old friends were making their farewells to her mother. She and Lord Robert had lingered in a dim corner of the drawing room. She couldn't recall how that had come about, but it was one of the rare moments when they *hadn't* been arguing. Indeed, they'd been in charity with one another, for once. And he'd looked down at her with admiration, and tenderness, and longing. She couldn't have mistaken it. His gaze had sent shivers through her body. She'd wanted to step into his arms and lose herself in a wild kiss and let passion take them where it would.

Flora blinked, and swallowed. She'd shoved that simmering desire away, out of sight, almost out of mind. She'd been so sure that he'd walk out of her life as easily as he'd walked in, that he would make a fool of her. Then, recently, she'd wondered if she was mistaken. Now, she faced a new version of this unfathomable man.

"Am I right in assuming this is your first house party?" Lord Robert asked.

"Yes." One word was all she could manage.

"I think you'll find the Salbridges' arrangements very pleasant. There'll be shooting tomorrow, I understand. Ladies often come along to observe."

"Observe men shooting? Isn't that unwise?" Flora pictured strolling groups straying into the line of fire. Shouting would be the least of it.

"Everyone stays behind the butts."

"The butts?"

Lord Robert shaped a waist-high barrier with his hands. "Short stone-and-turf walls."

"But how can they find any game if they just stand there?"

"The beaters flush the birds."

Flora realized she'd heard of this. Wasn't it just like the *ton* to have their targets hustled to them by servants? "I don't care to watch a lot of birds herded to slaughter," she answered.

"Yet you enjoy eating a fat partridge," Lord Robert said. "I've seen you do it. Very daintily too."

There was that warmth in his eyes. "When?" she challenged.

"The first time I was invited to dinner in Russell Square."

"You remember what we ate?"

"Yes, I do."

Flora couldn't look away. Their many conversations seemed to rush back into the space between them. "I have that article you wanted to read," she said before she thought. "The one by Stanfield. About the similarities between Akkadian and Aramaic."

"Ah." Lord Robert's blue eyes flickered with... something. She couldn't tell what it was.

"You were very eager to see it." When he didn't answer at once, well-worn words popped out of Flora's mouth. "You said. Back when you were claiming to be interested in Papa's scholarship." His jaw tightened. She'd always been able to goad him, if nothing else.

"Fl— Miss Jennings. Allow me to give you some advice. Talk of ancient inscriptions will do you no favors here. People won't understand. They'll find you odd. And that can make things difficult at a gathering like this one."

"I certainly wouldn't wish to embarrass you!" she replied, hiding hurt under an acerbic tone.

"This isn't about me," he said. "Everyone knows me. It's you who would suffer."

"Are you threatening me?"

"Of course not. Why would I do such a thing?"

"Because you wish I wasn't here and hope I will go away and leave you to your grand friends." Her voice sounded petulant and childish in her own ears. Flora flushed, mortified.

Lord Robert raised one auburn eyebrow. He gave her a disturbingly understanding smile. "No, I don't." With an elegant bow, he moved away.

Flora stood very still. She'd found that was the best way to contain a strong emotion. Especially when she didn't know what it was. Or, rather, what a bewildering mixture of things it was. She resisted closing her hands into fists, forced down her wish to follow him.

A young man behind her gave a shout of laughter. Flora started and turned. But no one was looking at her. She was not the focus of a battery of stares. In this opulent drawing room she wasn't the respected expert on her father's work, or the admired head of a charitable organization. She wasn't the least bit important. It was a kind of safety.

She encountered the gaze of the medium-sized man who'd smiled at her during the introductions. His name was Sir Liam Malloy, she recalled. He looked a bit older than the gaggle of suitors around Lady Victoria, somewhere between them and the host and hostess in age. When he saw that he had her attention, he approached.

"Miss Jennings," he said with a small bow. "How do you do?" His voice had a faint lilt. He was stocky and tanned by the sun, probably an avid sportsman in this place and time. "Looking at you, I wondered if we might have a bit of heritage in common. Are you by any chance black Irish like me?"

They shared black hair and light-blue eyes, she noticed. It wasn't a common coloring. "No, not so far as I know."

"It's a bit of a tale where the 'black' part came from," he began.

"The wreck of the Spanish Armada," said Flora automatically. "The foreign sailors washed up on Irish shores."

Her companion looked startled. "Well, you've

quite stolen my thunder, Miss Jennings. Not many people recall that bit of history."

Flora flushed. Despite her resentment, she knew that Lord Robert was right. No one here cared for learning, and they would find her strange if she paraded her knowledge. Not that she ever did. She wasn't some sort of pedant. Facts simply...popped out when you knew them. Was she supposed to *try* to reply stupidly? But she didn't intend to make a point of it either. Flora planned to slide into society unobtrusively, stealthily—a dispassionate observer, an explorer of new realms. That was the way to look at it, she thought. It wasn't all about *him*. "I just...happened to read of it somewhere," she replied.

"A great reader, are you?"

Flora met his bright, interested eyes. She would tell no outright lies. But there was no need to recount her entire biography either. "Not lately," she said. Indeed, it had been more than three hours since she had opened a book.

Three

ROBERT DIDN'T JOIN THE SHOOTING PARTY THE NEXT morning. Instead, he requested a mount from the Salbridge stables and set off early for the village of Hexham, some ten miles away. It was a longish ride for pleasure, but Hexham was the site of his brother Randolph's church, and he knew Randolph was eagerly anticipating a visit.

The ride also gave Robert ample time to mull over a topic that interested him deeply. Flora Jennings hadn't traveled all the way to Northumberland to criticize him. She wasn't insane. She hadn't come because she loved tonnish house parties either. Her distaste for "fashionable fribbles" had always been clear. Thus, she must have other motives. Which meant that he could have…revivified hopes.

All well and good, Robert thought as he rode along the banks of the River Tyne in the crisp October sunshine, but he did not intend to revive their continual disputes. He'd had quite enough sniping, an experience unique in his life so far. His unexpected fascination with the ancient Akkadian language had started it, he thought. Who would have imagined that he'd enjoy studying cuneiform symbols? But it had meant that he entered Flora's world as an apprentice where she was expert, and this inequality had colored all their relations. She'd felt free to doubt and dismiss him. But Salbridge Great Hall was a different matter altogether. And he meant to manage rather better.

Robert had a sudden memory of a summer evening when they'd sat together in her father's study, the windows open to the green scents of the back garden and the sound of crickets. They'd been struggling over a difficult bit of cuneiform, and he'd suddenly gotten an inspiration. When he told her his idea, Flora's eyes had positively flamed with triumph and delight. She'd nodded, and smiled at him, and touched the back of his hand with her fingertips. A mere brush, and he'd become so aroused he didn't dare rise from his chair for half an hour. Who could have predicted that a fine mind would be more stimulating to him than a daring neckline or a froth of petticoats? A reminiscent smile curving his lips, Robert rode on.

Hexham turned out to be a pretty village on the banks of the Tyne with quite a grand church in the center. The building's size and style surprised Robert; he'd gotten the impression from Randolph that it was a paltry place. Robert left his borrowed horse at an inn and asked directions to the rectory. He found it to be a neat house not far away. Knocking, he was admitted by a maid, immediately joined by a housekeeper, who introduced herself as Mrs. Yates. From this unusual courtesy, Robert deduced that the lady kept the village informed about everything that went on in Randolph's home.

Randolph appeared at the back of the hall and rushed up to shake his brother's hand. "Robert! I didn't look to see you so soon. Come in. You can help me—" Randolph broke off with an oddly furtive expression. "My study's back here," he continued, instead of whatever he'd been about to say.

In a few minutes, they were settled in a cozy book-lined room overlooking the green. The housekeeper, not the maid, brought a tray with wine and cakes. When she'd gone, trailing promises of luncheon, Randolph rose, tried the door, found it not quite closed, and remedied that lapse. He returned to his chair with a sigh and poured wine. "You can help me celebrate," he said as he handed Robert a glass. "I've had some good news."

"Which you don't wish to share with the whole village?"

"Nothing gets past you," replied Randolph with a smile.

It was always a little strange to see him in his clerical collar, Robert thought. Not that Randolph was unqualified for his position. But Robert could remember him as a small boy slathered in mud, with a collection of beetles.

"I have a new parish," Randolph said. "The bishop that Nathaniel found for me was very helpful. The letter came yesterday."

"Farther south?" Well, it would have to be, Robert realized. They were practically in Scotland up here.

"Derbyshire. And a larger town."

Robert raised his glass. "As you wanted. Congratulations."

"Thanks. I'll tell them here once my replacement is arranged," Randolph added, as if Robert had questioned his reticence.

"I wonder if you'll have as impressive a church."

Randolph shook his head. "Hard to match Hexham Abbey. It's Norman, you know, but there's been a church on the site for well over a thousand years, since Queen Etheldreda of Northumbria—"

"Was it built to ward off curses? As in Hexham?"

His brother only smiled at the interruption. It was an established joke in the family that if Randolph was let loose, he'd give you the history of a thing going back to Noah's flood. "Nothing to do with curses." Randolph's smile grew broader. "The word derives from Old English, *Hagustaldes ham*, related to the Old High German *hagustalt*, which refers to a younger son taking land outside the settlement."

"I see," Robert said.

"William Wallace burned the town in 1297," Randolph added. "The Scots patriot. As you know, of course."

"Naturally," said Robert.

"Various Scots kings marauded about as well." Randolph smirked at him. "Robert the Bruce, King David II."

"As they do, in these parts," Robert said blandly.

"King David sacked the Abbey. In 1346, I believe that was."

"I'm certain you're right." Robert pressed his lips together.

"During the Wars of the Roses—"

Robert threw up a hand. "I yield," he said. "No more."

They burst out laughing together.

"I enjoy following a trail of facts all the way to the end," Randolph observed.

"I know you do," replied Robert fondly. "I remember the family chronicle you assembled for Mama. A hundred pages."

His brother nodded, grinning. "And so I must tell you that Hexham is active in the leather trade, famous for gloves known as Hexham Tans."

"I must procure a pair," said Robert.

"I know several shops where you can do so."

They shared another laugh.

"It's good to see you," Randolph said then. "Of all my brothers. I'm going to want your advice particularly. I have some leave between postings, and I intend to go to London next season."

"Indeed?"

"I want a wife," added Randolph, sounding wistful. "The rest of us all have 'em. Nathaniel and Sebastian and James and Alan. And you have dozens of flirts."

Robert ignored the latter exaggeration. "Aren't you surrounded by, er, worshipful female worshippers?"

His brother moved restlessly in his chair. "That's tricky. Some women are self-conscious around a clergyman, and others are rather…strangely interested. I have to be careful not to rouse talk or expectations among the few young ladies in the village. It's difficult to get to know anyone with a whole parish watching."

Robert saw his point. "Why not ride over to Salbridge for a visit? Lots of girls about there."

Randolph straightened, blue eyes shining. "That's a splendid idea!"

Too late, Robert realized that he hadn't mentioned Flora's presence. Randolph would meet her, and he would certainly remember the twitting Robert had endured at Sebastian's wedding.

As if reading his mind, Randolph said, "Did you come all the way up here to get away from that bluestocking?"

"I'm not sure I—"

"The one Ariel thinks you're in love with?"

His youngest brother's wife was entirely too talkative, Robert thought.

"I must say she didn't sound like your type."

Robert scanned the room, searching for what Sebastian would call a diversionary tactic. As if he'd called on his military brother's spirit, Robert immediately spotted one. "Is that Sebastian's lute?"

Randolph started, glanced at the case in the corner and then away. He looked intriguingly self-conscious.

"What's it doing here?"

"It's mine, actually. Sebastian got it for me."

Robert scented a secret. "Why?"

Randolph cleared his throat. "I, ah, I had a strange experience last summer. A kind of daydream, you might call it. Brought on by an Indian gentleman's drum and Sanskrit chanting." His eyes grew distant. "I saw myself with a lute. It was unmistakably a lute. I was playing a ballad; the melody haunts me still. And I, er, returned from the daydream convinced that I had to reproduce that song. Precisely." He stirred in his chair again. "It isn't enough to pick it out on the pianoforte. I've tried that. It doesn't do. So I am learning to play the lute."

Robert examined his brother's face. He seemed perfectly serious. "I hadn't suspected you of mystical visions."

"Quite the wrong word!" Randolph protested. "Far too grandiose and…fraught."

"I suppose they go along with your profession," Robert mused. "Although…is that one quite orthodox?"

"This has nothing to do with my profession. I'm simply learning a song." Randolph cleared his throat again. "I'd appreciate it if you'd consider that a confidence, however. I wouldn't want it repeated, particularly to the Archbishop of Canterbury."

"The—?" Robert gazed at him, astonished. "I wouldn't know the archbishop if I tripped over him."

"All the more reason not to mention it," answered Randolph.

❧

Back at Salbridge Great Hall and changed out of his riding dress, Robert found the house quiet. He went to the library for a book, and observed a group of younger guests trooping past the window, Flora Jennings among them. Intrigued, he slipped through one of the glass doors and followed them to a bit of sheltered lawn near the edge of the shrubbery. The late afternoon was sunny and windless; the scene might have been placid if not for Philip Moreton, the younger son of the Salbridge household. Robert watched him rush about the grass like an inexperienced sheepdog herding…something less docile than sheep. Cats, perhaps.

A skinny lad of seventeen, still working on his full

growth, with gangling limbs and big, occasionally clumsy hands, Philip was brown-haired and brown-eyed like his sister, Victoria. Robert knew that his sporadic efforts to be sociable concealed shyness. Philip was slated go up to Oxford for the Hilary term after the holidays, and Robert had heard him express some unease about his level of preparation.

Robert watched the lad nearly trip over an invisible hummock and recover with a blush. He'd have to put Philip on to Alan, Robert thought. His collegial brother would certainly help if needed. Robert remembered what it was like to be on the cusp of manhood, at one moment convinced you were the smoothest, most sophisticated fellow in the world, and the next stricken with the certainty that you were an utter clod.

"It's a new sort of game," Philip said, directing two footmen who carried a large chest from the house. "Or an old sort revived." He opened the chest. "I found these in one of the attics." He pulled out an odd wooden mallet with a slender handle that reached the center of his chest. "I couldn't tell what they might be until I found a picture in *The Sports and Pastimes of the People of England*. It showed someone using a thing just like this"—he brandished the instrument—"to play a game called paille-maille."

"What, like the street in London?" asked one of the other young men.

"Exactly," said Philip. "The book said Charles the Second used to play it there with his courtiers. It was very fashionable, and the Mall in St. James's Park was named for it. It comes from the Italian words for *ball* and *mallet*."

He flushed again as the group began to cluster around him. Robert could practically hear him worrying that he'd sounded ridiculously pompous.

Flora stood on the other side of the group, her alluring figure not quite obscured by a knot of other young ladies. Robert was acutely conscious of her, as if she was a lodestone to his compass. It was a mystery as unfathomable as Randolph and his lute. Robert knew prettier ladies. Many were more vivacious, more sweetly attentive. But Flora Jennings compelled his attention.

"It's something like ground billiards," Philip continued. "See the arches I've set up?" He pointed, and heads obediently turned to observe the knee-high metal hoops dotted about the lawn. Robert hadn't noticed them till now. They were rather hard to see against the sod.

Philip bent and took a smooth wooden ball from the chest, holding it up for all to see. It was larger than a cricket ball and showed faded bits of red paint. "Each player gets a mallet and a ball," he said. "You hit your ball through the arches to reach that stake." He pointed again. Robert saw the sturdy stick of wood driven into the grass at the end of the lawn. It nearly blended into the trees beyond. "Whoever makes it with the fewest blows wins," finished Philip. "I thought we could give it a try."

As Robert's gaze shifted from the stake back to Philip, it caught Flora's. He could see a host of questions simmering in her vivid blue eyes. Of course she would want to know all about Charles the Second's games. She'd be imagining bewigged noblemen in jewels and brocade and lace mincing about the Mall, hitting wooden balls from one end to the other. That was the other thing about her. She was full to the brim with ideas and theories; she made his mind fizz like fine champagne. No one else in his life made him feel so energized. But she was *not* asking those urgent questions. Had she actually listened to his advice?

Salbridge Great Hall was no place for the kinds of conversation they'd had in London and Oxford, he thought with a pang. Long, lively…passionate discussions would draw attention and speculation and, eventually, spiteful comments. People would whisper that she was setting her cap at him. An alluring thought that he must nonetheless prevent. He looked away from her.

"What are the rules?" asked one of the young men. He'd taken a mallet from the chest and was idly swinging it in one hand.

"Nobody knows," replied Philip. "The book said the game had dropped out of use."

The young man looked speculatively at the mallet. The glint of mischief in his expression did not bode well, Robert thought.

Philip walked about handing out mallets. Some people drew back; others stepped forward eagerly. Robert took one. Victoria and Flora appeared, rather, to accept those thrust upon them. A stocky man about Robert's age examined his with interest. "It looks like a similar thing used in India," he said with a soft Irish lilt. "This is shorter, but that game is played on horseback."

"You've been to India?" Flora asked.

Curiosity must be nearly choking her by now, Robert thought, hiding a smile. Flora Jennings was used to pursuing any topic that caught her fancy as far and as long as she pleased.

"I have," answered the Irishman.

"You must tell me about it," Flora said.

"With great pleasure," was the reply.

Who was this fellow? Robert wondered. He recalled his name—Malloy. Sir Liam Malloy. He had an estate in Ireland. The usual crumbling wreck and pile of debts, no doubt.

Philip got the players lined up along the near end of the lawn. They started out taking turns, and people soon found that propelling the balls over the lawn was more difficult than they'd expected. The grass looked smooth, but it was in fact dotted with small lumps and tussocks that deflected shots in unpredictable ways.

As the hard wooden balls sped across the sod, it occurred to some of the players that preventing others from reaching the hoops was as effective a strategy as getting there oneself. These enterprising souls began using their shots to send opponents' balls careening into the shrubbery.

"Don't muck about," called Philip, looking irritated.

"You said there were no rules," was the laughing reply. The fellow whacked first one, then another ball into the bushes with resounding cracks.

Startled, Flora watched her ball fly off. She'd been waiting for her turn, though the rota seemed to have disintegrated into more of a melee. She could see no reason for the assault on her ball. She was about to go after it when another went zooming past her feet.

"Look out!" cried Lord Philip Moreton. "It won't be funny if someone is hit by one of these things."

Indeed, they made effective missiles. At least they weren't flying through the air, Flora thought as she walked across the grass. Lady Victoria came up beside her. "Mr. Trevellyn knocked mine right into the brambles," she said. "I'm not sure Philip was wise to suggest this game."

"He should have made up some rules," Flora remarked.

"That would have been clever," the younger girl replied.

She said it as if cleverness was a rare and suspicious thing, Flora thought. And immediately dismissed the idea. It made no sense.

They walked side by side to the fringe of bushes. Flora found her ball under a spreading evergreen, but Lady Victoria's was more elusive. They pushed through branches together until they spotted it near the roots of an arching berry bush.

"Oh dear," said the other girl, looking down at the delicate lace trimming her dress. Obviously it would catch and tear on the thorns. "I'd better call a footman."

"From the house?" said Flora. "No need. I'll get it." She wouldn't have to crawl, she decided, marking out a passage through the thorny growth. She could crouch and creep under an arched branch. Her plain gown would be in no danger.

"Really?"

"It won't be difficult," Flora replied. She bent and edged her way beneath the branch. At the center, she half knelt to pick up the ball, then made her way back out. She handed the ball to Lady Victoria.

"Thank you." The girl surveyed Flora with curious dispassion, and without visible gratitude, then turned to walk back to the game. "Mama says that Mr. Trevellyn teases because he admires me." Lady Victoria examined the wooden sphere she held. She shook her head. "It seems nonsensical to me."

Flora placed the name from the introductions. Edward Trevellyn was a large, boisterous young man, with pale-blond hair and a penetrating voice.

"So you are particularly well acquainted with Lord Robert?" Lady Victoria said.

Something in her tone brought Flora alert. Her companion's voice held much more than idle inquiry. "We are distantly related," she said, as he had yesterday.

Lady Victoria seemed to consider this as they stepped through the final screen of branches.

Up ahead, a young man shouted in triumph as he slammed his ball through one of the metal arches. It nearly struck Sir Liam Malloy's foot on the far side; the older man had to leap into the air to avoid it. A tangle of players contended in the middle, mallets swinging like claymores. Flora stopped to contemplate the seething mass. Most of the ladies had drawn back, clustering on the opposite side. Lord Robert stood near them with Philip, who was wringing his hands. "Poor Philip is so bad at games," observed Lady Victoria. "It is a continual trial to him."

Her brother did look distressed. "I think we'd best move to the side," Flora said. A ball sped past on their right. It crashed into a small tree, ricocheted, and disappeared into the bushes.

Lady Victoria nodded. They edged along the lawn toward the other young ladies. "I understand you're quite a bluestocking," she said.

Flora glanced at her. The word was almost always meant as an insult. There'd been a comic opera of that name several years ago, cruelly mocking.

Lady Victoria didn't look at her as they walked. "Mama said you were terribly learned," she added.

Her softness was all surface, Flora decided. There was something more complicated underneath. Which would have been quite interesting, if not for the whiff of threat that had, inexplicably, entered the conversation. Lady Victoria's tone was making Flora uneasy.

"I dislike books myself, and quite often don't get the point of a witty remark." The daughter of the household said this as if she was proud of it.

Mystified, Flora made no reply.

"I think gentlemen prefer it that way," Lady Victoria added.

"What way?"

Her companion stopped and faced her. The brown eyes that Flora had thought doe-like drilled into her. "They may be briefly diverted by smart talk and odd studies, but for their wives, they want *quite* a different sort of female."

The words sounded like a gauntlet thrown down. Flora was irresistibly reminded of duelists meeting at dawn, shots ringing out in morning mists. She wasn't sure whether to protest or laugh.

"When I was fourteen, I told Lord Robert I intended to marry him," Lady Victoria continued. "He said he would wait for me."

The intensity in her voice startled Flora. "But that was just a—"

"He may have been diverted by...something last season," interrupted the younger woman. "My first season," she added darkly. "Something that kept him from places where I might have seen him. But I made certain Papa would invite him here this autumn. To my home, where there will be plenty of time to remind him of his promise. And he is *not* married." She finished with the air of someone clinching an argument and a positively searing glance. "You had better not get in my way."

With that, Lady Victoria sauntered over to the other young ladies. Watching her go, Flora felt as if a pampered house cat had suddenly snarled and twisted 'round and bitten her hand, hard enough to draw blood. Only, no. Everyone knew that cats had abrupt changes of mood and might scratch. She'd thought Lady Victoria was another sort of creature altogether. Did she actually consider Lord Robert's offhand remark of years ago a promise? Flora would have wagered any amount of money that he had no memory of the conversation.

Flora kept to the edge of the group as they welcomed Lady Victoria and pointed out the antics of the gentlemen. Lord Robert stood on the other side of the lawn, a poised contrast to the schoolboy-like skirmish. He stepped forward as if he might come and speak to her.

"Did you crawl into the bushes?" asked a male voice at Flora's back. She turned to find Sir Liam next to her. "You have leaves in your hair," he pointed out.

She put a hand to her curls, found the leaves, and removed them.

"I wonder Lady Victoria didn't tell you," the man added.

In light of their recent exchange, Flora didn't. "That would have been kind," she replied.

Sir Liam blinked at her dry tone. "I saw you bend down," he said.

Flora wondered if she'd shown the whole party her petticoats.

"In a perfectly unexceptionable way. You're rather intrepid, aren't you?"

"It was hardly an expedition into the jungle." It came out more acid than she'd meant, but he only laughed. Flora realized she was still holding her retrieved game ball. She put it on the ground.

As she started to straighten, another ball hurtled by, two feet above the ground and only inches from her head. She felt the stir of air on her cheek as the hard wooden sphere hissed past. It bounced along the sod behind her like a stone skipping over water and disappeared into the shrubbery. A distant crack suggested that it had hit a tree trunk. Flora leaped backward, steadied by Sir Liam.

Across the lawn, Lord Robert grasped the arm of the young man who'd hit it. He took the mallet from him and set it, along with his own, back in the open chest. Flora expected an argument, but the younger man accepted the intervention with cordial deference. Lord Robert let him go and stepped into the dispute that had erupted over who'd won the contest. Flora watched him civilize a gaggle of shouting noblemen without apparent effort. In fact, they all appeared eager to hear his opinion and accept his judgment. Flora watched in wonder. Suddenly, all was good-natured raillery.

And with that, the game was over. People replaced their mallets and started back to the house. Lord Robert went surrounded by a jostling, admiring train of young men.

Lingering to avoid Lady Victoria, Flora found herself walking beside Lord Philip. "Well, that was a disaster," he said. "Why do I try? It always goes wrong."

"I think people had…fun," Flora said.

He stared at her. "Fun? They ran amok. Look at the holes in the lawn. As if it'd been attacked by an army of moles. Finch, our head gardener, will want my head for this." He looked desolate, and very young.

Flora was moved by a desire to reassure him. "Everyone will remember the game."

"As an utter debacle," he replied glumly.

"No, as something fresh and new. Never seen at a house party before." Flora was pretty sure this had to be true.

"Do you really think so?" Lord Philip perked up a bit.

"You might set a new fashion."

"For mayhem?" But he smiled.

"For originality and…ingenuity. For a wish to offer your guests novel entertainments."

Lord Philip considered this. Then he laughed. "You're out of the common way, aren't you?"

It was the third time she'd been called unconventional, and she hadn't been at Salbridge two whole days. Her notion that she could slide into the company with scarcely a ripple, just another young lady, an unremarkable creature of society, was proving dubious. "No," she said. But she very much feared that it was too true to be concealed.

Four

ROBERT'S VALET BRUSHED A TINY BIT OF FLUFF OFF THE shoulder of his evening coat and stood back to survey the results of his work. He said nothing; nor did Robert. Small, wiry, and taciturn, Bailey was an artist who didn't wish to be personally involved with his creation—any more than a painter wanted to converse with his canvasses or a sculptor with his busts. He didn't scorn an occasional word of praise, but otherwise he kept his distance. Which was fine with Robert. He didn't want a load of chatter when he was trying to achieve a grand effect with his neckcloth. Bailey went out, carrying the one Robert had spoiled before he got the look he wanted.

A stir at the fireside caught Robert's eye. From his blanket on the hearth, Plato was gazing at him. As he always was, whenever Robert looked. It was almost as if the dog was waiting for Robert to recognize some quite obvious fact. Robert leaned down to pat the small furred head. "It's true I am not quite sure of my next step," he told the dog as he straightened.

Plato responded with his weird curmudgeonly gurgle.

"None of it has made any sense, from the very beginning."

It'd been those fiery-blue eyes first of all, Robert thought. He'd walked into the Jennings' house in Russell Square, trailing his brother Alan on a quest for information, and there Flora had been, daughter of the house. Something in Flora's gaze had set him alight, right to his fingers' ends. A revolution that could not be explained. He'd had to pursue that irresistible connection. But he'd let it unravel into an argument. "I shall do better here," he declared.

Plato rose from his blanket. He was much steadier on his feet now that he'd had a few good meals. His unusual coat was already glossier. He approached, and for a moment Robert feared the little dog would put a paw on his polished shoe, an act that would further alienate Bailey. The valet had not been pleased to find a mongrel in his employer's bedchamber.

But of course Plato did nothing of the kind. He walked deliberately past, his uncanny gaze fixed elsewhere for once. Following it, Robert saw that a moth had gotten inside and was fluttering around the candle flames. Plato sat down just beneath the spectacle, watching.

"A tired metaphor," Robert said. "And quite inappropriate in this case."

Plato cocked his head.

"Unless I'm the flame," Robert said.

The small animal gazed up at him. It was alarmingly easy to see skepticism, and perhaps even amusement, in those dark eyes.

Robert snuffed the candles. "You'll have to make

do with firelight," he told Plato, and possibly the moth, as he left the room.

Flora stood in the crowd of guests waiting to go in to dinner and tried not to feel self-conscious about her evening dress. There was nothing wrong with it. The cloth was good; the color and cut became her. Harriet's superior dresser had helped with her hair. But she didn't have the kind of sumptuous, extremely fashionable garments the other young ladies here wore. Most of them looked as if they'd stepped right out of a pattern book.

Also, she had only two formal ensembles, and as of this evening, she'd worn them both. Harriet had suggested tricks to make them appear slightly different—a shawl, a branch of artificial flowers. But these would fool no female in this house, and Flora was finding the thought of Lady Victoria's scorn surprisingly irritating. Was she actually going to begin caring about this sort of thing now? After a lifetime of disdaining fashion and all it represented? She'd vowed before she came that she would visit here on her own terms. The trouble was, she hadn't been completely clear on what those terms were.

Lord Robert strolled into the room, rivetingly attractive in his evening dress and, unlike her, completely at home. Flora saw the envious glances he attracted from many of the younger men and the admiring ones from the ladies. The distance between them felt far greater than a stretch of parquet flooring. There was so much more to him than she'd realized. She hardly knew how to approach him in these…foreign surroundings. Had he been as uncertain when he plunged into a discussion with her father's crusty old scholar friends? Flora wondered. She hadn't thought of that before.

The countess gave the signal, and the party went in to dinner. The dining room was huge, and yet nearly filled by a long table sparkling with crystal and silver and gleaming with candlelight. Flora found her place about halfway down, between Mr. Edward Trevellyn and Lord Philip. In Flora's newly acquired geography of dinner parties, this suggested that Mr. Trevellyn was not a favored suitor for Lady Victoria's hand, since he was far from her. Yet he was not out of the question, because Flora couldn't be seen as a rival. He was the son of a baron, lower in rank than many here but much richer. Lord Robert was many seats away, near Lady Victoria but not at her side. Sir Liam Malloy sat on the other side of the table.

"I asked to sit beside you," Lord Philip confided, "because you were so good about the game."

Soup was put before her. As the guests ate, footmen placed a vast variety of foods down the center of the table—from great roasts ready to be carved to all manner of side dishes.

Flora wasn't accustomed to such a feast. She and her mother had much smaller meals, even when entertaining. Mr. Trevellyn clearly had no such qualms. He finished his soup in record time and accepted a great portion of roast beef from the earl's carving, then piled his plate from every dish within reach. Each time, he held heaping serving spoons over Flora's plate, saying, "Have some of this, Miss…er?" She told him her name three times and then gave up, concentrating on fending off small mountains of food.

At last, he seemed satisfied and dug in with a gusto that would have gratified the cook. If he kept this up, Flora thought, he was going to become one of those fat, red-faced Englishmen who wheezed when they exerted themselves. Rather like the Prince Regent, as she had heard him described.

"So you're a great friend of Lady Victoria's?" Mr. Trevellyn asked when he had made significant inroads on the first course.

"We've only just met," Flora replied.

"Ah." He looked disappointed and returned to his dinner.

Clearly, he had no interest in her except as a way to get closer to the daughter of the house. Flora didn't care in the least. But his rudeness did not excuse her from social duties. "Do you live in Northumberland, Mr. Trevellyn?" she asked.

"No, Cornwall," he replied, emptying his wineglass and signaling for more.

He'd come the whole length of the country to be here. Flora was impressed. "Cornwall is very beautiful, I believe."

He shrugged.

Really, he might make some effort. For all he knew, she had delicate sensibilities. "I suppose you met our hosts in London?" she said.

He nodded, drinking from his refilled goblet. Gazing down the table, he said, "Caught sight of Lady Victoria across a ballroom. Felt as if somebody had heaved a rock at my head."

"You were struck by her beauty," Flora said.

Mr. Trevellyn turned to look at her, which was

more than he'd done up to now. "Struck by some-thing," he replied. "There are prettier girls. I daresay *you* are prettier, by some people's measure. But there's just something about her." He shook his head like a bull goaded by pesky flies.

Flora forgave him, wryly, for the way he said *you*. It was mildly insulting, but then, she didn't want his admiration. And perhaps there was more to him than was immediately apparent, which was interesting.

Still, conversation remained hard going, and she was grateful when the table turned as the servants set out the second course, as rich and various as the first.

"Are you enjoying your visit so far, Miss Jennings?" Lord Philip asked her.

Flora found herself absurdly grateful that he'd remembered her name. "Of course," she replied, plac-ing courtesy above absolute honesty in this instance.

"I shan't be arranging any more 'special' entertain-ments," he added, seeming younger than his tall frame would suggest. "One mob scene was quite enough for me."

"Did you see me whack Lady Victoria's ball right across the lawn?" put in Edward Trevellyn across Flora. "That was jolly funny!"

Lord Philip seemed startled at this breach of eti-quette. He blinked, his mouth a little open.

"Sending her off into the brambles in a lace gown?" Flora said, saving Lord Philip the necessity of answer-ing. "She didn't think so."

Trevellyn gaped at her. "Eh?"

"A chivalrous man might have fetched it for her," she added. And now that she thought about it, why hadn't some of the gentlemen rushed to do just that? Too involved in the chaos of the game, she supposed. "Even if he was the one who hit it."

"Chivalrous," said Trevellyn, still staring.

"You could have managed a bit of private conversation with Lady Victoria at the same time," she pointed out.

He blinked, finally closing his mouth.

"I would like some of that blancmange," declared the young lady on Mr. Trevellyn's other side, pointing to a dish out of her reach. Her tone was openly irritated. When the man continued to ignore her, she elbowed him in the ribs. He gave out a surprised *uff* and turned to her in astonishment. "Blancmange," she repeated.

Flora searched her memory. Frances Reynolds—that was the girl's name. She looked younger than the other young ladies, more Philip's age than Victoria's.

The second course was cleared away and replaced with nuts, fruits, sweetmeats, and dishes of ice cream. By the time the countess gave the sign for the ladies to withdraw, Flora was sick of racking her brain for suitable remarks. "Making" conversation was worse than knitting. Wistfully, she remembered her talks with Lord Robert last summer. *Those* had swooped and dipped and…crackled. Her mind had flooded with words. And she'd wasted so many of them.

Later that evening, Robert found himself passing Mrs. Runyon in the spacious drawing room. She nodded and smiled. He grasped the opportunity. "A pleasant party, is it not?"

The older woman agreed that it was.

"I hope Miss Jennings is enjoying it. I know she has…reservations about the *ton*. Did you persuade her to come?"

"I wouldn't say *persuade*," Mrs. Runyon replied, her gray eyes glinting.

Here was a woman who appreciated a verbal joust, Robert saw. But not, he thought, an adversary. "Coax," he suggested. "Cajole, urge, wheedle?"

She laughed. "Perhaps those terms apply more to you, Lord Robert?"

"Oh, I am a fixture at house parties. Miss Jennings is the novelty."

"She is certainly distinctive."

Robert looked across the room. Flora sat on a sofa talking to a very young lady with pale-blond hair and a look of being unformed somehow. They seemed engrossed. "Undoubtedly." The word came out a bit too strongly.

"As are you, of course," said Mrs. Runyon.

Meeting her shrewd gaze, Robert saw understanding and amusement there. Definitely not an adversary; quite possibly an ally, under the proper circumstances.

"I am here to support her," she added, confirming his conclusions.

"And advise her?"

"Should she need, and want, my opinion."

"She is fortunate." He gave her the bow of a worthy sparring partner. Mrs. Runyon nodded acknowledgment and moved on.

Robert surveyed the chatting guests, noting budding flirtations, knots of gossipmongers, a hint of gentlemanly jostling. He'd always had a greater talent for society than any of his brothers. James might sail the seven seas. Sebastian could very well command his regiment one day. The others had worthy tasks—on the ducal estates, in the church, pursing elusive scientific knowledge. But Robert knew this world. He started toward Flora.

Young Victoria caught his arm as he passed her. "Oh, Lord Robert," she said, "do tell Susan that story about the balloon. She is *longing* to hear it."

She tugged at him like the child he'd first met five years ago. He smiled and conceded.

❧

A grand house party was more like a theatrical performance than a simple visit, Flora thought as she got ready to go down to breakfast the following morning. She felt as if she was preparing to go onstage. Life at Russell Square and in Oxford had been much more like…life. She rejected an impulse to sigh and headed downstairs.

There was the question of what to do next. She didn't want to go out to the hunting stands. Even if she was placed with Lord Robert, which was extremely unlikely given Lady Victoria's attitude, they'd be surrounded by booming shotguns and dying grouse. Did people actually talk in such circumstances?

Flora passed the half-open door of an elegant parlor. From inside, a cultured voice declared, "She invited herself, Gerald."

It was her hostess speaking. She sounded irritated.

"Well, you must write back and tell her it isn't convenient," replied the earl.

"Would that I could. She sent word from the

road, giving me no opportunity to refuse. They arrive tonight."

"What insufferable cheek!"

Flora couldn't help slowing a little, curious at this peek behind the scenes of an aristocratic household.

"She is *your* aunt," Lady Salbridge replied.

"She is married to my uncle. Barely."

How could one be barely married? Flora wondered.

There was a momentary pause, then the earl added, "I don't suppose we can turn her away at the door."

"No," said his wife heavily. "But they don't fit with the group we have staying. At all."

"I expect they will keep each other...entertained."

The Countess of Salbridge uttered a quite unlady-like oath.

Startled, and a bit amused, Flora moved away. She didn't wish to be caught eavesdropping on a conversation that had nothing to do with her.

She found the breakfast room sparsely populated. The hunters had gone out earlier, and others were still abed. She was helping herself from the row of silver chafing dishes when Frances Reynolds entered. The younger girl's face lit up, and she hurried over. "Oh, Miss Jennings, you didn't tell me that you were a great scholar. You must know that I have ambitions in that direction myself. I hope you will tell me all about your studies."

Meeting her glowing eyes, Flora felt a strange disorientation. It was like looking into a mirror and seeing not her present face, but her younger self—ardent, opinionated, determined. "That is an exaggeration," she said.

"But I heard Lady Victoria telling Miss Forster that you are terribly learned."

Making certain the information would reach all the guests, Flora thought. "My father was the great scholar," she said. "I learned a little from him."

"How I envy you!" Miss Reynolds cried. The beginnings of hero worship shone in her face. "Is it true that you can interpret hieroglyphics?"

"No." In other circumstances, Flora would have explained the difference between ancient Egyptian writing and cuneiform. She would have pointed out that her skills applied to a much earlier period. She would have been a bit of a pedant in fact, she thought wryly. Now, she took her plate to the table and began to eat.

Miss Reynolds would not be discouraged, however. She didn't notice that others in the room looked bored and supercilious. Flora did her best to balance opposing interests, but as soon as she finished her meal, she rose and excused herself.

Slipping from the room, Flora walked down the corridor and straight out a glass door that led into the gardens. Circling behind a line of shrubbery, she stopped and took a deep breath of the fresh autumn air. It was chilly, but not intolerably so.

Feeling liberated, Flora wandered, and marveled at the grounds surrounding Salbridge Great Hall. Her enjoyment of nature had been limited to London squares and parks—verdant, pleasant places, but crowded and tame compared to this. She gazed at beds of autumn blooms, swathes of trees gone golden or orange. Each new vista seemed lovelier than the last.

NOTHING LIKE A DUKE

She turned a corner and came upon Lord Robert strolling toward her, a small, odd-looking dog at his side. She stopped short. He kept walking. "You're not out shooting," she said.

"I am not." Though he *was* hunting, in a sense, Robert thought. He even had a faithful hound. The idea made him smile slightly. "You have no wrap. You'll be cold."

"I'm all right."

Robert knew there were high sticklers here who would criticize her for walking outdoors without a pelisse, and a bonnet and gloves. Such people lived on disapproval, and if they decided to snub her, they could make her visit quite unpleasant. How to tell her this without having the storm of her wrath break over him? Actually, he had missed that fiery onslaught, a bit. "I know how low you rate fashionable folk," he began. "You've said it a hundred times. But—"

"Too many times, I believe." Flora stood straight, her hands at her sides. "I'm sorry for that."

Robert blinked. Had he heard her correctly?

"I regret the…repetition of my opinions. And their…intensity. I may have overstated the case."

She looked away. Robert eyed her appreciatively. Those phrases had sounded as if she'd wrenched them from reluctant depths. Still, an interesting development. Flora rubbed her arms. He could see gooseflesh on her skin. "You are cold," he said.

"Very well! You were right. I'm cold. I'll go in." She whirled in a flurry of pale skirts.

Her left foot encountered Plato, who had somehow made his way directly into her path. Flora jerked sideways to avoid kicking him. Plato moved with her. She tripped and threw out her arms as she started to fall. Without thinking, Robert stepped forward and scooped her up.

Time ground to a breathless halt.

He held her against his chest, in a froth of petticoats. Heat spread through him from every spot they touched. Robert could feel the curve of her breast and the lovely roundness of her thigh through the muslin. The many words they'd thrown at each other over these last months evaporated. Their eyes met, two variations of intense blue. Her lips, just slightly parted, seemed to call him, as if they were meant by nature to be his. He would scarcely have to move to sink into a kiss—a kiss he'd wanted for quite some time.

Flora's breath caught. Her right hand gripped the collar of his coat. She leaned across the last few inches to meet him, and then those lips were his.

The kiss was every bit as riveting as he'd imagined it would be. The soft sound she made set him afire. His arms tightened around her. Indeed, every bit of him tightened as desire flashed through his veins.

Flora felt as if she was melting. Here, at last, was a kiss, she thought. This tender, urgent caress that sent heady demands shooting through her whole body. She'd known there must be more to kissing than the mechanical pressing together of lips, which was all she'd experienced when she'd allowed one of her father's students to kiss her. Purely in a spirit of experimentation. This was to that as a mud puddle was to a seething volcano. This was…bliss.

She'd come to Salbridge for this, Flora realized as

the kiss deepened. She'd been wanting it, and resisting the longing, for months. When Lord Robert had gone away, and it seemed as if she might not see him again, subterranean desires had pushed her to travel, to discover this searing moment.

She laced her hands behind his neck and pressed closer, giving herself up to the embrace. She didn't want it to end, ever.

There was a curious sound, like the harrumph of a grumpy old man clearing his throat. One of her father's oldest friends, in every sense of that adjective, had grumbled just that way when one of his pet theories was questioned. But he couldn't be here. Actually, he was dead.

Robert stopped kissing her. Flora tugged him close again. Then she heard footsteps.

Before either of them could move more than a few inches apart, a figure in an elegant blue pelisse rounded a clump of evergreens, stopped short, and gaped. "Whatever are you doing?" exclaimed Lady Victoria Moreton.

Robert's body cried out in frustration. Desire stronger than he'd ever felt before fought his innate good breeding. The conflict held him immobile for several tumultuous heartbeats. Then he set Flora carefully on the gravel. She wobbled briefly, then stepped back. "Miss Jennings tripped," he said. "I was assisting her."

"Assisting? Is that what you call it?"

Robert had never heard Victoria screech like that. He thought of her as a sweet child, his friend's little sister. It had been amusing to see her grow into a young lady surrounded by a crowd of society's young sprigs.

"*This* is why you did not go out shooting today?" she asked.

She sounded like a judge accusing a criminal.

"So you could sneak out with *her*?" she added, glaring at Flora. "You told me you'd meet me. Last night, in the drawing room, you said we'd go for a walk together!"

Robert supposed he might have done so. One talked idly of such things. He was sure he'd made no specific appointment.

"And now, instead, I find you with this…hoyden. Showing her petticoats, outside without so much as a shawl."

"Victoria!"

"Pretending to trip, I daresay, so that you would have to—"

"Victoria," Robert repeated. "Stop this at once."

She responded as the child she still was, fixing him with wide brown eyes.

"Miss Jennings tripped, and I kept her from falling. That is all there is to this." He avoided Flora's gaze. Protecting her was more important than strict honesty just now.

"*You* may think so," responded the daughter of the house.

He wouldn't have thought she could sneer like that. She'd always been such a gentle little thing.

"But why was she out here, half naked, *tripping*?"

"Naked!" exclaimed Flora.

"Nothing of the kind." Robert shot Flora a glance, asking her to leave this to him.

"She was lying in wait for you," Victoria insisted.

"Olivia says men hardly ever notice such snares until they are trapped into marriage."

"Well, Olivia, whoever she is, is an idiot," said Flora. "As is anyone who would believe such nonsense."

Victoria looked shocked. Robert sighed. There were ways to avoid social embarrassment. Best was to laugh off the incident, make people feel they were faintly ridiculous for bringing it up. Next was to appear bored, as if the topic was just too tedious. Nobody wanted to be thought dull. Arguing was not advisable.

"Are you calling me an—?"

"Really," said Robert before Victoria could complete this doom-filled sentence, "we are making a mountain of a molehill. Miss Jennings is eager to get back to the house. If you want a walk, Victoria, I am at your service." He offered his arm.

His friend's little sister hesitated, then marched over and took it. Her possessive grip confirmed his concerns, as did the glare she aimed on Flora. He'd known Victoria since she was in pigtails, however. He was practically an uncle to her. He would deal with this complication.

Flora turned and walked away without another word.

"What is that?" Victoria asked.

He followed her gaze. "Oh, that's Plato. My dog."

"Yours? Why do you have a dog like…that?"

"He has many special qualities."

Victoria examined the little animal. "He's quite odd-looking," she said finally. "Why does he stare so?"

"I believe he has a deep interest in human foibles."

Victoria frowned at him. Flora would have laughed,

Robert thought. Or thrown back some caustic, but exhilarating comment.

"Are you trying to set a new fashion?" the girl asked.

Robert choked off a laugh. It was a perfectly understandable inquiry. People did far odder things in order to make a splash. He had a sudden vision of a troop of young fashionables scouring the streets of London for mongrels. Flora would have enjoyed that picture as well.

"Is something wrong?"

Robert shook his head, and they set off on what he feared would feel like a very long walk. He would have to make certain it was not lengthy in actuality.

Five

As the guests at Salbridge Great Hall waited to go in to dinner once again, Flora stood off to the side, observing, her mind drifting back to the morning, to the garden.

Sir Liam Malloy strolled over to join her. "Good evening, Miss Jennings. Have you had a good day?"

A silent narrative flashed through Flora's mind. *I kissed Lord Robert Gresham. Passionately. And enjoyed it very, very much. I was caught in his arms by Lady Victoria, who considers him hers by right, and made an enemy.* Flora knew a declaration of vendetta when she saw one— and she had, in the girl's no-longer-soft brown eyes. *I almost called my hosts' daughter an idiot,* her inner voice continued. Actually, there was no *almost* about it. As Lady Victoria was well aware. Flora didn't care; she wouldn't have missed that kiss for anything. But Sir Liam was waiting for an answer. "Some of us walked into the village in the afternoon," she said aloud. "How was the shooting?"

"Splendid."

"Oh, good."

There was a stir near the door. Looking sour, the butler moved out of the opening and announced, "Mrs. Lydia Fotheringay and Mr. Anthony Durand."

There was a general murmur as an older couple entered. The lady looked perhaps forty-five. She was quite thin, which made her luminous hazel eyes seem larger. Richly dressed in garnet satin, she had a pointed chin and beautifully dressed brown hair, glinting with gems. She moved forward with languid grace.

Not as gracefully as her companion, however. Anthony Durand came into the room like a great predatory cat. Though not particularly tall, he was well muscled for a man in his fifties. He had craggy features, a swarthy complexion, and hair and eyes as black as midnight. His evening dress was impeccable.

They nodded to the group like sovereigns greeting their subjects. The earl and countess moved forward to receive them without visible enthusiasm.

"I wouldn't have expected to see them at this gathering," said Sir Liam.

"You know them?" asked Flora, through lips that felt stiff.

"Only, er, gossip," he replied. "I wouldn't befriend them if I were you."

As if Flora didn't know. Lydia Fotheringay had treated Flora's mother shamefully; she'd heard about it all her life. And she knew Anthony Durand's name. A powerful man with a very bad reputation, he'd been a close friend of the late, unlamented Lord Royalton.

Flora suppressed a shudder of revulsion. She hadn't thought of Royalton's murder, or her inadvertent involvement in it, for weeks. She hadn't meant to get him killed, even if he richly deserved it! To keep from thinking about it, she'd used a method her father had taught her to help remember complicated linguistic forms. He'd had her imagine her mind as a chamber lined with cupboards and drawers. Each particular piece of knowledge could be placed in its own compartment, where she could find it whenever she pleased. It worked remarkably well.

And so she'd taken her nightmares about being tied up and shut away in the dark and shoved them into one of the far cupboards, securing it with rows of mental locks. She didn't know what Papa would have thought of that use of his system, but it had succeeded. Until now.

Here was another part of the reason she'd come here, Flora saw then. She'd wanted a break from her previous life. The chance to be away from London—far from any connection to events that had happened in the past and were all too often revisited in her dreams—had appealed.

Flora turned away from the sight of Anthony Durand, hardly aware of Sir Liam by her side. She noticed that Lord Robert was looking at her, too. That wouldn't do.

Durand moved through the crowd. People simply got out of his way. Flora's heart beat a little faster. But he wouldn't speak to her. They hadn't been introduced. Social conventions had their uses after all.

Lydia Fotheringay was monitoring the man's progress with little darting glances, perhaps thinking she was being subtle. Harriet had said the woman had the brains of a pebble and the heart of a rabid stoat. The Duchess of Langford had added that she had the morals of a Covent Garden abbess. That had been quite a moment, Flora remembered, one of those conversations that turned your preconceptions on their heads.

The countess gave the signal to go in to dinner. A woman nearby took Sir Liam's arm. He looked as if he would much rather have escorted Flora to the dining room.

People moved toward the door. Flora couldn't seem to follow. She told herself to walk, but her body refused to take a step nearer to Anthony Durand.

From across the room, Robert could see that the new arrivals had distressed Flora. Lovers who scarcely bothered to hide the fact, they weren't the sort of people he'd have expected the Salbridges to invite, particularly to a party arranged for their daughter.

Flora was starting to draw glances, standing alone as the others moved to the dining room. He went over and drew her arm through his. She was trembling. What could be the matter?

Robert made himself into a shield, returning curious looks with bland discouragement. Or not so bland, if necessary. Silently, he got Flora moving. He escorted her down the corridor and guided her to her place at the table. Her chair was far from the newcomers, he was glad to see. She was seated between two young men who wouldn't notice a mood unless it had a tail like a fox.

He looked down. Flora smiled at him. It was the sweetest smile he'd ever seen on her face, and it went straight to his heart.

"I'm astonished to see her here," said Harriet Runyon. Flora sat beside her in the drawing room, watching Lydia Fotheringay talk to one of the countess's older friends. "I cannot believe Anne invited her."

"I don't think she did," said Flora. She told Harriet about the conversation she'd overheard between their hosts.

"Well! It's never clear whether Lydia is shameless, or simply too stupid to realize she's being outrageous."

Across the room, Mrs. Fotheringay's companion looked startled, then laughed.

"Talking scandal, no doubt," Harriet added. "Lydia has no other interests." She sighed. "I'm very sorry she's here, but we don't have to take any particular notice of her."

Flora nodded. She'd recovered her balance during dinner. For once, she was glad it went on so long.

"You should avoid the man she came with," Harriet continued. "He is…rather notorious."

Flora would be only too glad to do that.

A few minutes later, the gentlemen began to stroll in. Durand looked like a raven among crows, Flora thought. Nearly the same, but in fact larger and more dangerous than his fellows. He joined a group of older men setting up a card game at the far end of the large room.

Lord Robert appeared in the doorway—handsome, utterly assured—and surveyed the scene. Flora could still feel the echoes of his touch. Here was a limitation of social conventions. She couldn't rush across the room and repeat that kiss. The idea did make her smile, however. What gasps and fluttering that would cause!

Lord Robert walked over to Lady Victoria and spoke to her. Her answering smile was brilliant. She took his arm as if it belonged to her, and they moved over to the pianoforte in the corner of the large room. Lady Victoria sat down and opened it. Robert leaned against the instrument.

The younger woman started to play. "Naturally she's quite good," Flora muttered. "She would be."

"What?" Harriet turned to her.

"Nothing." Flora had never learned the pretty accomplishments of a noble lady. If the group wanted a lecture on the intricacies of declension and inflection rather than a song or a sonata, well, she had *that* at her fingertips.

"I wonder why Robert is flirting with Victoria," Harriet said.

Mr. Trevellyn and two other young men had gravitated to the pianoforte. The corner was getting crowded. "That's the question," said Flora.

"I also wonder why you're muttering."

"Do you?"

"Are we reduced to oblique remarks and grim hints?" replied Harriet with some asperity. "Do I try to guess what you mean while you glower and mumble darkly?"

Flora was startled into a laugh.

"Because, really, I find that sort of thing so tedious," Harriet continued. "It is why I rarely converse with 'sensitive' young gentlemen. And it is not at all like you."

It wasn't, Flora acknowledged. So far, this visit had felt more like being tossed hither and yon by a storm at sea than a reasoned reconnaissance mission into the *haut ton*.

Lady Victoria moved on to a tender ballad. She sang well, too. She probably excelled at everything she was supposed to do, and did nothing that she wasn't, Flora thought. But that was just spiteful. She wasn't spiteful. A sensation that might have been exasperation, or heartache, assailed her. She'd never seen Lord Robert flirting with anyone else, she realized. His attentions had been all for her.

She didn't like it.

Was she right, after all, about the shallowness of society? Could he kiss her so meltingly and then forget all about it?

"Flora?" said Harriet. "You're looking tragic again."

Flora turned to face her. Harriet had treated her with great generosity. Flora owed her a good deal and didn't want to let her down. But she had to be honest. "I don't think I can be anyone but myself," Flora said. "I've tried, but I'm failing miserably."

"Well, stop it at once," came the tart reply.

Flora blinked.

"Is that why you've been hanging back and moping?" Harriet added.

"I haven't been moping!"

The older woman frowned at her. "You've been thinking that you had to be…what? A simpering, wide-eyed miss? A sweet little doormat?"

"Well, I…not quite that, but—"

"Like me?"

"You've never been anything like that!"

Harriet waited, gazing at her.

"Not at all," Flora said slowly.

"You are so intelligent, Flora, so exact and analytical. I assumed you would see more clearly than that."

It was too kind to be a reprimand, but Flora felt foolish anyway.

"Let me assure you, then. You can be yourself. You must, really. It's the only viable choice."

That was a relief. "But things are getting into a tangle," Flora said.

"They tend to, at house parties. I've never been to one that wasn't seething with undercurrents. Sniping and overindulging and bedroom doors stealthily opening and shutting in the night."

"Doors. So that they can—?"

"Carry on their love affairs. Yes, Flora. You are not seventeen. Now, what is your tangle?" Harriet cocked her head, waiting for an explanation.

Flora looked around. No one was too close to them. "Among others, Lady Victoria considers herself…destined to marry Lord Robert," she said. "She told me he promised to wait for her, when she was fourteen. Her 'definitive' argument was that he is *not* yet married." Flora decided not to mention the kiss.

Harriet raised her eyebrows. She did not turn to look at the group around the pianoforte. "She confided in you?"

"It was more a warning than a confidence," Flora said.

"Indeed?"

"She sees me as her rival, an enemy."

"Ah, that explains Robert's behavior then."

"Explains it?"

"Well, he is going to have to maneuver her, isn't he?"

Before Flora could pursue this interesting topic, a fluttering movement in the corner of her eye made her turn. She found Lydia Fotheringay standing before the sofa where they sat. Her large hazel eyes were focused on Flora. Her hands moved restlessly and constantly, patting the air, fingering a bracelet.

"Are you indeed Agatha, ah, Jennings's daughter?" she asked. "Yes, Jennings, that was the name."

Flora sat straighter and raised her chin, braced for a sneer or a snub. And for a fight, if necessary. This was the woman who had given her mother the cut direct after Mama married outside her aristocratic circle. "I am," she replied defiantly.

"We used to be great friends, you know."

Of course Flora knew. That fact was part of the lore of her childhood. But it was so far from what she'd expected to hear that she had no reply.

"Best of friends, really," the thin, bejeweled woman continued, her hands smoothing the folds of her gown. "Before you were born. Did she never mention me? I am Lydia Fotheringay, you know."

"This is Miss Flora Jennings," Harriet put in.

"Flora." The newcomer smiled. "A sweet name. Agatha was always very fond of flowers."

Flora stared at her, searching for any sign of the rancorous history she knew.

"I haven't met Agatha in years," Mrs. Fotheringay went on. "She quite dropped out of society for some reason."

This was too much. Flora started to stand. "Because of the way *you*..."

Harriet's hand on her arm stopped her.

Mrs. Fotheringay waited a moment. When Flora said no more, she added, "Is Agatha coming up to join you here? It would be so delightful to see her again."

With Harriet's fingers tight on her wrist, Flora simply shook her head.

"Ah, too bad. Send her my dear love, won't you?" And with that the woman flitted away, trailing garnet satin and a heavy scent.

Flora was practically sputtering. "What the— How could she speak to me that way after what she did?"

"She's forgotten it ever happened," said Harriet, letting go of Flora's wrist.

"Forgotten! How could she? She must have seen that Mama was devastated."

"Lydia Fotheringay rarely sees beyond the end of her own nose. And people forget the most extraordinary things. I've often observed it. Memory is an untrustworthy tale."

"Mine doesn't!"

"How would you know?"

That was an unsettling idea. Flora shifted in her seat.

"Your mind is particularly acute," said Harriet. "Others aren't so quick, and Lydia Fotheringay is much stupider than most."

"Does she think I will be her friend now?" The idea revolted her.

"Oh, I don't believe she spends much time thinking."

Bewildered, Flora watched her mother's enemy flutter onto a sofa on the other side of the drawing room. What would Mama say when she wrote her about this? Would it be better or worse for her to hear that her old friend didn't recall the incident that had so wounded her? Flora watched Mrs. Fotheringay chatter and gesture, bright as a magpie. It was a picture to hold up beside Flora's image of her mother, a representation of two sorts of people—those who only skim the surface of emotion and do not really care, and the opposite. Looking around, Flora felt that the room was filled with the former. This was Lord Robert's world.

Robert had let his attention wander, wondering what the deuce Lydia Fotheringay might be saying to Flora. Victoria shot him a sharp glance. Who would have guessed that his friend's little sister could be so fierce? Still less that she harbored a crackbrained notion of marrying him? Right now, she was giving him languishing looks as she sang a song in Italian. This wouldn't do.

He looked over the younger men in the vicinity. Trevellyn was glowering at him in a promising way. Another, the heir to an earldom, had tried to elbow into Robert's current position. A couple of others were jostling in the background. Robert moved a step to the left. The young heir surged triumphantly forward, displacing him. Carrick...that was his name, Robert recalled.

"Allow me to turn the pages for you," the youngster said. "I read music perfectly."

Stepping back, Robert moved away from the pianoforte. Victoria pouted a little, but Carrick's shower of compliments on her skill soon had her smiling again.

Robert drifted down the room. Not directly to Flora, even though her presence pulled at him. Not like a moth, however. He had no doubt Victoria's

eyes were on his back. It would be maddening if
Victoria got Flora sent away just when he'd finally
kissed her. He needed to take what Sebastian would
call evasive action. The perfect answer came to him
at the same moment as a sharp exclamation from the
card table at the end of the drawing room.

Salbridge walked by, gathering Robert with a
jerk of his head. Happy to support him, Robert
walked down the room beside his host. The nearer
they got to the card table, the more tension he
felt in the air. Indeed, that corner had a whiff of
gaming hell about it. One fellow—a neighbor,
Robert thought—had the look of a man who'd lost
more than he could afford. Another seemed furious.
It was odd. Deep play did occur at some country
house parties, but not so early in the evening or in
the hostess's drawing room. And not, to his knowledge, at the Salbridges'.

Robert noted a litter of vowels in front of
Anthony Durand. His presence accounted for it.
Durand spent most of his nights in London hells,
and people said he always won more than he lost.
Which was unlikely, unless he cheated. He claimed
it was skill, of course, and no one had proven dif-
ferently. Robert remembered his father mentioning
an ugly incident. A fellow who'd accused Durand
of cheating years ago had been attacked by footpads
and nearly died. Papa had warned all of them off
playing with the man. But some here didn't know
his reputation, and others probably hadn't expected
high stakes. Robert wondered again how Durand
had gotten this invitation.

Salbridge's grim expression only heightened that mystery. "Perhaps enough cards for now, gentlemen," he said.

"Mr. Silvan may want a chance to recoup his losses," replied Durand.

He really was unpleasant—from the drawling sneer in his voice to his lounging posture, Robert thought. Durand made it aggressively obvious that he didn't care what anyone thought.

"Not me," said the neighbor. "I acknowledge I'm beat."

"Intolerable," muttered the angry man. Robert couldn't place him. But he knew Salbridge well enough to see how greatly the situation galled him.

"I'm sure the ladies would welcome your company," said their host, his tone clipped and terse. It was clearly a command.

Men rose from their chairs and began to move away. "I suppose we must do our duty and entertain them," replied Durand, languidly joining them.

Robert met Salbridge's eye, and saw his own response mirrored there. The idea of Durand entertaining the ladies held absolutely no appeal. Robert nearly asked why the deuce the man was here. Then he didn't need to. As soon as Durand left the card table, Lydia Fotheringay drifted over to him like a bit of flotsam. She didn't drape herself over him, but she gave a clear impression of doing so. Off to the side, Lady Salbridge watched, her customary serenity marred by a frown. The Fotheringay had pushed in, Robert concluded, and brought her lover with her. She was the sort of silly, stupid woman who would do that. Why, or if, Durand wished to be here was a mystery.

In the next moment, Durand shed Mrs. Fotheringay like a man scraping a bit of mud from his shoe and went to join a group of men by the fire.

Robert dismissed him from his mind. It was a large party. There would be no need to speak to Durand. He passed behind a chattering group; skirted a game of bouts-rimés, resisting pleas to join in; and ended up beside Flora. She smiled up at him, and for a moment, he lost himself in those blue depths.

"Did something go wrong with the card game?" she said.

Of course she'd noticed. She was quicker and more intelligent than anyone else in this room. He started to answer, and was interrupted by a crashing chord from the pianoforte. Heads turned throughout the room.

"I beg your pardon," called Lady Victoria with a glittering smile and a glare in their direction. "My hand slipped."

This was ridiculous, Robert thought. It had to be stopped immediately. Oddly, he found himself imagining a backing troop of brothers. But what did he imagine they could do? Sebastian was better at charging with a drawn saber than drawing-room maneuvering. James said straight out that he'd rather face a storm at sea than navigate social shoals, and Alan wouldn't be torn away from his laboratory. Nathaniel was tired of rescuing his younger siblings from their follies. Not that he'd said *follies*. And not that this was one. Still, he'd get Randolph over here sooner rather than later, Robert decided. Why not? Randolph wanted a wife.

Perhaps he could offer for Victoria. The thought made Robert smile.

Flora smiled gloriously back.

"Meet me in the corridor outside the dining room in ten minutes," he told her.

She blinked. "Is there a secret password?"

Blessedly, delightfully quick. "I want to show you something." Turning on his heel, Robert walked out. Let Victoria chew on that.

Flora joined a nearby group and listened to three young men try to top each other with tales of the tricky shots they'd managed and the number of birds they'd bagged. When ten minutes had passed by the mantel clock, she went out. She did not make a show of yawning to give the impression that she was off to bed. She did not slink furtively around the edge of the room and then slither through the doors. The best way not to be noticed was to be commonplace. She found Lord Robert where he'd said he would be. He held a branch of lighted candles.

"Come." He beckoned with his free hand and set off along the hallway.

"Where are we going?" This expedition was not strictly proper, but Flora didn't care.

"It's a surprise."

"What sort of surprise?" Her mind filled with thoughts of kisses.

"You'll like it, I promise." He turned into a crossing corridor, moving toward the east wing, which was older than the central part of the house. After a while, he turned again into a short, narrow hall with tall double doors at the end. He opened one, passed through, and held up the branch of candles. Flora stepped in just behind him into…magnificence.

It was a huge library.

Lord Robert went about lighting more candles, like a wizard illuminating further bits of a magical cave.

The paneled chamber was two stories high, with a narrow balcony running around it halfway up, reached by a fanciful spiral stair. There were armchairs, worktables, cushioned window-seat nooks, and a large, empty stone hearth. And it was positively enwrapped in books. Flora turned in circles, taking it all in.

"I understand this room hasn't been much used since the old earl died last year," Lord Robert said.

"What a waste." She walked over to the nearest bank of shelves, running her eyes over the contents.

"The family isn't bookish." Robert set down the candles and came to stand beside her. "And they're still settling in. I believe Philip comes here now and then, when he remembers his studies." He looked around. "They'd probably appreciate your expert opinion on the collection."

"But then they'll think I'm odd," countered Flora with raised eyebrows. "And it will ruin my visit."

"I did say that, didn't I?" His expression was rueful.

She nodded. The nearest books seemed to be histories, though many of the spines were hard to read in the low light.

"I worry about you, you see."

Flora met his eyes. His gaze was warm. A shiver that had nothing to do with the chill in the room went through her. At the same time, it occurred to her that she hadn't worried about him when he entered their small circle in Russell Square.

"You can sit here whenever you like. I'll ask them tomorrow to light the fire."

"Just for me? That's too much trouble, if they don't use the room."

"Nonsense. Gerald and Anne love to please their guests. Nothing they like better."

It was too tempting to resist. Flora nodded. In the silence that followed, she grew increasingly conscious of his tall figure—so near. This was the kind of place where everything had started between them, although intellectual discussion was the last thing on her mind just now. If she moved her hand just a few inches, her fingers would twine with his. If she leaned a little, she could rest her head on his shoulder. And he would kiss her.

"You're unlikely to encounter Victoria here," he said.

Flora's thoughts thudded back to Earth. "No. She dislikes books. She told me so."

"Did she?" Lord Robert shook his head. "Her fascination with me won't last. I've known Victoria since she was a schoolgirl and—"

"When you told her you'd wait for her to grow up and then marry her."

He looked at her with raised brows. "When I nodded without really paying attention, perhaps."

"That will teach you to listen."

"Oh, I've learned. I had a superb teacher."

Where had these knee-melting gazes come from? Flora wondered. He hadn't looked at her this way in

London. Or…there had been some occasions. She'd run from them. She wasn't going to do that anymore.

"I'll soon divert her," he said. "There are plenty of more alluring young men for her to choose from."

"Not really," replied Flora. Could her eyes smolder like his? She experimented, and achieved a very satisfying reaction.

Lord Robert cleared his throat. "More suited to Victoria," he added. "It may take a bit of time. I can't just dump her in some fellow's lap, you see. She's my friend's little sister. I want her to be happy. Loved."

The final word vibrated between them— portentous, breathtaking—and a mark of his innate kindness. Even in his new, masterful guise, he was still kind, Flora thought.

"So you can leave this to me. Be assured I won't let Victoria annoy you."

"I don't need rescuing!"

The fierceness of her reply startled Robert. "It isn't a matter of rescue. I'm simply better at social…adjustments than you are."

Flora appeared to be grappling with some strong emotion.

"As you are better at cuneiform than I," he said. "And always will be."

"You admit that?"

"Did I ever deny it?"

She stared up at him, an arrested look on her face. "You never did. Not once. Unlike my father's old friends, and his pupils."

"A mark of my greater intelligence," he suggested.

In the next moment, her arms were laced around

his neck, she was pulling his head down to her, and Robert had what he'd so fervently desired. To take up where that earlier, interrupted kiss had left off. He pulled her closer and did so.

She pressed against him. His lips coaxed and teased. Her body softened all along the length of his. The combination of demand and surrender was incendiary.

Robert let his hands rove a bit, tracing delicate contours, delighting when he made her breath catch. But as his fingertips feathered down her arm, the skin felt chilled. Her gown was far too thin for this cavernous, unheated room.

"You're cold." He tried wrapping his coat around them both. It didn't reach. He would have to speak to his tailor. "I'll order a fire here every day, all day," Robert declared.

Flora laughed. But she also shivered. He could give her his coat, but…it was time to go. They'd be missed eventually. And he couldn't answer for his control if this went on much longer.

Six

SOMEWHAT TO HIS SURPRISE, ROBERT FOUND THAT HE enjoyed having Plato with him at the house party. The little dog was uncannily good company. Something in his solemn gaze seemed to stimulate Robert's thought processes. Robert most often walked the dog himself, rather than fobbing off the task on a footman. Their rambles through the autumn vegetation never became the dead bore he'd anticipated.

"My brother Randolph is coming for a visit tomorrow," he told the dog as they moved through the gardens the following morning. "I think you will like him. He is also quite philosophical." When consulted, the countess had been delighted to invite Randolph, dispatching a groom at once. Randolph's enthusiastic acceptance had come back with the man. "He'll stay for the middle of the week, which fits with his clerical duties."

They passed a bed of Michaelmas daisies. Robert allowed Plato a thorough sniff among the roots. "You don't suppose Randolph *would* take Victoria off my hands?" Robert mused. "They both play the pianoforte."

Plato huffed at an iridescent beetle. It scurried away.

"No, of course not. She hates books. Randolph loves them. And also—" After Victoria's recent bouts of temper, it had occurred to Robert that termagants like Nathaniel's fearsome grandmother-in-law did not come from nowhere.

"I never imagined myself as a matchmaker," he told Plato. The irony of his position did not escape him. "More accustomed to evading lures than setting them."

They rounded a pretty copse and entered a pergola draped with grapevines. The broad leaves had turned bright yellow with the frost, and they seemed to intensify the sunshine.

Plato turned left at the end of the bright tunnel and trotted along a gravel path like an animal who knew where he was going. Past a clump of shiny holly, Robert spotted Flora and Mrs. Runyon on a garden bench. They were huddled together, and their faces suggested they were engaged in a serious discussion. Robert decided to loop around and come back later to see if he could separate Flora from her chaperone. And here was the other side of the coin, he thought wryly. "Plato," he said quietly. "This way."

The small dog did not precisely obey. He appeared to consider the command, evaluate its implications, and agree. They turned and moved along a side path.

"I must tell you something about Anthony Durand," Flora was saying to Harriet. She'd debated whether to broach this topic, and then decided that one didn't engage the help of an expert and then keep her ignorant.

Harriet frowned. "I hope he didn't presume to speak to you."

Flora shook her head. She tried to decide just what to say.

Harriet raised her eyebrows and waited.

"We both…have a connection to something that happened last spring. I'm sure you remember Lord Royalton's murder."

The older woman looked startled. "At the Prince Regent's card party. Of course. It was a nine days' wonder."

"Mr. Durand was a good friend of Royalton. And I—" Flora didn't want to think of this. She'd had one of her bad dreams in the wee hours. "Did you know Lord Royalton?"

"To bow to in passing. I never cared for the rumors I heard."

Flora drew a breath and continued in a rush. "Lord Royalton had a perverted desire for children. He entrapped and…used street children." Bitterness crept into her voice. "Because no one watches over them or minds what happens to them."

"That's horrible," said Harriet, clearly shocked. "Are you sure? How could you know such a thing?"

Flora sighed at Harriet's response. Disbelief was society's usual attitude to news like this. "A few years ago, I set up a refuge for such children in London. After a ragged little girl tried, very ineptly, to steal my purse. And I saw how thin she was, and how desperate. And then I began to see her counterparts everywhere. All around the city. Why I hadn't truly noticed before…" Flora shook her head. "At any rate, I established a place where they could have a bit of…respite."

"That's admirable, Flora." Harriet's gaze was fixed on her face.

"It seems no more than common decency to me." The next part was more difficult. "And so, I began to hear these children's stories. They are, for the most part...terrible." That was an understatement; a long litany of tragedies that had been poured into her ears haunted her. "And I came across some of the youngsters Lord Royalton had...despoiled and discarded."

"Ah." Even the imperturbable Harriet Runyon looked at a loss.

Flora left out the failure of the law, Royalton's bribes and threats, and the magistrates who could see him only as a peer of the realm, a member of their clubs, related to their wives. None of that mattered now that he was dead. "One of them used a bit of information from me to get into Carlton House and kill Royalton." No need to add that he'd made sure she couldn't stop him by tying her up in darkness.

Harriet sat back, frowning. "One can see the... motive, if not condone the action."

"The boy is long gone. There's nothing to be done." Flora didn't want to argue ethics right now. She just wanted this particular conversation over. "But it's possible that Mr. Durand might connect me with the matter. Royalton's friends were furious that the killer wasn't caught."

Harriet considered for a long moment. "He's unlikely to know about you, I would think."

Flora nodded, reassured. Although she thought the same, her stirring fears weren't external. Durand's arrival had rattled her locked mental doors. Behind them yawned a world of darkness, where things were done that fortunate people never imagined.

To admit that felt like weakness. She was not going to be weak! "I just thought you should know," she finished.

"Very wise." Harriet patted her hand. "I'm sure nothing will come of it."

Flora shoved the whole matter back into its interior cupboard and reinforced the mental locks.

A figure appeared at the curve of the path on their left and walked toward them.

"Ah, Lord Robert," Harriet observed.

Flora watched him approach. How did he stroll as if he ruled the Earth—and at the same time found that idea exquisitely humorous? Did he know he did that? She couldn't look away. She could still feel his kisses on her lips.

"With his much-discussed little dog," Harriet added.

It wasn't the sort of dog anyone would have expected him to have, Flora acknowledged, watching the little animal trot along beside him. Its parentage was a mystery, though the slashes of brown fur along its black flanks were distinctive. The large pointed ears, flopped over at the tips, ought to have been comical, but somehow weren't. They gave the dog a look of great... *Sincerity* was the only word that occurred to her.

From the look of things, he'd timed it right, Robert thought as he walked over to the bench and greeted the ladies. He got none of those "We are exchanging confidences and need no gentlemen" glares. "A fine day," he said.

"They say there'll be rain later," answered Flora, then blinked and bit her lower lip.

Her arguing was a reflex by this time, Robert observed with amusement. "Aren't we wise to be out before the weather turns then?" he responded.

"Your new pet has become a source of fascination among our fellow guests," said Mrs. Runyon. "One camp claims that it is a calculated eccentricity. Another that he is a sly joke. Both groups scorn the ladies who wax sentimental over your noble act of charity in taking him in."

"Good lord," said Robert. He hadn't heard that last bit.

"Why do you have him?" said Flora.

"I believe I would have to say, rather, that Plato has me."

"Plato?" Flora looked down at the dog. The two exchanged a long gaze. "I suppose you've forgotten that you tripped me, Plato," she said. When she raised her eyes to Robert's, he knew she was remembering the delicious moment that came after.

"Why is he staring at me?" asked Mrs. Runyon.

Plato had planted himself at the older woman's feet, and he was gazing up at her as if her fashionable form hid the secrets of the universe. "He just does that," Robert replied.

"How extraordinary," Mrs. Runyon added. "He looks as if he's weighing every virtue and flaw I possess."

"Doesn't he?" Robert was gratified to have his observations about the dog confirmed. "I met a Hindu at Sebastian's wedding who said that people can be reborn as animals after they die. They call it reincarnation."

Plato kept staring at Mrs. Runyon. The two women looked at Robert and then back at the dog.

"Are you saying that you believe he was human in a…a previous life?" asked Flora. She seemed torn between doubt and curiosity.

"I don't," Robert answered. "But there's a large country full of people who might."

Without shifting his gaze, Plato stood and took a step away from the bench. Then another. "It's as if he wants me to come with him," said Mrs. Runyon.

"We passed a fine bed of autumn roses back that way," Robert insinuated. "Perhaps he wants to show you."

Mrs. Runyon gave him a satirical look. "A few minutes," she said. "No more."

Robert gave her a smile and his best bow.

"Come then, Plato, unveil your mysteries," the older woman said. The dog started off as if he understood, and she followed.

Robert took her place on the bench. It was pure pleasure to sit beside Flora in the autumn sunshine. He wanted nothing more at the moment. But dog walking wasn't the chief reason he'd skipped the shooting again this morning. "I've remembered that Anthony Durand was a friend of Royalton's," he said. "I didn't think of it at once, probably because I dislike thinking of either of them."

She stiffened and drew slightly away from him.

"I know you don't like to speak of the murder." In fact, she'd frozen him out the one time he mentioned it, despite his crucial role in the aftermath. "But if Durand's presence should make you anxious, know that I stand ready to help."

Flora turned away. "I've told you I don't need rescuing," she replied, her voice flat.

"So you have. But should you ever need…not rescuing, you know you can call on me."

She turned back to frown at him. "Not rescuing? What is that supposed to mean?"

"That I offer you whatever my poor wits—"

"A stupid *tonnish* expression," Flora interrupted. "We both know your wits are quite keen."

"And yet you have had complaints," Robert murmured, fascinated and rather touched. He also felt a spike of pride at the compliment, an unanticipated triumph.

"I said you were insincere. Not unintelligent."

"So you did."

"And I apologized."

"More or less."

"So don't speak to me of poor wits."

"Very well." Robert suspected a conversational diversion. "You know you can trust me," he said. "For anything."

Abruptly, Flora's fierce blue eyes gleamed with a film of tears. She blinked, swallowed, looked away.

The reaction was startling, and deeply affecting from a woman so outwardly reserved. Robert wanted to sweep her into his arms. He wanted to guard her from all harm. Flora, being Flora, would rather pretend the instant of emotion had never happened, he thought. And their current situation was very public. Setting his own impulses aside, Robert stretched out his legs and leaned back on the bench. "My brother Randolph is coming for a visit," he remarked.

Flora glanced at him, and away. Her stiff posture eased a bit. "In-indeed. He is the one I have not met."

"The clerical Gresham," Robert said. "His parish is nearby."

"Is that why you came all this way?"

She was relaxing, as he intended. "One of the reasons."

"I always wanted a brother. Or a sister. I envy you your large family."

"Would you say so if you'd always been the fourth to arrive at dame school, at Eton, on the town? There was once a catchphrase in London—*Not* another Gresham."

She laughed, as Robert had meant she would. It was as satisfying as entertaining a drawing room full of fashionables.

"Randolph is quite a scholar, though he hasn't your focus."

"My limit to one arcane subject, you mean?" Flora sounded completely herself again.

"I do not. I think you'll like him."

"Oh my," said a tinkling voice nearby. "Not again?"

Robert's jaw tightened. Victoria Moreton stood at a curve of the path, frowning, arms akimbo. "What the deuce?" he muttered. "The girl is everywhere."

"I suspect she's following you," murmured Flora.

He stood. "Hello, Victoria. Did you see Mrs. Runyon? She's with us." He spoke loudly, hoping Flora's official chaperone would hear and return.

"Indeed?" Victoria made a show of looking all around, and finding no one. "Wherever can she be?"

"She walked on to look at some roses," Flora said.

"Really?" The girl marched over and plumped herself down on the bench. "I can stay with you until she *returns*."

His friend's little sister had developed a real penchant for sarcasm, Robert thought. And a hard glint he'd rarely seen in her soft brown eyes.

"We can have a *cozy chat,*" Victoria added. She made the two words sound quite threatening.

Robert sat. Victoria half turned away from him. There were moments when being a pink of the *ton* did not seem quite sufficient, he thought with a touch of amusement.

"It won't help to ignore me," Victoria said to Flora.

"What? I wasn't. I was thinking."

"Well, don't expect that to do you any good," replied the younger girl.

"We were discussing my brother's visit," Robert said. "I don't believe you've met Randolph. He's practically a neighbor now that your family is settled in Northumberland."

Victoria turned to him. "Olivia says he's the handsomest of you all. I told her that he couldn't possibly be handsomer than *you.*"

"Oh, he is." He couldn't place this Olivia. She might be worth meeting.

"You just say so?" Victoria blinked in surprise.

"Good looks aren't everything," said Flora.

"Is that what you have found through your wide *experience*?" Victoria retorted.

Flora snorted, in a soft ladylike way. He couldn't ask her to keep quiet, Robert thought. And it probably wouldn't help, even if she would do it.

"Of course, you're *much* older than I am," Victoria added.

"Practically in my dotage," Flora said before

Robert could speak. She cocked her head at Victoria. "Do you ever wonder where those terrifying old dowagers come from?" she continued. "They can't spring into life full blown at age fifty."

Victoria looked confused, while Robert was nearly surprised into a laugh at this echo of his own earlier thought.

"What do dowagers have to do with anything?" the younger girl said.

"A great deal, if you ask them," Flora replied.

Robert met Flora's eyes over Victoria's head. But just briefly. This conversation could only get worse. "May I escort you back to the house, Victoria? We're losing the sun." Clouds were thickening in the east.

The younger girl hesitated. Flora watched her consider the relative merits of remaining to get in a few more digs or walking off with the object of their…rivalry. Finally, Lady Victoria nodded and rose, taking possession of Lord Robert's arm. As they walked away, she threw a triumphant look over her shoulder—victor on the field of battle.

Several minutes passed before Harriet emerged at the turn of the path. "I beg your pardon," she said. "I swear this wretched dog led me around in circles."

Plato delivered her to the bench and then trotted off like an animal who has done his duty.

"I suppose he'll find his way back to the house," Harriet said.

"Plato seems capable of a good deal more than that."

The older woman nodded. "How unlike Lord Robert to leave you all alone."

"Lady Victoria *happened* upon us," Flora said.

"Oh dear."

"Only she didn't just happen, of course. I'm sure she's trailing after him."

"Is she?" Harriet pursed her lips. "I wouldn't have expected that, and I've known her all her life. But one can be acquainted with a young person and still be astonished at how they turn out. I've noticed it before."

The clouds were thicker. "We should go in."

"I shouldn't have left you alone," said Harriet as they headed back to the house. "We'll have to take more care."

She was obviously no good at that, Flora thought. She'd known Lady Victoria wouldn't understand, or appreciate, her remark about dowagers. But she'd gone right ahead. And she wasn't sorry. Fitting into the *haut ton* seemed less and less worth the effort. It offered none of the rewards she found in solving an intellectual problem, for example. She could go whenever she liked, Flora thought. She could head home, leaving it all behind.

"Where have you gone?" asked Harriet.

Flora turned to her friend. "You know, I could have invited Lord Robert to call in Russell Square, instead of coming here." She felt a sudden, intense longing for things to go back to the way they'd been. Or, not quite. She would keep things like kisses. "We could have avoided this silly business with Lady Victoria. I don't want to fight with her."

"Would you ask him to choose you over his world?"

"Choose?"

"Have you really considered, Flora? Robert Gresham has carved out a place for himself among the *ton*, over a number of years. He's admired, valued. Whatever you think of society, you must see that this is an achievement."

Her stern tone made Flora blink.

"And then, he worked very hard to enter your quite different social circle. Without much complaint, as I understand it. Or a great deal of encouragement."

Almost none at all, Flora thought. "It just seemed so unlikely that he meant it. At first." Her mother had also wondered what they offered the son of a duke.

"It was a rare gift, my dear. Very few men would do as much. Indeed, I can't recall another."

Flora looked up. Harriet's expression was quite serious.

"One of the reasons I was glad to bring you here," the older woman continued, "was to give you a chance to reciprocate. To show him that you are as…flexible as he was."

She hadn't thought of it this way. Flora had been good at her studies, the thing her father valued most in the world. She'd helped many street children. She'd been a steadfast companion to her mother, a bulwark against her anxieties. But here at Salbridge, she was a novice. She made mistakes. "What if I can't?"

"You can do whatever you set your mind to," replied Harriet.

"Not lawn tennis."

Harriet gave her a sidelong glance.

"I could never get the knack of lawn tennis," Flora added. And so she'd dismissed it as a waste of time. She so hated to fail that she abandoned things she wasn't good at, she realized.

"I don't think lawn tennis will be required," said

Harriet dryly. "But perhaps you would like to give Lord Robert some reasons to be proud of you. Here, and now. As he did for you?"

He had, Flora admitted silently, and she hadn't appreciated that sufficiently until the tables were turned. Lord Robert Gresham had made a vast and valiant effort to adapt to her way of living. If she refused to work as hard, if she gave up and went away…what did that say about her? Nothing she cared to hear.

Flora looked up, her jaw firm. For example, she was certain that it was going to be more difficult than Lord Robert thought to divert Lady Victoria Moreton. She'd better help him.

"Good girl," said Harriet.

Seven

As Flora was removing her hat and pelisse in her bedchamber a little later, a maid knocked with a summons. "I'm to bring you, miss," she said.

"Where?"

"Lady Victoria's orders," was the only reply.

Curious, and a bit wary, Flora followed the girl. They went upstairs rather than down, as she had expected. The maid led her along a Spartan corridor to a half-open door. A babble of female voices could be heard beyond it.

Flora entered to find Lady Victoria and all the young women guests clustered in the center of a large chamber filled with trunks and boxes. "Ah, here is Miss Jennings," said Lady Victoria. "That is everyone. Now I can reveal my scheme. We are going to enact tableaux this evening to entertain everyone."

"Tableaux?" Flora inquired, amid a chorus of delighted murmurs. She knew the word, but wasn't certain how it applied in this case. She was also a bit surprised to be included in Lady Victoria's plans with her friends.

"You don't know them?" Lady Victoria asked with condescending pity. The implication was clear: Flora was ignorant and countrified.

"They're silly," said Frances Reynolds, springing to Flora's defense. "People dress up to reproduce scenes from history or old paintings," the younger girl continued. "Then they just stand there. No one *says* anything."

"It's much more fun than charades," declared one of the others.

"If you don't want to use your wits."

"You certainly needn't participate if you don't wish to, Miss Reynolds," said Lady Victoria, moderately cutting.

"It sounds amusing," said Flora before Frances could dig herself in any deeper. She felt a strong desire to protect the younger girl from herself.

Lady Victoria went over to open one of the trunks, revealing a swath of lovely sapphire brocade. "We have all sorts of old things to use," she said. "We shall do two scenes. It's hard to manage more than that, what with changing clothes and hair."

Flora noticed that Victoria had a list. Clearly, this was not to be a democratic process.

"And ladies only," their hostess added.

"The gentlemen can admire us from the audience," said another girl with a giggle.

That was the idea, Flora realized.

"The first shall be the nine Muses, from ancient Greece."

Flora blinked. She wouldn't have expected Lady Victoria to know such a thing.

"Philip has written out a list for me," Lady Victoria went on, answering that question. "We can represent their…talents in our costumes." She consulted the page, read slowly and carefully, and pointed to one of her friends with each name. "Calliope represents epic poetry. Clio, history; you must take her, Miss Reynolds. You are so fond of history. Eu-euterpe, flutes and lyric poetry. Olivia, you can use your flute. Thalia, comedy and pastoral poetry. Mel-po-mene, tragedy. Terp-sichore, dance. I shall portray her. I love to dance! Erato, love poetry. Polyhymnia, sacred poetry, and Urania, astronomy. You must each think of ways to represent your subject."

"I could play a short piece," said Olivia.

Flora looked at her with some interest. Here was the fabled Olivia, the source of Lady Victoria's societal pronouncements. Small and slender, she looked more elfin than oracular.

"Tableaux are *silent*," Lady Victoria declared. Olivia subsided at once.

Flora waited. They were out of Muses, and she hadn't been assigned one.

"And you can be the Muses' mother, Miss Jennings, as you are older than the rest of us and much more *experienced*." Lady Victoria smirked at her.

Some noticed the dig; others were oblivious. "Did the Muses have a mother?" Flora couldn't help but ask. "Officially, I mean?"

"Mnemosyne, the goddess of memory," supplied Frances Reynolds. "I have studied *Greek*," she added when the others stared.

"We shall wear classical draperies of course," Lady

Victoria directed. "And wreaths of leaves and flowers in our hair."

"We can show off our arms," commented one of her friends.

Much of the group exchanged satisfied, sidelong glances.

"Our second tableau will be the Faerie Queen and her court," Lady Victoria continued. "I shall be the queen. We have masses of old gowns for that one." She pulled the brocade from the trunk and shook it out. It proved to be a sumptuous dress with a square-cut bodice and yards of skirt.

"Ooh, can I have wings?" said Olivia.

"If you can manage it in time," their hostess replied. "You may each decide on the sort of fairy you wish to be."

A babble of ideas filled the room.

"And Miss Jennings will be the wicked witch," said Lady Victoria over it.

There was a brief silence. The trend of her role assignments was now obvious to everyone, Flora thought. She felt increasingly amused. "I don't recall a wicked witch at the Faerie Queen's court."

"Oh yes," her unwanted adversary replied. She gave no explanation. The constraints of logic and the requirement that one must prove assertions clearly had no hold on Victoria. She said it, and so it was truth. "We have the most cunning false nose here somewhere," she added.

"There was not a witch," said Frances Reynolds.

Flora heard echoes of the bright, stubborn child she must have been in the words.

"Oh, keep your bookish quibbles for your governess," Lady Victoria retorted. "It will be very dramatic. I'm sure Miss Jennings welcomes the chance to display her *acting* ability."

Miss Reynolds looked ready to storm the barricades in Flora's defense. Flora couldn't let the girl expend her social credit in a futile battle. "Certainly," she declared, rather loudly, and was gratified to see that she'd managed to startle Lady Victoria.

There was a brief, uncertain pause, and then the room descended into happy chaos. Trunks and boxes were flung open and despoiled of their contents. Gowns of all sorts and eras were spread out for examination, a rainbow of color. A cache of elaborate powdered wigs was greeted with delight. The chamber rang with exclamations and laughter.

Flora soon found herself laughing with the others. Their excitement was contagious, and it was more and more amusing to find that she got no choices at all. For the first tableau she was provided with a shapeless tunic and a long, dark veil. The mother of the Muses hid her face, apparently. Perhaps all that memory depressed her spirits. Or bearing nine girls to Zeus, whom Frances Reynolds had identified as their father. Alliances with Zeus were not known for their happiness, Flora recalled. Lady Victoria decreed that Flora would not require a wreath of flowers in the first tableau. She would sit, it seemed, in a corner and contemplate her bevy of daughters.

For the Faerie Queen's court, Lady Victoria indeed unearthed a false nose for Flora. It was long and pointed, complete with a wart, and fastened about her head with a pair of ribbons. She also found her a stringy, gray wig and a black gown that resembled a bag more than a tailored garment. A bit of soot rubbed on her face would complete the picture perfectly, she assured Flora with false kindness.

It was irritating, and ridiculous, and increasingly funny. As Lady Victoria piled on the detail, Flora mostly thought about how young the girl was. Did she imagine anyone would care if Flora was dressed up as a witch? That it would matter a whit? Was Lady Victoria expecting magic? Did she see everyone—or more properly, Lord Robert—staring and pointing and murmuring, "Ah, Miss Jennings is evil and ugly."

Flora shrugged and began helping the others think of ways to accessorize their Muse costumes. It was actually rather interesting. Representing the different genres of poetry presented a challenge. How could epic poetry be differentiated from pastoral or sacred poetry? After some back and forth, they hit on the idea of combining a slender book with a boar spear, a sprig of greenery, and an attitude of prayer, respectively.

The Muse of love poetry declared she would simply fix the audience with a loving gaze. Exchanged glances suggested that she had a particular target in mind. The putative Melpomene stated that she would have no trouble at all looking tragic because Grecian draperies did not become her type of figure at *all*. She said it with good humor, however, and the others reassured her.

A small telescope was found. Frances Reynolds said she would use a scroll to stand for history. With rising enthusiasm, she decided to make it herself, in the style of an illuminated manuscript. Promised the use of ink and paints, she hurried off while others were still debating their choices.

Flora's aid was appreciated, and she enjoyed the intellectual exercise. Indeed, it was a relief to have a task, vastly preferable to aimless chatting. She also noticed, gradually, that these girls were not as vapid and shallow as her prejudices had led her to expect. Several were quite clever; most knew more than they perhaps even realized, absorbed from their better-educated male relatives, she supposed. They simply hadn't been given much opportunity, or reason, to learn.

On the contrary, they'd been discouraged from undertaking serious studies or projects—any endeavor that Flora's father would have defined as useful. Which was…a pity. At least, she saw it that way. She also saw that she had a tendency to judge fashionable people based on criteria that she'd accepted without personal observation. That was an eye-opening moment. In the end, Flora couldn't call the time wasted when it had been so educational and…rather fun.

Still, she was happy to slip away to the library when the group broke up. As soon as she walked through the tall double doors, a familiar peace descended. Warmed by a fire in the great stone hearth, the chamber enveloped her. It was empty—except for the sight, the promise, the *scent* of yards of books. Flora found the one she'd been reading right where she'd left it and curled up in an armchair to lose herself.

She felt a surge of disappointment when the door opened half an hour later. But it was Lord Robert, leading another gentleman.

"Oh my, what a perfectly splendid room," said the latter.

Flora stood. This must be Randolph, she thought, examining him. The resemblance was unmistakable. And he *was* better looking than his brother. Put Lord Randolph in a portrait frame, and you could present him as the epitome of the Duke of Langford's sons. He was a supremely harmonious combination of two handsome parents—the auburn hair, the piercing blue eyes, the classical features, the rangy, muscular frame. His clothes were much simpler than Lord Robert's. He wore no clerical collar; perhaps he just used it in his parish.

As Robert introduced them, he hoped that Randolph had listened to his explanations. He'd balanced the idea that Miss Jennings was a good friend—a cousin, surely he remembered—with mockery of the family rumors of unrequited love. Things were developing nicely with Flora. Brotherly commentary was not required, much less interference.

Randolph tore his gaze away from the shelves long enough to offer a bow. "Miss Jennings. So pleased to see you again after all these years."

So he had heard the part about her childhood visits to Langford, Robert thought. Good.

She acknowledged him with a smile. "Lord Randolph."

"And of course we find you in the library."

"Of course?" she replied with raised brows.

"Your father would sit nowhere else when your family visited us." Randolph's eyes strayed back to the books. "He had a favorite spot in the Langford library, a nook with an armchair hidden behind the antiquities section. Where no one ever went."

"He did?" Flora looked bemused.

Randolph nodded. "He dragged a little table in there, quite blocked it off. Just as I'd done with the west corner. If we happened to come in at the same time, we pretended not to notice each other, so we could go directly to our studies, without talking."

"That sounds like Papa." She sounded both fond and elegiac.

Randolph nodded. "I remember one day, the dinner gong rang, and we both came out. Nearly gave my father's secretary an apoplexy. He'd been working at the writing desk for an hour without realizing there was anyone else in the room."

Flora laughed. Robert met her dancing eyes. She looked lovely when she laughed. Of course, she always looked lovely.

Randolph wandered over to the shelves. "I wonder if they have any volumes on Sanskrit."

"There's a section on languages over by the window," Flora replied, pointing.

Randolph turned, clearly delighted. "You know Sanskrit?"

"Well I know what it *is*," she said. "No more than that. Are you interested in ancient Indian tongues?"

Robert wondered if his brother would tell her about the vision, and the lute. *He* couldn't. It had been a confidence.

"I met a Hindu gentleman at our brother Sebastian's wedding," Randolph said. "We had a number of fascinating talks."

An adroit answer that was not an answer, Robert thought.

"You could try here." Flora led him to a bank of shelves.

They became engrossed in book titles, throwing suggestions back and forth. "What an extraordinary girl you are," Randolph exclaimed at one point.

A bit later, he made Flora laugh again. Fleetingly, Robert wondered if he'd made a mistake, inviting Randolph. He was not, of course, jealous. But he and Flora had first come together in study. He thought of it, of the library, as theirs.

"I shall never leave this room," Randolph declared dramatically.

"You'll have to venture out to meet the other young ladies," Robert pointed out.

"Yes, of course." Randolph came away from the shelves, looking every bit as eager as he had in pursuit of Sanskrit.

"There's a fine pianoforte in the drawing room," Robert added. Randolph was justly proud of his musical talent and enjoyed showing it off. "Randolph has a splendid singing voice," he told Flora.

"You should arrange a duet with Lady Victoria, our hosts' daughter," she said. "She's quite good."

Randolph rubbed his hands together. "A fine idea."

Robert met Flora's eyes, alight with humor and mischief. So much information could be exchanged without words, he thought. He'd seen his parents do it for years. The comparison startled him. And then it transfixed him. And then it gratified him deeply.

"We've bored Robert," Randolph said. "He cares nothing for scholarship."

"That isn't true," replied Flora at once. "He has a very acute intellect."

All would be well, Robert thought, savoring his brother's surprised expression.

❦

This weather won't last, Robert thought, as he took Plato for his second constitutional late in the day. Golden light slanted across the path, gilding the trees and garden plantings. The breeze was refreshing, practically astringent, bringing intermittent flurries of colorful leaves. Undoubtedly it would be less pleasant to walk with the dog in an autumn rain or a cold snap. For now, though, he was filled with a great sense of well-being as they strolled, Plato trotting along beside him on his far-shorter legs.

Passing a pretty little gazebo, Robert thought of showing it to Flora. The same idea surfaced when they came upon a waterfall fringed with fern. She'd begun to figure in every train of thought he had. "I must settle things between us," he said aloud.

Plato stopped, sat down on the path, and looked up at him, for all the world as if he understood.

"Yes, there are a few trifling obstacles," Robert said. He made a dismissive gesture.

The little dog cocked his head. One ear flopped over.

"I shall take that as an offer of assistance," Robert said with a smile.

As if he'd made his point, the dog rose and moved on. At a junction in the path ahead, Plato went left.

"Not that way." Robert reached the crossing and

indicated the right-hand turn. "Come along." He took a few demonstrative steps.

Ignoring him, the dog continued in the opposite direction. He walked like an animal who had a definite goal in mind.

"Plato! We're going down here. It's time to head back."

His supposed pet disappeared around a curve.

"Plato, come," Robert called.

There was no response. Plato did not reappear.

Robert strode after him. "There seems to be a misunderstanding," he said when he caught up. "You are a dog, and I am your master."

Plato glanced back over his shoulder.

It was not a sneer, Robert thought. His canine... liege was simply going where he wished to go. Others' desires were not a consideration. "Or he's a dashed dog," Robert said aloud. "Without a thought in his furry head. And now I'm talking to myself as well as to an animal. It's all downhill from here, my lad. Soon you'll be addressing trees and rocks, and people will begin edging away from you with nervous sidelong looks. Plato! Come here!"

The dog trotted around a bend and out of sight.

Robert nearly left him to his own devices. Plato would come crawling back when he was hungry. But the park at Salbridge Great Hall, and the lands around, were home to foxes and badgers and, who knew, great hawks and owls that could carry off a small dog in their talons. Robert went after him. He'd *carry* him back to the house.

Robert wasn't quite within grabbing distance

when he heard voices. Plato slipped off the path into
a stand of evergreens. At the other side, he stopped
and sat.

Moving up beside him, bending to snatch him
from the ground, Robert saw Lydia Fotheringay and
Anthony Durand through the interlaced branches.
She was sitting on a bench in a small clearing. He was
pacing the turf in front of her.

If it had been anyone else, Robert would have
sneaked away at once. But the arrival of these two had
shaken Flora so deeply. Robert gave in to temptation
and stayed to listen. Plato maintained an undoglike
silence beside him.

"This place is a dead bore," said Durand as he
paced. "Salbridge has declared there's to be nothing
but low-stakes play."

"It's a coveted invitation," replied Mrs. Fotheringay.
"All society longs to be here."

The man made a slashing gesture as he moved. "You
know I care nothing for that." Every line of his stocky
body expressed restlessness. "I don't know why you do.
The Salbridges don't like you."

"Why would you say that?" She sounded hurt.

"Because I don't bother with polite fictions, my dear."

"I think you are mistaken," the thin woman protested. "Anne greeted me quite kindly."

"Oh, she's well-bred." Durand looked savage.
"How the devil am I to occupy myself? Play is intolerable with chicken stakes."

"You can hunt," offered his companion.

"Careen about the countryside with a crowd of
shouting idiots chasing furred vermin? Risk my neck

over the suicidal jumps they choose to call 'regular raspers'? I think not. Christ, I hate the country!"

"You often say you're fond of exercise."

Lydia Fotheringay's voice dropped easily into a kind of whine, Robert thought. He wouldn't have been able to endure it for any length of time.

"Proper exercise," Durand said. "Boxing. Or fencing with a decent opponent."

Robert suspected that the man just liked to hit things.

"There are some pleasant people here," Mrs. Fotheringay said. "I encountered the daughter of one of my oldest friends. I haven't seen her—my friend, I mean—in twenty years."

"Hardly a friend then." A branch brushed Durand's shoulder. He snapped it off and tossed it away.

"You're always so cruel," she complained.

Durand whirled, strode over, grabbed her upper arms, and pulled her to her feet. He loomed over her.

Mrs. Fotheringay didn't protest. But she said, "You're bruising me."

He pulled her closer, until their foreheads nearly touched. "Am I?"

Robert was reluctantly deciding that he would have to offer assistance when she pressed herself against her captor, slipping her hands under his coat. Half-seen movements suggested she was undoing the fastenings of his trousers.

"Someone might come by," said Durand. He sounded amused rather than concerned.

"I know," answered the lady.

Not wanting to see any more, Robert stepped away. He forgot to pick up Plato, but when he looked down, he found the little dog at his heels. "So you wanted to see that?" he said when they'd put some distance between them and the scene. "I fear I must deplore your taste, Plato. And your manners. None of our business, eh?"

The little dog watched him as they walked along the path. He never stumbled, even though his eyes were so often fixed on Robert rather than the terrain. It was uncannily distracting.

They came to a crossing. Robert took the right-hand path. Plato continued straight.

"Not this time. I won't be led astray again."

The dog trotted off.

"If you see a badger, run," called Robert.

As he was incapable of speech, Plato said nothing.

Within a very few minutes, Robert realized he'd made the wrong choice. This part of the grounds was a maze of twisting walks. Just when he felt he was going in the right direction, the path would turn back on itself. It was a good twenty minutes before he glimpsed rooftops through a gap in the branches, pushed through a thicket, and discovered a wider track. He strode quickly along it. A mental picture of Plato trotting up to the kitchen door and being regaled with a bowl of scraps didn't improve his temper.

Robert rounded a final clump of yew and found Anthony Durand standing on the terrace outside the house. "Come sneaking back, have you?" the man said.

"I beg your pardon?"

"Did you think I didn't see you crouched in the bushes? Like to watch, do you? Lydia puts on quite a show."

He hadn't crouched. He'd simply bent down to pick up his dog. And he hadn't watched the show. But Robert knew his position was awkward. "I came upon you quite inadvertently," he said. "I'm sorry."

"Ah, that galls you, doesn't it? Nothing worse than being forced to apologize when you don't want to. Your father taught me that. There's nothing like a duke for arrogance and effrontery."

There was nothing like a duke for learning how to handle blackguards, Robert thought. Unconsciously, his jaw firmed and his usually amiable blue eyes hardened. His resemblance to his formidable father became suddenly marked. He supposed Durand was referring to the cheating incident he'd heard gossip about. He didn't particularly care.

"You needn't pretend Langford didn't tell you," the other man added.

Robert gave him a raised brow. "We don't discuss you, actually."

Durand scowled. His hands closed into fists. "You sounded just like him there. That insufferable tone—as if it's such a bore that you're never wrong." He bared his teeth in a parody of a smile. "Suppose I send the almighty duke a note about your spying? Or your mother. Yes, Her Grace might enjoy the story more."

"Feel free," said Robert with a careless wave.

"You think they won't care that one of their precious sons likes to watch?"

"I know that they would consider the source," Robert replied.

For a moment it seemed that Durand would try to hit him. Robert braced to repel a blow, confident the fellow couldn't land one. But then Durand controlled himself. He took a step back and resumed his habitual bland sneer. "You Greshams, so damnably high-nosed. Think yourself invulnerable, don't you? Perhaps I can do you a bad turn on this visit."

"Unlikely," said Robert. "And unwise."

"Yet who would have expected me to be here? I'm not much invited into the *haut ton*. Any longer. The wolf in the fold, eh?" The man's dark eyes glinted. "I've always felt an affinity for the wolf," he said. Turning away, he walked into the house.

Robert waited a few minutes before following. He'd had enough of the man. He wondered whether he should write to his father and get the details about their past encounter. Perhaps. But he didn't really need them to decide his approach to Durand.

Eight

WEARING HER DRAB, BAGGY, NON-GRECIAN TUNIC, but not yet her veil, Flora watched Lady Victoria direct a team of Salbridge footmen, as uncompromising and efficient as a general laying out the plan of battle. A cunning set of doors had been unfolded in the large drawing room, shutting off one end for their purposes. Having shifted the furniture, the footmen were moving hefty wooden blocks about this space. They'd been constructed years ago for tableau participants to stand upon, Flora discovered when she asked. "They elevate people at different heights to create a pleasing impression," Lady Victoria told her.

The other young ladies bustled about, whispering and laughing, juggling the items they'd chosen to represent their Muses. They looked exotically lovely in their flowing draperies, with colorful wreaths of autumn leaves and flowers in their hair. They would remember this all their lives, Flora thought. As ancient grandmothers, in whatever varied places they ended up, they would tell the tale of impersonating a Muse during an elegant house party in Northumberland. She found the idea surprisingly touching. And then she laughed softly as she realized how well the thought fit with her role as the goddess of memory.

When the blocks were arranged to her satisfaction, Lady Victoria began filling them, directing one girl after another to her place. Two had to step up from a chair to their high perches, helped by their friends; Olivia looked distinctly nervous. Lady Victoria pointed at Flora and then at a low ottoman at the edge of the tableau. Flora went and sat. She draped her veil over her head, hiding a smile, and settled her unappealing skirts.

Last of all, Lady Victoria moved to her spot, the most prominent, and posed, one arm curved above her head, the other flung out to the side, her head back—a dancer frozen in an instant of ecstasy. With a flick of her fingers, she signaled the footmen.

The doors were drawn back, revealing the rest of the guests sitting and standing about the drawing room. Murmurs rose, along with a general movement toward the tableau. It was actually rather comfortable to be wearing a veil, Flora thought, as they gazed and pointed. She wasn't used to having so many eyes fixed on her. Not that they were. Their attention was focused on the Muses. Applause began at one end and spread through the group.

Where is Flora? Robert wondered as he clapped politely. She'd left with the other young ladies to prepare for the tableau, but he didn't see her among them. He ran his eyes over the draped figures once again. Those old Greeks had some good notions about the female form. The soft draperies flattered their youthful curves, except for the one brandishing a dagger with bared teeth. He didn't blame her for looking Friday-faced. The dress wasn't suited to her thin frame.

Then he spotted Flora, sitting on a stool at the side, nearly covered in a dark veil. What was she supposed to be? He counted the figures. Nine Muses, and there were nine young ladies in various poses. Flora made ten. Which made no sense. Except that she was clearly meant to be set apart, her loveliness obscured.

He watched her, trying to see beyond the gauzy fabric over her face. You could cover her with a sack—well, Victoria had done pretty much that—and still he was drawn to her. He had the feeling she was looking back at him, though he couldn't really tell. As the applause died away, footmen closed the folding doors, and she was gone.

The latch clicked, and all around Flora the tableau dissolved into mayhem. Girls jumped or were helped down from their perches. They rushed toward a door at the end of the room, causing a brief scuffle in the doorway as everyone tried to be the first through. In a parlor that had been set aside for their purposes, a team of housemaids waited to help ten young women change their clothing and hair and ornaments at top speed. Flora had to laugh as she joined the melee. The excitement and enjoyment were contagious.

"Here's your nose, miss," said one of the maids. Flora turned to find her holding out the false append-age, ribbons dangling. "Lady Victoria said to be sure you found it."

"I wager she did," Flora replied as she took it, but

she felt no real rancor. This playacting, even the petty spite, felt like a children's game of dress up. She'd played very few games as a child. Unless you counted her father's imaginative play to help her learn Akkadian symbols, which she knew most people wouldn't. She'd enjoyed those, but they hadn't had the lighthearted quality of this romp. There was no risk of disappointing a revered parent here, or failing to achieve an important goal. She could simply…be silly. It was fun.

An hour later, the next tableau was ready, orchestrated and approved by Lady Victoria, resplendent in the sapphire brocade gown. Flora had thrown herself into her witchy role. She wore the lumpy, pointed nose, stringy, gray wig, and shapeless black dress with all the panache she could muster. She'd even put the soot on her face. From her obscure corner of the scene, she posed scowling, with her fingers crooked into claws and a secret giggle. The footmen went to the folding door and awaited Lady Victoria's nod.

The doors opened. Robert took in the new scene, and laughed.

"What is it?" asked Randolph at his side.

"Sheer appreciation."

His brother gave him a quizzical look. When Robert said no more, he added, "Lady Victoria makes a credible fairy queen."

"Marvelously autocratic," answered Robert.

"I'm not sure about those wings on…Miss Townsend, is it? That sort of fairy doesn't fit with this scene. And why is there a witch?"

"I suppose they wanted one." There was no supposing about it, Robert thought. Victoria was trying again to make Flora look bad. This gambit had a touch of the ridiculous. He caught Flora's gaze and saw his conclusions laughingly mirrored there. They exchanged a long look full of amusement.

"Well, the witch is an intrusion from quite another tradition," Randolph declared. "Fairy tale and fairy court—totally different things." He looked offended. "I'll explain the mistake to Lady Victoria."

"I doubt that would be well received," Robert told him.

"Miss Reynolds seems to be holding some kind of magic wand," said Randolph, giving no sign of having heard. "Not really proper either. I'm certain Lady Victoria will wish to know. For any future tableaux she organizes."

"I don't think so," Robert said. It was amazing how much could be conveyed in a look. Flora couldn't move a muscle, and yet they were in secret communication across the long room. Amusement shifted into something deeper. The crowd faded into irrelevance around him.

"The gowns and wigs are interesting," said Randolph, continuing his assessment. "A sort of last-century reinterpretation of a classic theme."

The applause started up, and they both joined in. And then doors folded back over the tableau, and the crowd returned to their flirting and gossiping. Or, in Randolph's case, critiquing.

Flora followed the other young ladies into a second melee in the parlor. This one was far more competitive than the last as they vied to be first into the drawing room in their customary clothing. Unsurprisingly,

Lady Victoria won. The maids had been instructed to attend her first, Flora suspected. She waited for the room to clear out a bit, and for a servant to bring her a basin of hot water to clean off the soot. By the time she made it back to the others, Lady Victoria was surrounded by a complimentary circle. Flora joined a cluster of her fellow posers nearby.

"You did very well indeed," young Lord Carrick was saying to Lady Victoria.

Flora examined him. He was the son of an earl, if she remembered Harriet's descriptions correctly. A handsome young man—not tall but well set up, with regular features and reddish hair nearly the color of Lord Robert's. That might be an attraction for the daughter of the house. His eyes were ivy green, sparkling with conviction just now. Clearly, he took this business of posing just as seriously as Lady Victoria did. He'd been very enthusiastic about her musical skills, too. Perhaps he'd make her a good husband?

Lord Robert came up beside him. "Fond of tableaux, are you?"

Flora sidled a bit closer.

"I enjoy all sorts of theatricals," Lord Carrick replied. "Last year we put on an entire play at my parents' home. Well, a shortened version. *The Rivals*—Sheridan, you know. It was great fun, and very much admired by my mother's guests."

"Indeed?" said Lord Robert. "You know, I daresay the two of you could organize something like that here."

Lady Victoria and Lord Carrick gazed at each other. Flora could see possibilities dawning in their eyes.

"You'd be so good at that," Flora put in. Lady

Victoria shot her a suspicious glance, Lord Robert a warning one. She subsided.

"It would give us fellows a chance to show our mettle before an audience," Lord Carrick said.

"It might be amusing." Lady Victoria looked at Robert. "You would join in?"

Flora hid a smile at his expression. He hadn't counted on that.

"Not really my forte," he murmured.

"Choosing the right person for each role is the greatest challenge," declared Lord Carrick. "One cannot simply assume—"

"We'd have to include all our *friends*," Lady Victoria interrupted. She gave Lord Robert a militant glance.

He made a gesture that might have been a concession. Flora didn't think he'd be evading a role, if there was a play.

"I would have to ask Mama, of course. But I should like to try it."

The group fell into a spirited discussion about what kind of drama would be best. Lord Robert faded unobtrusively back, making his way to her side. "So, a witch, eh?" he said when he reached her.

His blue eyes brimmed with humor. A dozen other occasions when they'd shared a joke came back to her. She hadn't valued that gift enough, until now. "By special request," she replied.

"Was that soot on your face?"

Did anyone else smile with that combination of irony and warmth? "It was. For verisimilitude."

"I suppose witches are continually leaning over cauldrons."

"Dropping nasty ingredients into their potions and getting smoke in their faces," she replied.

He laughed.

She'd always enjoyed making him laugh, Flora realized. Even when they were arguing. Perhaps especially then.

"You must consult with us, Lord Robert," called Lady Victoria.

His face showed reluctance. Flora nodded to show that she understood. "We should ask my brother's opinion," Lord Robert suggested as he moved back into the fray. "Randolph has staged some quite elaborate pageants."

Aware that their ploy of promoting amateur theatricals would go better without her presence, Flora walked down the room. She looked around for Harriet, and was waylaid by Lydia Fotheringay. "There you are," the latter said brightly. As if Flora hadn't been in plain sight for some time. "We must have a good talk." The thin woman took Flora's arm and led her over to a vacant sofa. There was no escaping her without blatant rudeness. "I have been thinking so much of your dear mama," she said. Settling her amber satin skirts, she fixed her eyes on Flora. "You don't resemble her greatly."

"I look more like my father," said Flora stiffly. She didn't know how to talk to this woman. It was so hard to believe that she could have forgotten snubbing her mother.

Mrs. Fotheringay nodded. "We met when we were only five years old, you know," she went on, as if Flora's father hadn't been mentioned. "Our families were neighbors."

Flora did know. How many times had her mother marveled at the wreck of such a long friendship?

"We were sent to school together," said Lydia Fotheringay. "Agatha was such a scholar. And I was always a perfect dunce."

Her glancing look and titter invited Flora to laugh with her. Feeling as if she'd wandered into a phantasmagoria, Flora forced herself to smile back, and not to flinch when her companion leaned closer.

"Sometimes, she did my assignments for me," Mrs. Fotheringay confided. "If I begged her long enough."

Flora didn't understand how her mother could have been friends with this woman in the first place.

"The teachers were so cruel. They seemed to think that I failed to understand what they were telling me on *purpose*."

Against her will, Flora felt a thread of sympathy. What would it be like to be unable to learn? What if she'd failed to absorb her father's instruction? Because she simply *couldn't*. That would have been dreadful in so many ways. But this woman had treated Mama badly. What had happened? She couldn't help herself. "The last time you and Mama met, you were not glad to see her," she said.

Mrs. Fotheringay looked blank. "Impossible."

"It was at the Lansdownes' evening party." Flora had heard the story a hundred times. "Twenty-five years ago. She came over to speak to you, and you turned away from her."

"Oh, I couldn't have!"

"You gave her the cut direct." Flora held her hazel eyes, refusing to back off.

"You must be mistaken." Lydia Fotheringay squirmed in her seat like a child accused of naughtiness. "That was a lifetime ago."

Flora nodded. It was… Her lifetime.

Mrs. Fotheringay's fingers plucked at her skirts. She made a petulant face, then went still. "Twenty-five years?" she said then. "In the spring?"

"It was during the season," Flora said. Her mother had ventured into her former haunts among the *ton* despite the storm of disapproval over her "lowly" marriage.

"Ah." Her companion looked away. "I was rather… distracted that year."

"But you were at the party," Flora said.

"Yes. I was just married, and…well, you are not such a very young lady. I can tell you that I had found my husband sadly wanting in…the physical aspects of matrimony." She made a vague gesture. At the same time, she was gazing out at the chattering crowd, smiling brightly.

Flora gazed at her, unwillingly fascinated.

"I was puzzling what to do." Mrs. Fotheringay tittered. "I soon found quite a number of gentlemen with ideas about *that*."

What had this to do with the matter? Flora wondered.

"So, you see, I think you *must* be wrong," the older woman added. "I would have loved to have seen Agatha right then. I was sorely in need of advice."

Had her mother been so certain she'd be rejected that she mistook her old friend's distraction for a snub? Flora felt guilty thinking it. Yet she didn't believe Mrs. Fotheringay was lying.

The other woman sat straighter, as if shaking off

an unwanted cloak. "And if I didn't see her, it can't matter now, after all this time."

What would her mother do when she learned that her years of social exile were based on a misapprehension? Should Flora even tell her? Which regret was worse—a lost friendship or years of unnecessary resentment? No, Mama would want to know the truth.

"I found my way," Mrs. Fotheringay said. Her tone had changed, become sly and caressing. "Other friends. Allow me to present one." She beckoned, and Mr. Durand came over.

Flora was caught by surprise.

"Miss Jennings, may I make Anthony Durand known to you? Anthony, Miss Flora Jennings."

He gave her a slight bow, his gaze running over her form before fixing on her face. "Jennings, is it? Jennings. Have we met?"

She wasn't certain how to refuse an introduction to the man, a sanctioned guest, standing right in front of them. "No," she said.

"Ah, I thought I had heard the name."

"It isn't uncommon." Pinpoints of candlelight glinted in Durand's dark eyes; they felt like drills boring into her.

"I mentioned her," Lydia Fotheringay said. "Miss Jennings is the daughter of an old friend."

"That must be it," he agreed.

The older woman tossed her head flirtatiously. "He doesn't listen to a word I say."

Flora could believe it. He was ignoring her right now, and he hadn't been attentive at other times either.

Flora became aware of an approaching figure. Sir

Liam Malloy was moving toward them as fast as was decent in a countess's drawing room. He stopped beside Durand.

"Ah, a knight in shining armor," murmured the latter, obviously amused.

"What was that?" said Mrs. Fotheringay. "I didn't hear you."

Sir Liam greeted them all with a small bow. "Miss Jennings, I wondered if you would care to take a turn about the room?"

"Charging in, lances ready?" Durand's tone was openly mocking. "Can you do no better than that, Malloy? Where is your address?"

"Pardon a bluff Irishman," Sir Liam replied. The way he locked eyes with Durand said something quite different.

The man gave him a small ironic wave and turned away.

"You're not going?" exclaimed Lydia Fotheringay.

"I am clearly de trop, my dear."

"No, you're not!" She looked around their group, her large eyes indignant.

"I'm afraid you're mistaken. As you so often are. But you may come with me, if you like." He offered an arm.

Mrs. Fotheringay hesitated, frowning. Then she rose and took it. "I don't see why *we* should go," she said as they moved away. "He interrupted. Rather rudely, I thought."

Sir Liam Malloy sat down beside Flora. "She shouldn't have introduced you to that fellow," he said.

"You know him?"

"Not personally. I'd heard of him, I think. Certainly I've learned a good deal more here."

"People talk about him?" Flora was relieved to be out of Durand's looming presence.

"I should say they do. He won four hundred pounds at cards the other night. From a neighbor who can't well afford such an amount. Salbridge is furious."

"That's a great deal of money." Even in circles like these, it was a significant sum. Modest households lived a year on less.

"I shouldn't have mentioned that," said Sir Liam.

"Are only gentlemen to know about it?"

"Something like that." He smiled at her.

It was interesting how you could sense a good deal about people without words, Flora thought. Sir Liam "felt" kind and open and…balanced. She smiled back. "Thank you for stepping in."

He sketched a seated bow. "A privilege to be of service."

Flora noticed that Lord Robert was frowning at her. She wondered if something had gone wrong with the plan. As he turned back to his brother, she couldn't help comparing her impressions of him and Sir Liam. One sensed kindness in Lord Robert, yes, and intelligence and the engrained manners of a nobleman, but there was also a…thrill. His presence stirred her. It had since he walked into her home in the spring. She hadn't recognized the sensation at first. Or she'd refused to. Did anyone welcome a force that turned life upside down?

"Miss Jennings?"

Her companion had said something. She didn't know

what, which was not acceptable. "Tell me more about India," Flora replied, pulling her attention back to him.

Chafing at the tedious discussion of theatrical details, Robert told himself that all was well. Malloy had gotten rid of Durand. Rather adroitly, as far as he could judge. However, the fellow was leaning close to Flora now, looking for all the world as if he was about to take her hand, blast him.

"Do you think so, Lord Robert?" asked Victoria.

"I believe I am rather more familiar with the process," Carrick replied.

"I've no doubt about that at all," Robert answered.

An elbow in the ribs was his reward. "You're not paying the least attention," said Victoria. "You are ignoring me…us. I thought a pink of the *ton* was supposed to have exquisite manners."

His friend Laurence's little sister appeared to know very little about manners. "I was deferring to Randolph for, er, well-honed aesthetic opinions."

Randolph fielded this unexpected lob with aplomb. The twinkle in his eyes suggested that he understood a bit more than Robert might have wished, however.

"We can do quite well without help," Carrick said before Randolph could answer. His expression suggested that he wanted no interference from that quarter.

"Indeed." Robert offered an encouraging smile. "You and Victoria seem to make a splendid team. I'm sure the two of you will create—"

"The three of us," said Victoria, taking possession of Robert's arm. "We shall put on the play together." She looked complacent, like a cat who has not only found the cream pot but cornered the market on it.

Nine

THE FOLLOWING MORNING, FLORA ROSE EARLY, breakfasted before most of the other guests, and went to the library in search of solitude. She was accustomed to more of this commodity than the other people here. At home, she was often alone for hours, reading or writing. A legacy from her scholarly father, solitude was a habit in her family. And so she craved it, now and then, as a balance to the activities of the house party. But she didn't wish to simply sit in her bedroom.

The library wasn't empty, however. Lord Philip hunched over the large worktable, books piled around his elbows, head in his hands. When Flora came in, he stood at once, looking delighted at the interruption. "Grinding along on my Greek," he said, clearly ready to drop all thought of study and talk to her. "I'm off to Oxford in the new year, you know. Been preparing for ages. For all the good it does me."

Flora hid her disappointment and walked over to him, waving him back into his chair.

"I don't want to look like a fool," he went on. "I've had quite enough of that." Lord Philip waved his hands as if batting away bothersome insects. "Flailing along after Laurence and Victoria. You have no idea what that's like."

Flora hadn't met his elder brother, but she could see that Victoria must be a challenging sister. "You'll be on your own at Oxford," she suggested. "No comparisons. You can forge a place for yourself."

"I usually flub it," he replied gloomily. "Think of the paille-maille game. What a debacle."

His expression was so woebegone that Flora felt sorry for him. She didn't see how she could help, though. She knew no Greek. Then an idea occurred to her. "You should ask Lord Robert for advice." The more she thought about this, the more sensible it seemed. Robert had been to university. He had three older brothers and must know what it was like to feel overshadowed. Though she couldn't quite imagine that. "One of his brothers lives in Oxford. I'm sure he'd be glad to introduce you."

"I don't know." Her young companion looked dubious.

"He's extremely intelligent," Flora retorted. "A fine scholar, as I can attest." She hadn't asked Robert about his university career. No, she'd been too busy thinking about herself.

Lord Philip looked startled at her tone. "Oh, I'm sure. It's just…he mightn't want to bother with me."

"Why not? He's a friend of your family."

"Of Laurence, mostly. And Lord Robert is… He just never puts a foot wrong, does he? He's rather intimidating."

"Do you find him so?" Flora gazed at this young son of an earl, gauging the respect in his brown eyes.

"Well, yes." Lord Philip shrugged. "He's all one wishes to be."

It was like turning around on a forest path and discovering that the way looked entirely different from the opposite perspective, Flora thought. The Robert she thought she'd gotten to know was only one facet of a remarkable individual.

When she thought of him now, it was Robert, not Lord Robert, she realized. Which was odd, here among the nobility. Shouldn't it have been the other way around?

Her young companion was frowning at her. She'd speak to Robert about helping him before she made any promises, Flora decided. Then, feeling she'd done enough, she left the lad to his books, despite an expression designed to melt a heart of stone. She was not abandoning him to a dreadful fate, she told herself. He needed to study.

Fetching her bonnet and pelisse, Flora set off for a walk. The Salbridge grounds offered plenty of scope for solitude. She'd heard her hosts describing a "wilderness" they'd had especially planted. It sounded like just the place to find…nobody.

The October day was gray and chilly, with scudding clouds above but not much wind at ground level. The last leaves were dropping from the trees. Glad of her gloves, Flora walked quickly across the perfect lawn, through a border of trees, over another less-manicured stretch of grass, and onto a path that twisted into tall bushes. Their branches were so thick and intertwined that the absence of foliage made no difference; they screened the outer world completely. From that point, the landscape on either side grew wilder with each step.

As she walked, the history of her association with Robert Gresham passed through her mind. But this time the scenes looked different. Robert had skipped various fashionable events of the season to spend hours at her side, poring over dusty clay tablets. He'd read an entire book on Akkadian religious epithets. Why had she been so blind? And so stubborn?

With a rustle of fallen leaves, a small dark creature shot from the bushes on her left. Flora jumped back, heart pounding, and nearly tripped. It took her a moment to realize that Plato stood on the path before her. She looked around for Robert but saw no sign of him. "Hello?" she called.

There was no reply.

The little dog stared solemnly up at her. "What are you doing out on your own?" she asked.

Flora had heard some of the young gentlemen visitors talking of a badger sett in the park. Badgers sometimes hunted, and caught, rabbits. Plato was not a great deal larger than a rabbit. "You should go back to the house."

As if he understood, the dog walked a little way back along the path. Then he stopped and looked over his shoulder as if waiting for her to join him.

"Go on," said Flora. She made a shooing motion.

Plato sat and stared at her.

It was so easy to imagine intelligence in his expression. "I want a walk," she said. "Will you force me to carry you back to the house instead?"

Plato harrumphed.

"You are the oddest dog," Flora commented. She stepped forward, reaching for him. He moved just enough to evade her grasp. Flora went quickly after him; he veered away. She lunged. He hopped over one of her hands and trotted a little way down the path, then waited for her again. "Plato! Come."

The little dog tossed his head, as if signaling, "We are going this way."

"Well, I am not," declared Flora, a bit irritated by his antics. "And it seems to me you are clever enough to escape any badger ever born." She turned her back on him and strode away.

Spotting a narrower walk, she plunged into it. There were no signs of cultivation here. Shrubs and saplings crowded forward as if eager to overrun the path. She might have been miles from civilization.

Something caught at her skirts. Turning to look, Flora found that Robert's eccentric dog had followed her and was tugging at her pelisse with his teeth. "Plato! No." She pulled at the cloth with one hand and reached for the scruff of his neck with the other. Plato let go and danced back along the path. "You are the most vexing creature. Return to the house at once!"

Not bothering to see if he obeyed—because she was certain he wouldn't—Flora strode on. One side of the path was now a wall of brambles, rising well above her head. A few dried-out berries clung to the inner reaches, behind a barricade of thorns.

A protruding bit of bramble caught the side of Flora's pelisse. She twisted to reach for it, and a whole raft of briars shifted with her, entangling the other side of her skirts, her right arm, and the brim of her bonnet. If she pulled away, it would rip the cloth. She struggled a little; more thorns dug in. "Blast it, I suppose you were right, you wretched dog," she exclaimed, and discovered that Plato was gone.

Flora lifted a hand to free her hat. The movement tipped another part of the bush, which swayed and seemed to grab at her. A second branch lodged in her bonnet. She felt several claw at her back. A stem lashed across her neck. That one drew blood. She tried to step back, and was pricked by more thorns, through her clothes, from all directions.

Flora went very still. She saw that the path petered out just ahead. Or perhaps this hadn't been a path at all, but merely a deceptive opening in the vegetation. She hadn't been paying attention. She tried again to move. She was trapped in a sea of briars. The thorns were long and wickedly barbed. They pricked the skin of her neck, her arm, her back, her side.

Flora stopped moving. It did no good to be exasperated, much less afraid. If she was very careful, she'd soon be free.

But no matter how meticulously she worked, for each thorn she managed to pry loose, another dug in. She could get out, of course, if she was willing to ruin her clothes and slash her skin. She could feel blood trickling down her neck. She imagined returning to the house looking as if she'd been savaged by a pack of mad cats. Doubtless she would encounter an immaculate Lady Victoria on the doorstep, all too ready to sneer.

She became aware of a rustling in the leaves near

her feet. What next? The badgers? Snakes? No, of course not snakes. It was far too cold.

A small black-furred head poked through an opening at the base of the briars. Evading the thorns with no visible effort, Plato emerged and stared up at her. "Oh, you're back, are you?" said Flora. He sat down at her feet. "Come to gloat? Point out that if I'd followed you, I wouldn't be in this predicament?"

Plato looked at her. Not judgmentally, because that was impossible.

"Go fetch help," commanded Flora.

The dog didn't move.

"Some clever gardeners. A footman from the house. Anyone. Go!"

"Plato? Where are you, you dratted animal?" called a voice nearby. "There are badgers in here. Salbridge told me. A half-grown badger could tear you limb from limb without breaking a sweat."

Great minds move in similar directions, thought Flora. "Lord Robert?" she called.

There was a short silence. "Flora?"

"Yes. I've, ah, become entangled in some brambles."

"Keep talking so I can find you," he answered.

"I'm quite stuck," said Flora. "In these thorn bushes. Plato doesn't appear to care in the least. Or, actually, he's staring at me as if it was all my fault." She frowned down at the dog. "Does he ever blink? He's really a bit uncanny, don't you—"

Robert appeared on the path. "Good God!" He started forward.

"Be careful! It's very easy to get caught. If you touch one branch, the whole mass moves."

"I see." He examined the arching stems. "You really *are* caught, aren't you?" His lips twitched.

"If you laugh, I'll…make you sorry," Flora promised. Plato made one of his odd grumpy gargling sounds. "And you! I'll *find* a badger and hand you over to him."

Robert choked. "So, would you say you're in need of rescue?"

"Just get me out!"

Robert moved a few steps closer. He could see that the thorns had barbs like fishhooks, ready to rip and tear if not removed very carefully. There was a trickle of blood on Flora's neck. After a moment of calculation, he eeled between two branches. He had to stop once and detach thorns from his sleeve before he reached her side.

"These things are diabolical," she said. "When I turned to pull loose, they seemed to…sort of lunge at me."

Robert nodded as he evaluated her plight. She was likely to become even more entangled if he attempted to work the thorns out here. He'd probably suffer the same fate. Reaching carefully inside his coat, he slipped his penknife from the pocket of his waistcoat and opened it. "I'm going to cut the branches that are stuck to you," he said.

"Then I can move to a clear spot to remove the thorns. Good idea." When Flora nodded, she pulled at the briars on her bonnet. Another sprig latched onto the brim.

"Stay very still."

"I know!" She let out a huff of breath. "I beg

your pardon. This is…rather irritating." She smiled an apology.

Robert felt a catch in his chest, as if his heart had stumbled briefly. "Right then. Move back, Plato," he said. For once, the little dog obeyed him, slipping easily out to a more open spot.

He began on the closest branch, embedded in the skirts of Flora's pelisse. He had to kneel to reach it properly. His knife was small for the tough fibers. The bush swayed as he sawed at the branch. A spray of thorns rasped across his hair, but didn't catch hold.

Robert soon pricked his skin. There was no way to hold the branch still without being stuck, and he'd left his gloves indoors when he'd seen Plato shoot wildly out of the bushes and then go haring off again.

Blood made the blasted thing slippery. Robert got out his handkerchief, used it to wrap the branch, and went back to work. At last, he was through. The severed stem sprang back a little, he was glad to see, giving him a few inches of working room. He looked up. "One down," he said with a smile.

The heated gaze he encountered went through him like a thunderbolt. He was suddenly acutely aware of his position, right in among her skirts. His shoulder rested against her thigh. The scent of her—flowery perfume and sheer female—enveloped him.

"You've hurt yourself," she said.

"It's nothing." Intensely aroused, Robert eased to his feet. Flora smiled at him again. Her fierce blue eyes raked him. He knew, absolutely, that she was remembering their kisses.

Robert turned to the stem that lay across her

neck—the worst of them, because the thorns had broken her skin. He had to move very carefully, or they'd both be shredded. His hand couldn't tremble.

The sawing of the knife inevitably moved the thorns. For all his care, they dug in a little as he worked. Robert gritted his teeth when a droplet of blood ran down to the collar of her pelisse. Then the briar was severed, no longer pulling at her.

The next branch was wrapped around her far sleeve. He had to press close to her to avoid the briars at his back as he reached for it. And stay there while he cut through the stringy fiber of the bramble. The feel of her—curve of breast and hip, her cheek resting on his chest—made him clumsier. At one point a thorn drove deep into the pad of his index finger, and he stifled an oath.

"I'm sorry," she murmured, her voice a vibration in his body as well as a musical sound.

"Don't be silly." The words came out rough with yearning. He heard it, and he was sure she did, too. Without moving from his intoxicating position, Robert lifted his hands to the briars twisted in her bonnet.

Flora was having trouble breathing. She could feel his heartbeat, so near her ear, accelerating in tandem with her own. She could feel his muscles shift against her as he cut at the brambles. If she looked up, carefully, she could see his face—handsome, intent. The lips that had thrilled her were only inches away. But she couldn't move enough to offer her own again. She had to remain very still, plastered against him.

She felt her bonnet come free from the thorns. Then his hands were on her shoulders, turning her slightly, and her side was pressed against him as he dealt with the branch snaked along her back. She was in his arms. It felt very good.

Robert sawed at the final stem, wondering if the pressure of her hip on his groin would drive him mad. All the fingertips on his left hand were bloody now, but he didn't feel it.

The last fibers parted. The branch sprang back. Leaving one arm around Flora, Robert carefully guided her out of the brambles. Plato still sat there, watching them like a builder supervising a tricky construction job.

Robert wiped the blood from his fingers. The pulse of desire was so strong that they trembled a little. "I should remove the thorns at your neck," he said.

Flora nodded, her eyes fixed on him in a way that further enflamed him.

She stood still as he detached the barbs as gently as possible, one by one, his fingers repeatedly brushing the silken skin of her neck. At one point, her breath caught. "Did I hurt you? I'm sorry."

"No. You didn't hurt me." She raised a hand and touched his cheek.

Finally, the last thorn came away from her neck. Robert refolded his handkerchief to the cleanest part and pressed it to the line of tiny wounds. "Hold this for a bit." Their hands touched as Flora complied.

And then he kissed her. He didn't pull her close. He simply lowered his head and took her lips for his own. Her mouth was warm and pliable under his, eager and encouraging. She leaned into the kiss with equal fervor.

Robert felt as if he might go up in flames. Irresistibly, his hands started to rove, and caught on a line of thorns along her back. With an impatient exclamation, he drew back.

Flora supposed she could have removed the rest of the barbs herself. Most of them. But she didn't want to move away from him. Indeed, she leaned closer, dizzy with his kiss and the clean masculine scent of him. His hands were gentle and authoritative as he detached the thorns one by one—from her shoulder, her arm, her back. He knelt again to deal with the branch twined in her skirts. Her throat tightened as she looked down on his bent head. She wanted to twine her fingers in his auburn hair. When he finished and stood, she felt oddly bereft.

"Best take off your bonnet, I think," he said.

She untied the ribbons and pulled it free. Strands of her hair came loose and blew out on the breeze, black streamers. Despite the brisk autumn weather, she felt hot.

Robert took the hat. "This may spoil the trimming," he said, starting to detach a thorn.

"I can do that later," she said, taking it back. She dropped the bonnet on the ground and laced her arms around his neck.

She wanted a kiss that went on and on. She wanted more than kisses. She wanted everything. Months of denied desire flooded through her.

Robert responded ardently, gently, fiercely. As Flora melted against him, her defenses crumbled and fell. All the yearning she'd locked away rushed out. She pulled him closer.

And without warning, a tide of very different emotion roiled and twisted and shook Flora as a terrier does a rat.

It wasn't the first time he'd freed her. Last spring, he'd found her imprisoned in darkness, left there by the youngster set on killing Royalton. He'd dashed in, bringing light and exclamations, and untied the ropes knotted around her. The rescue had been an immense relief, and a humiliation—to have made a stupid mistake, to have been caught, to be helpless. She hated the idea of the damsel in distress. And the complacent fellow who plucks the poor creature from her folly. She was not that witless girl; she was intelligent, self-sufficient, strong.

Flora looked up into Robert's handsome face. She'd been pushing him away partly because of that past history, she realized. It wasn't only wariness about the difference in their stations in life. She didn't wish to feel less, to owe a humble gratitude.

Concern showed in his expression, warring with the heat in his blue eyes. "Are you all right?" he said. His embrace had slackened. "What is it?"

How could understanding one's behavior be more unsettling than ignorance? Flora wondered. Her father had taught her that it was always better to know. But she was profoundly shaken. She had to step back.

Her expression had gone tragic, and he had no idea why. Robert resisted his impulse to enfold her in his arms again. She took another step back. "I should go back to the house," she murmured.

"I'm very sorry if I've offended you," Robert couldn't help saying.

"You have not *offended* me!" she cried, as if the complete opposite was true.

It wouldn't do to press her now, Robert thought. And

whatever had gone wrong, a wilderness of thorns was not the place to mend it. He would get to the bottom of this later. He bent and picked up the discarded bonnet and his handkerchief, which she'd dropped.

She took the bonnet from him. Ignoring the spray of bramble that still swayed on its brim, she jammed it on her head, pushing loose strands of black hair under the edges. Her hands were shaking as she tied the ribbons.

He knew she'd enjoyed kissing him. There could be no doubt about that.

At their feet, Plato offered one of his curmudgeonly grumbles.

Robert grasped the opportunity. "We'll hear nothing from *you*," he said to the dog. "You have a ruined bonnet and a stained handkerchief chalked up to your account, sir."

Flora choked out a laugh.

"And we both know what Bailey will say about these." Robert bent to show his dog five bloody fingertips. "Bailey is my valet," he told Flora as he straightened. "He and Plato are not friends. Not even remotely."

"I-I begin to think you're right about Plato being reincarnated," said Flora, picking up his cue.

"The return of Oliver Cromwell, perhaps?" suggested Robert. "Or Louis the Fourteenth? Caligula?"

She laughed wholeheartedly this time, which had been his goal. He offered his arm. She took it. They walked back along the path. Plato paced them.

"It's…it's odd, the way he moves and stares at the same time," said Flora.

"It's more than odd. It's bizarre. And I've never seen him stumble."

"He has the strangest expression. As if he would solve all one's problems if he could only speak."

Plato trotted along, eyes on them.

"An idiotic idea," Flora added.

"Oh no, I've often thought the same." Robert looked at his dog. It occurred to him that Plato didn't stray. Every time he'd run off, he'd taken Robert to some quite particular location. Perhaps he was, rather, Machiavelli reborn.

At the edge of the thicket, Flora paused. "What if someone—Lady Victoria—sees us coming out of the shrubbery together? Disheveled." She put a hand to her ravaged bonnet.

Robert didn't want to let her go. He'd had some idea of slipping into the library, he realized, and having a quiet talk. But she was right. Reluctantly, he stepped back. Flora walked quickly, back straight, clearly hoping she could reach her room without encountering any of the other guests.

He watched her hurry into the house. "Nothing goes easily with her, Plato."

The door closed. She was gone.

"And yet, would I want it to?" Robert mused. "Her complexity is surely part of the…fascination."

He turned back. "We will loop around and come out elsewhere."

When Robert finally emerged from the trees, two strolling couples on the other side of the lawn waved to him. He acknowledged the greetings cordially.

Ten

AS SOON AS ROBERT ENTERED THE DRAWING ROOM after dinner that evening, Victoria pounced. She'd clearly been lying in wait, a lurker in pink satin. She grasped his arm with both hands and tugged, obviously intending to drag him to her lair—a sofa in the corner—and monopolize his attention.

It wouldn't do. Her behavior was starting to be marked; much more of this, and people would whisper. He didn't want that for his friend's little sister. He was also rather weary of Victoria's conversation. She was very young and not well informed. So rather than allow himself to be maneuvered, Robert deployed his reinforcements. "I hope you are going to play for us," he said to the girl. A gesture brought Randolph to his side. "I know my brother would welcome the chance to join in. His singing voice is much admired, and I've told him of your talents."

Victoria preened a little as Randolph bowed. "I'd be delighted to try a duet," he said.

She nodded. But Robert was not to be allowed to escape so easily. "Come and help choose a song," Victoria said to him.

She was going to have to learn, soon, that not everyone could be commanded, he thought. But he went along for now. He had no intention of approaching Flora in this setting.

They walked over to the pianoforte. Randolph and Victoria rifled through the sheet music kept nearby. Their tastes did not match.

Robert turned from the escalating dispute to watch Flora brood. He had no doubt that she was. He knew her face in many moods. He'd traced them over weeks in Russell Square as they worked together. He missed that time far more than he'd ever thought he would. How surprising to learn something new about himself at his age! That was the point, he thought. The person who showed you new parts of yourself was the one you—

"Oh no," said Randolph forcefully.

"Lord Robert likes *this* one," Victoria declared.

They turned in tandem to face him.

"You said it was a pretty melody," Victoria added, exhibiting the music for a tune called "Evermore."

Like anyone else, he sometimes spoke absentmindedly, Robert thought. But he was certain he hadn't said this.

"Sentimental tosh," Randolph objected.

"How can you say that?" exclaimed Victoria.

"Because it is the truth. The phrasing is trite. The—"

"Lord Robert is choosing!"

They crowded closer. Robert faced his dilemma. Lose a bit of his brother's aesthetic respect, or prolong this tedious argument. "Yes, sing that one," he said. He could mend matters with Randolph later.

With a triumphant glance, Victoria sat down at the

instrument. Randolph stood beside her. To one who knew him well—a brother, for example—it was clear that he was irritated. He'd best woo a lady who shared his musical sensibilities, Robert concluded.

"Ladies and gentlemen," said Robert. "A duet."

People turned to the pianoforte. Robert stepped back, then faded further into the mass of guests. Victoria played some introductory notes, and then they began to sing.

They sounded quite good together, Robert thought, watching Flora drift toward the door. Lingering conversations were dying down. Some were moving closer to the singers. It was easy, in the general shift, to move unnoticed to the entry.

There was a sudden discordance. The music stopped. "You can't change the key in the middle of a song," Randolph said loudly.

"I did no such thing!" cried Victoria. "You were flat."

"Flat!"

Carrick rushed over to offer his opinion. Trevellyn waded in to say that he was sure Lady Victoria was right. The crowd focused on this new form of entertainment.

Aware that Randolph could hold his own, and more, in any musical discussion, Robert slipped out of the room on Flora's heels.

"Are you on your way to the library?" he asked as he caught up with her.

"I— Yes, I was."

"We've been very comfortable in such rooms, haven't we?"

"I have been," she replied with a touch of her old acerbity. "You seem comfortable anywhere."

Gently, he drew her hand through his arm. She was stiff as they walked along the corridor.

"You want an explanation," Flora said as they entered the library. She pulled away.

"We can talk as we used to," he replied. He sat down on the small sofa beside the fire, so as not to loom over her.

She laughed without humor. "You want to have an argument?" She didn't settle. She paced. The skirts of her gown swished in the quiet chamber. "One moment I'm kissing you, and the next I'm pushing you away," she went on. "You must think me erratic, or a tease."

"Never that."

"It's about last spring," she blurted out. "When Royalton's murderer tied me up and left me."

Puzzled and concerned, Robert watched her face. He wanted to pull her into his arms, to banish all distress. As if that was possible.

"I was alone and afraid. You came and found me." She said it as if it was a shameful admission.

"Rescue." Was this why the word had such weight for her?

"Yes, I couldn't do it myself."

"None of us is—"

Flora rushed on, words pouring out as she kept pacing. "And then you just…went on, as if nothing had happened. You chatted and laughed, the same as ever. But I had nightmares." Her blue eyes evaded his.

"I suffered one day of anxiety as I searched for you," Robert said. "Not so very much to bear. It was quite different for you, imprisoned. And you've listened to the sad stories of street children for years."

Flora stood still, staring at him, her lips open in astonishment.

"Trying to soothe the ones who woke screaming in the night," Robert added. "To comfort the ones who wept, pale and silent. Ease those who lashed out in fury."

"How do you—"

"Did you think I didn't listen?" Robert asked her. "When you told me about the work of your refuge?"

"But I never... I didn't say all that." Flora was deeply shaken. The phrases he'd used captured the terror of the streets so exactly.

"The details were there between the lines," he said. "In your tone, your face. In passing remarks from those who worked with you."

Flora found her hands were shaking. Her eyes filled with tears. "But you were strong. I was weak."

"I would *never* use that word about you."

She didn't quite hear him. "I pretended to take it as easily as you did. I tried to shut it all away." The locks on her inner fortress rattled and strained.

"So that's why."

"Why what?" Flora tried to interpret the look on his face.

"Why you said it was intolerable to think of the matter, when I asked if you couldn't bear to think that I'd done you a service."

She remembered the humiliating way her voice had wavered. "I don't want your pity." Or worse, disappointment, she thought.

"You'll get none." He looked thoughtful. "Durand's presence can't be helpful."

"No. He's another reminder of Royalton and… all that."

"Another? Ah, you mean that I am one as well." Robert's expression went wry.

Flora was desperately afraid that she'd really hurt him, this man who'd seemed invulnerable. "No. You aren't! All your actions were admirable." Her throat tightened. "Only today…after you'd freed me again…" Her hands closed at her sides. She forced out a difficult admission. "The dark comes rushing back sometimes. I can't tell when it will happen. And I can't seem to stop it."

"So this lies between us," he murmured. "Actually, I'm relieved. It's more logical than those endless disputes about pretense."

"Logical?" Flora cried. "It's supremely illogical. Ridiculous. The murder happened months ago. I should be over it!"

"Should." He shrugged. "You'll find your way. I've never met anyone with more tenacity." He smiled at her.

There was such warmth in that smile. It held none of the impatience and contempt she'd lavished on herself. Flora caught her breath on a sob.

"It occurs to me that we should examine this difficulty together," Robert went on. "We have much better ideas that way, after all."

Flora gazed at him as the mantel clock clicked off several seconds. Then she sank down on the sofa and threw herself into his arms.

Robert held her. She was trembling. There could be no question of more just now, and he found he didn't mind. How many different sorts of embrace might one discover over a lifetime? he wondered. His father would know something about that.

After a while, he felt her trembling stop. Flora relaxed against him. Matters grew more complicated then. He wanted her desperately. And he was not made of stone.

Robert made the sacrifice of letting her go. He didn't allow the disappointment in her face to sway him. Some truly precious things in life could not be hurried.

❧

The amateur theatricals were approved by Victoria's parents, igniting a flurry of conversation and activity. All the young ladies were entranced by the idea, and a number of the young gentlemen were lured away from the hunting by the thought of performance—or spending hours in the close company of pretty girls. Older visitors and men addicted to the chase reacted with disbelief, amusement, or indifference, according to their temperaments and interests.

"I'm sorry I won't be able to join in," Randolph said as Robert saw him off the following morning. "But duty calls." He mounted his horse. "I'll be back to see the play. Lady Salbridge was kind enough to invite me."

"I imagine Victoria will have forgiven you by then," Robert couldn't help replying.

"She? What of me? I've never hit a flat note in my life."

"You're a man of the cloth. Forgiveness is obligatory."

Randolph looked down at his brother with a sardonic quirk of his eyebrows. "Fortunate for you, as you so often require it."

Robert laughed. He felt remarkably well this morning. Strolling back inside as Randolph rode away, Robert wondered where Flora was at this moment. Their first meeting after the confidences of last night was a matter of some delicacy.

"There you are!" Victoria came up from behind and took his arm. "Where did you go last night?"

This really must end, Robert thought. Beyond the present irritation, he had far more important things to do in pursuit of his... Dare he call it courtship? What else?

"After you made me sing with your brother." Victoria pouted prettily. She waited for a reply. He made none. It would have been enough to discourage any other girl. Victoria merely tugged at his arm. "Come along. We're beginning on the play. The performance is set for two weeks from today."

"So soon." Robert allowed himself to be chivvied one more time. He must find an opportunity. It was past time to detach Victoria once and for all.

"Lord Carrick is promised to another house party in Lincolnshire after that. And he refused to leave his copies of the play with us. So very disobliging of him."

It had been decided that the group would put on *The Rivals*, the play that had been so successful at Carrick's home. He'd sent for the copies they'd used, and seemed poised to take over the entire endeavor.

Victoria led Robert to the drawing room, where those interested in theatricals had gathered. The group came alert, like a pack of hounds catching a scent, when they arrived. Amused, Robert watched people eye each other in uncertain rivalry—some shy, others avid for a role. It soon became apparent that their hopes were irrelevant. Victoria intended to hand out the roles, and Carrick had his own plan, as well as the instincts of an autocrat.

"It is my home providing the stage and costumes and so on," Victoria sweetly pointed out.

Carrick gave her a courteous bow. "I have the experience and skills to make the play go smoothly."

"A gentleman always defers to a lady," she replied.

"Clever ladies are guided by gentlemen's wider knowledge of the world," he suggested.

Their voices increased in volume with each exchange. If they'd been navies, the knives would have come out next, Robert thought.

In the end it was decided that Carrick would hold auditions for some of the roles during the afternoon, while Victoria would decide others by her own methods. As the latter included consulting Robert on every point—and then ignoring his responses—he couldn't slip away to the library. Or, he could have, certainly. But escape wasn't the problem. If Victoria trailed after him, as she had been doing, that book-filled refuge would be lost. Robert set himself to make use of the play for his own purposes instead, much as he begrudged the time.

The final disposition was set for the following morning, in the ballroom of Salbridge Great Hall, which had been given over to the play. The huge chamber was chilly, even with fires lit in the great hearths at each end. It was meant to be warmed by crowds of dancers, Robert thought, as he sat in one of a circle of gilt chairs. Rain trickled down the glass doors that lined two sides of the room. The young ladies needed their thick shawls. He rather wished he'd worn his greatcoat.

"Be quiet, please," said Victoria.

Her voice was crisp and authoritative. She held a list. Carrick, in the chair beside her, looked sullen. She would rule her future family, and country neighborhood, with a rod of iron, Robert thought.

"After extensive consultation—and Lord Carrick's auditions, of course—we have decided on a list of players." Victoria smiled like a queen certain of her power, and relishing it. "I shall play the chief female part—Lydia Languish, a young heiress."

She made no apologies for appropriating the main role. Indeed, the idea clearly had not entered her mind.

"Lord Carrick will play the hero," the daughter of the house continued, "Captain Jack Absolute, disguised as Ensign Beverley."

She had tried to foist that role onto Robert. But he'd refused. After a quick look through the play, he'd agreed to do the hero's father.

Victoria turned graciously to Carrick, handing him her list. He took it with poor grace but perked up as he became the center of attention. "I would like to say, first, that some of our number have exhibited a real talent for acting," he began. "I was most pleasantly surprised. That is to say, impressed. For example, Miss

Frances Reynolds showed quite a gift for pathos. She will take the role of Julia Melville, a young relation of the Absolutes."

The young, fair girl sitting across from Robert looked astonished, then delighted.

"And also Mr. Edward Trevellyn, who had an unaffected ease in his reading. He will play Bob Acres, a friend of Jack Absolute," Carrick continued.

Robert eyed the stocky, bluff Trevellyn. He would have expected the fellow to mock their efforts and bluster off hunting. Then he noticed the way he was watching Victoria, like a cat at a mousehole.

"We intend to ask Sir Liam Malloy to portray Sir Lucius O'Trigger, an Irish baronet," Carrick said. "He's Irish, after all. And a knight."

Victoria nodded. Robert wondered if Sir Liam knew about this. He wasn't here, and hadn't shown the least interest in acting.

"Wrentham shall play Faulkland, a friend of Jack Absolute," said the earl's heir.

It made sense that he would choose one of his cronies, Robert thought.

"And Mrs. Malaprop, Lydia's middle-aged guardian will be played by Miss Flora Jennings," finished Carrick.

Robert hid a start of surprise. Victoria hadn't told him this. Flora hadn't applied for a role, and she wouldn't like being given one by fiat. Carrick didn't seem very pleased at his own announcement, either.

"It's too bad that some of our number are not here," said Victoria severely. "I shall speak to them afterward."

"The remaining four parts, the servants, will be

played by different people in successive scenes," Carrick went on. "This will allow everyone who wished it to have some time on stage."

"But that will be confusing," said Victoria, clearly hearing this for the first time.

"The audience will follow along."

"No, they won't."

"They did so when we put on the play before."

"That is nonsensical."

"We don't wish to leave people out," Carrick said. Looking around, Victoria saw that the group's opinion was against her. "Everyone must begin learning their parts right away," she said in a bid to regain the upper hand.

"We will start rehearsals tomorrow," Carrick put in.

There were murmurs of dismay.

"You can read from the pages at first. Until you have the speeches by heart." Carrick picked up a cloth bag that sat at his feet. "If you haven't yet gotten a copy of the play, I will give you one now."

People rose and surged forward. Victoria snatched three of the copies and started toward the ballroom door. He'd have liked to warn Flora, Robert thought. But he had no hope of getting to her first.

"What?" said Flora a few minutes later. "No, I am not going to act in the play." She stood before Lady Victoria, who sat on a sofa by the drawing room fire like the queen receiving supplicants at court. Lady Victoria had sent a footman to fetch Flora on this wet day.

"It is all decided," replied the younger girl. "You can't cry off now."

"It's not crying off if you never agreed to something in the first place."

Lady Victoria thrust a sheaf of paper at her with a steely glint in her brown eyes. "People are expected to join in and be entertaining at house parties," she said. "I suppose you may not know, since you are never invited, but it isn't done to hide and sulk."

"Sulk?" The girl really was exasperating. Had the footman said where she was? The thought of Lady Victoria hunting her down in the library was unpleasant.

"Everything can't be arranged for *your* amusement," Lady Victoria said. "I'm sure you wouldn't wish to ruin the play for everyone else."

"I would not, of course. But I have no doubt one of your friends would be glad to take...whatever role you've assigned to me."

"Oh no. It's simply meant for you."

The smirk on her face told Flora the story. "Am I to be a witch? Or a heavily veiled mythological parent?"

"You were so good in the tableaux at portraying old—"

"Hags?"

"Older ladies, I was going to say. And you can't be so rude as to refuse when I ask you to join in one of our...communal activities." Lady Victoria held out the sheaf of paper again, shaking it a little.

"Why do you want me in the play? You dislike it whenever I come near Lord Robert." Curiosity over-came Flora—one of her chief strengths, or besetting sins, depending on who you asked. "Why do you wish to marry Lord Robert?"

The girl blinked, as if startled once again by Flora's frankness.

"I mean, why him, especially?" Flora wondered. "You have a number of suitors."

"He is the son of a duke," said Lady Victoria.

"True, but he's not the eldest. He will have no title. Not like Lord Carrick or Lord Fanshawe."

"He is in the first stare of fashion. He knows exactly how to go on in society. I shall set fashions myself. Everyone will envy me." The girl's brown eyes grew distant. "We'll go to all the best parties. You can't say anything to discourage me. I shan't listen."

Lady Victoria wasn't thinking of Robert the man, Flora realized. She saw only the leader of the *ton*. She knew nothing of his intelligence, his kindness. She didn't even seem moved by his dizzying physical attractions. And Lady Victoria hadn't considered that Robert's fortune was modest, that he would have no great country estate like Salbridge, no neighborhood for her to rule.

"Have you stopped listening to me again?" her companion demanded.

"Sorry. I was thinking."

"How can he like you, when you are so very annoying?" Lady Victoria flapped the pages at Flora.

"Another consideration for you. Is his taste infallible?" Flora felt a laugh bubbling up. She swallowed it. "I really don't wish to be in the play."

"As a representative of the family, your hosts, I insist."

What was she going to do, go to the girl's parents and complain about being asked to join in a "jolly" project? Flora took the sheaf of paper.

With a sound very like a triumphant *ha*, Lady Victoria turned her attention to her pile of lists.

She was spoiled, Flora thought as she walked away. The only daughter of the family. It occurred to Flora that she was also an only daughter. An only child, actually, and she wasn't spoiled. Was she? Had Papa given her too high an opinion of her intellectual abilities? He'd been a hard taskmaster, never lavish with praise. Had her mother coddled her? No. More often it had been the other way around. With a sigh, Flora found a chair, opened the play, and began to read.

Eleven

SOFAS AND COMFORTABLE CHAIRS HAD BEEN MOVED into the ballroom, with small tables to hold branches of candles, a welcome light on this damp, dreary day. Flora had taken a seat to finish reading the play, but she was diverted by the buzz of activity, and reminded that the tableaux had turned out to be good fun.

Not far away, a mixed group of eight sat in a loose circle reading out bits of dialogue to each other and laughing. They were to alternate playing the servants, Flora had been informed, and they clearly meant to enjoy doing so.

Lady Victoria and Mr. Trevellyn occupied a sofa on the other side of the room. They were bent over their copies of the play, talking quietly. At the far end, near one of the blazing fireplaces, Lord Carrick supervised Frances Reynolds and Mr. Wrentham as they read through a scene they shared. He scarcely let them finish a sentence without interruption, Flora noticed. It must be quite irritating.

Sir Liam Malloy walked in. Spotting Flora, he came

and sat down beside her. "My fellow conscript in a troop of volunteers, I understand," he said.

"You were also…persuaded to join in?"

"Persuaded? I was press-ganged by our hosts' imperious daughter," he replied with a wry smile. "She gave me to understand that only an unbearable slowtop would refuse her."

Flora laughed. "It may be amusing after all. The character I've been assigned is…unusual. Listen to this." She read from the page before her. "'Oh! It gives me the hydrostatics to such a degree. I thought she had persisted from corresponding with him; but, behold, this very day, I have interceded another letter from the fellow; I believe I have it in my pocket.'" She looked up to meet Sir Liam's acute blue eyes. "What is *hydrostatics* meant to be, do you think?"

"Still water?" he ventured. "That is what the Latin roots would suggest."

Flora nodded. "But it makes no sense in context. Nor does 'had persisted from.'"

"Oh, context." He shrugged. A shout of laughter from the servant group made him turn to look at them.

"Here's another," said Flora. "'There's nothing to be hoped for from her! She's as headstrong as an allegory on the banks of Nile.'" She met his eyes, smiling. "It seems it should be *alligator*, should it not? Or to be correct, *crocodile*, for the Nile. Yet *allegory* calls up such a funny picture."

"I'm glad you're pleased," replied Sir Liam. He tapped the pages he held. "My role is dashed offensive. This Sir Lucius O'Trigger embodies every prejudice and cliché about the Irish. He is, in a word, a buffoon."

Thinking about what she'd read, Flora had to acknowledge the truth of this.

"If I'd looked at it before I agreed to participate… but no, Lady Victoria was not to be denied."

"No one could confuse you with such a person."

"I hope not! But I don't expect to enjoy strutting about and spouting stupidities."

"You need not strut," Flora suggested.

"No, no, no," declared Lord Carrick. His voice carried throughout the room. "You must speak with far more emotion at this point."

Sir Liam cocked his head in that direction. "You think not? I believe our guiding lights will insist I do precisely that. And more. I shudder to think how they will dress me."

"Lord Carrick does seem keen on supervising," Flora replied.

"Dictating, rather. He's autocratic as a Russian tsar. Or one of his own illustrious ancestors, I suppose. No doubt they excelled at oppressing their peasants."

"Perhaps you are exaggerating a bit," said Flora, amused.

"You think so? He's already told me that I needn't think I can do as I like with my role just because I didn't audition for him."

"Oh dear."

"And on top of it all, I must get this drivel by heart," Sir Liam complained. "As if I was back in school learning lines of poetry. I hate memorizing."

"Miss Jennings will have no difficulty with that," said a familiar voice from above.

Flora looked up to find Lord Robert standing next

to her chair. Reaction crackled through her. She'd been more aware of him than ever since their last conversation in the library. And less certain of what to say.

"She has a finely trained mind," added Robert, sitting down with them.

"I'd noticed."

It was no wonder that Malloy was taken with her, Robert thought. Any discerning man would be. That didn't mean he enjoyed the sight, however.

"Perhaps she can aid me," Sir Liam said. "I've never found it easy to keep set speeches in my head."

"There are some techniques that help," Flora answered.

Robert didn't care for the picture this conjured—the two of them bent together, collaborating.

"I would be delighted to put myself in your hands," said Sir Liam.

The amusement in the man's voice, and the glance he gave him, made Robert lower his eyelids.

"I daresay you would be a splendid teacher," said Sir Liam.

The fellow was goading him, Robert concluded with a certain amount of sardonic appreciation. His grandfather would have been able to leap up, declare that he found Malloy's tone damned offensive, and challenge him to a duel. But dawn meetings were not only illegal now, they were dashed bad *ton*. A silly idea. "I think Mr. Trevellyn wished to speak to you," he told Sir Liam instead.

The Irishman raised his dark brows. "Really?" Robert was about to urge him on when he rose with a smile. "It seems *The Rivals* may be an apt title for our little endeavor," he said. With a smile and a small bow, he at last went away.

He'd have to keep a sharp eye on Malloy, Robert thought. He was quick.

Flora indulged in a moment's gratification. She'd never had two gentlemen contending over her before. The young men who flocked around her father were far more interested in academic debate. "I've never seen Mr. Trevellyn talk to Sir Liam," she observed dryly. She watched over Robert's shoulder as the two met. "He seems rather surprised at Sir Liam's arrival."

"The play will give them an opportunity to get to know each other," Robert answered, equally dryly. "I had to get rid of him so that we could plot."

"Plot?" Flora's heightened self-consciousness lessened as they exchanged a smile.

"Ways to shift Victoria's interest onto a suitable young man," he explained. "And make her forget her idea of marrying me. All the reasonable candidates are part of this play, I believe."

"*You* are matchmaking?"

She was laughing at him, and he was glad. Anything to lighten the shadow he'd seen on her face in the library. "What next, eh? I thought at first that she and Carrick were a good fit."

"Oh no, they would…eviscerate each other."

"A grisly image." They watched Victoria stride over to dispute some point with Carrick. His face blazed with anger. He waved his hands as he contradicted her point by point. "Disputes can be a sign that one cares," Robert added. "Very much indeed."

His eyes locked with Flora's. It seemed to him that

the fire he knew, and loved, in hers was dimmed. He longed to take her hand or put an arm around her. It was frustrating to be surrounded by others. He missed the times they'd pored over arcane texts, minds alight, thoughts chiming together. Despite the differences in their upbringing and experience, they were kindred spirits. Their bodies had leaped in tandem.. But now this shadow of the past had fallen between them.

"I, uh, I think Mr. Trevellyn is a more likely candidate," Flora said.

Lost in thought, Robert only half heard her.

"Lord Robert, we need to consult you," called Victoria across the large room, her tone commanding.

Robert rose. They might as well have been onstage already, with all these observers around them. Conscious of Victoria's glare, Robert gave Flora a jaunty smile and turned away.

Over the next few days, the play took over the lives of those involved in it. Looking around the ballroom on a sunny afternoon, Flora marveled at the degrees of application she could see. It was more than she'd expected of the fashionable set. As far as she knew, only she and Lord Robert had ever applied their intellects to such masses of words. But these young people were struggling to memorize great rafts of text, and then learn to speak them with natural emotion. Even though the play was rather silly, their dedication wasn't.

Those who were good at it—Frances Reynolds and, to everyone's continuing surprise, Edward Trevellyn—enjoyed themselves. Others had a harder time. Flora saw Lady Victoria scowling over her pages. The daughter of the house was finding it impossible to learn her speeches. She still read from the page whenever they rehearsed bits of the play. It was making Lord Carrick frantic and leading to a great deal of shouting.

Frances Reynolds came over and sat down beside Flora. The younger girl looked far more relaxed and happy than she had in the early days of Flora's visit. She'd found her social "feet" with the play. "Who would have predicted that Mr. Trevellyn would be so helpful?" she said quietly. "I could hardly get him to give me a spoonful of blancmange."

The gentleman in question had joined Lady Victoria. He'd made it his business to aid her with her role. His face as he bent toward her was both ardent and kind.

"I admit he has surprised me," replied Flora. "I'd put him down as a dull countryman." She'd already suggested that Robert could point up the contrast between them.

"Do you think Mr. Wrentham is very handsome?" said Frances.

Flora turned to the younger girl. Her budding assurance and increased animation made her prettier. "You do know that he is only acting your beau," she replied. "In the play."

"Of course!"

"Unless there is more happening when you two go off in the corner to *review your scenes*," she teased.

Frances blushed. It was very visible on her fair skin.

"Aha!" said Flora.

"No. I'm not sure. I don't expect… We must see when the performance is over."

"Ah, there he is now." Mr. Wrentham had entered the ballroom. It certainly seemed to Flora that he searched at once for Frances Reynolds. Their eyes caught, and the girl hurried over to join him.

Flora's smile lingered as Robert took the girl's place next to her. "Matchmaking might be easier if they were the ones in question."

"I think you're doing quite well."

"Victoria is growing increasingly annoyed with me," he agreed. "You seem to be enjoying your own part."

"I am rather. Mrs. Malaprop is ridiculous, but the wordplay in her speeches is funny." Flora struck a pose. "'There, sir, an attack upon my language! What do you think of that? An aspersion upon my parts of speech!'"

"I would never cast an aspersion on your parts of speech," Robert put in, smiling.

"'Was ever such a brute!'" Flora continued. "'Sure, if I reprehend anything in this world, it is the use of my oracular tongue, and a nice derangement of epitaphs!'"

Robert burst out laughing. "Derangement of epitaphs?"

"I know."

"One pictures dancing gravestones."

"Or wandering, muttering ones. Cemetery bedlam."

"Oracular tongue, indeed," he murmured.

"And then there's this one: 'But the point we would request of you is, that you will promise to forget this fellow—to illiterate him, I say, quite from your memory.'" Flora leaned toward him. "I think one should say *ill-it-er-ate*, don't you? Rather than *il-lit-er-ut*? So that one gets *obliterate* as well as unable to read."

"Precisely," said Robert.

"Sheridan's wordplay is delicious. Did you ever meet him? I believe he died just a few years ago."

"I did. He was nearly as witty in person as on the page."

Lord Carrick swooped in then and snatched Robert, organizing him, Sir Liam, and Mr. Wrentham to repeat one of their scenes together. Flora watched wistfully. She didn't want to think of dark episodes from the past when she saw him. Was there no escape? They'd had no time to speak of it again.

"Flora?" said Frances.

She started and pulled her mind back to the present. The girl was standing before her. "What?"

"Will you listen to my speeches and correct me if I go wrong?"

"Of course." She took the pages Frances held out and followed along as the girl recited her lines. Frances was well along at memorizing them all.

It was too bad that Randolph couldn't be here, Robert thought a bit later, as he finally escaped Carrick's oversight. His brother would enjoy this play far more than he did. Randolph would fling himself into the drama, only now and then remembering that he was a parson and injecting a touch of solemnity. His eyes would twinkle as he did, though. On the other hand, Randolph's enthusiasm would most likely collide with Carrick's lofty pronouncements and Victoria's demands. Fleetingly, Robert wished for Sebastian. His military brother would mock their prancing and posturing with a curled lip. Sebastian had a curious vendetta against anything to do with words.

Robert wouldn't have minded seeing how Carrick liked that.

The younger man was lecturing one of the gentlemen playing a servant on the proper humble posture. He moved on to scolding Frances Reynolds for reading speeches from the printed page. Carrick could declaim all of his, with considerable verve, from memory. Of course he'd done this whole thing before, Robert thought. People forgot that when they praised Carrick to the skies for his skill. He was better than the rest of them in the way a seasoned cricket player was better than a tyro. He had, one might say, cheated. Robert rather enjoyed addressing him in his character as irate father and calling him feckless and insolent. But the lad was clearly not for Victoria. Flora was right about that.

Flora came up to do a scene next. Her Mrs. Malaprop soon attracted attention and set people laughing.

"'Since you desire it, we will not anticipate the past!'" she declaimed. Like Carrick, she had no need to consult the written page. "'So mind, young people—our retrospection will be all to the future.'"

Victoria had made a mistake in shoving Flora into that part, Robert thought, smiling. Victoria could glower all she liked. She could lumber Flora with a stringy wig and dowdy dress. But the audience was going to love her. And Victoria was not going to make a good showing unless her memorization skills showed miraculous improvement.

"Well done," said Carrick when Flora finished. "You have Mrs. Malaprop to the life, Miss Jennings."

Others clustered around her, adding their compliments. Robert watched, filled with admiration and…love. Yes, it was past time to admit it. He loved her with all his heart. He believed she cared as much for him. He'd felt it in her kiss, seen it in her eyes, heard it in their shared laughter. The rest ought to be easy. An offer, a wedding, and the rest of his life spent in a sweet, invigorating dance with this amazing woman. He—they—had to find a way through or over or around the thing that kept them apart.

An elbow in his ribs brought him back to the ballroom. "You are not listening to me," Victoria said.

Robert looked down. "Miss Jennings might be able to give you pointers on how to keep speeches in your head," he replied.

Victoria shot him a look laden with gratifying fury.

Miss Frances Reynolds and Mr. Wrentham came forward. Somehow it had come about that they must all demonstrate their progress to Carrick today. These two were playing the secondary set of lovers in the play.

"'I never can be happy in your absence,'" declared Miss Reynolds with a remarkable degree of fervor. "'If I wear a countenance of content, it is to show that my mind holds no doubt of my Faulkland's truth. If I seemed sad, it were to make malice triumph; and say, that I had fixed my heart on one, who left me to lament his roving, and my own credulity. Believe me, Faulkland, I mean not to upbraid you, when I say, that I have often dressed sorrow in smiles, lest my friends should guess whose unkindness had caused my tears.'"

She rolled out the playwright's words as if they were her own. The girl really was doing a fine job, Robert thought, both in learning them and saying them.

Wrentham sneaked a look at the written page. "'You were ever all goodness to me. Oh, I am a brute, when I but admit a doubt of your true constancy!'"

Miss Reynolds gave him a melting look before going on. It was returned full measure. Well, Wrentham was not for Victoria either, Robert thought. Either these two were deep into their roles, or…they were deep into something else.

⁓

Two weeks could pass frighteningly quickly when you had to stand before an audience at the end and risk making a fool of yourself, Flora thought. With the performance just two days away, the group around her in the ballroom thought of little else. Indeed, they scarcely saw their fellow guests except at dinner. She'd spoken no more than a few words to Harriet in days.

"You are aware that you cannot read from a manuscript on stage," Carrick said at the other end of the large chamber. His tone was cold and cutting.

"We don't have a stage," snapped Lady Victoria. She'd been stumbling through one of her long speeches, with frequent references to the copy of the play she held. She looked near tears—angry tears, but tears nonetheless.

"The point is, you will ruin all unless you *learn your part*," Carrick said.

Robert had made a rare misjudgment there, Flora thought. These two both wanted to be in charge—of everything, all the time. It was fortunate they'd had a chance to become better acquainted. Lord Carrick had come to the house party as one of Lady Victoria's suitors; he would be leaving as...well, not an enemy, perhaps. But less than a friend.

Edward Trevellyn stepped between them. "It is impossible for Lady Victoria to ruin anything," he said. "And have I not heard that actual theaters have a person, er, designated to stand at the side and supply the words, should an actor forget a few."

Here it was again, Flora thought—Mr. Trevellyn revealing unexpected facets of character right before their eyes. Perhaps he'd known of the existence of prompters, but she suspected that he'd made a point of inquiring. When she first met him, she wouldn't have thought him capable of the idea or the efforts he'd made lately.

"A sort of human crutch?" Robert said. "For the orally feeble?"

Flora choked. If she hadn't known that Robert was trying to put Lady Victoria off, she'd have been shocked at his unkindness.

The younger girl whirled on him. "You are... horrid, utterly horrid! How could I have thought you charming? Or admirable? I've never been so mistaken about a person in my life."

She launched into a tirade, enumerating his many faults. Though Flora recognized that it was provoked, and that the girl was taking out her fear and frustration about the play on Robert, it was still uncomfortable to witness. Others in the room turned away or laughed nervously or observed with a connoisseur's enjoyment, according to their different temperaments.

Flora met Robert's eyes and saw her thought

processes mirrored there. They shared one of those moments of perfect understanding that made him so very…riveting.

Lady Victoria strode out of the room in a froth of muslin. Edward Trevellyn started to follow, but Lord Carrick called him back. "We must work out the movements in your last scene," he insisted. With obvious reluctance, Mr. Trevellyn came back.

Robert strolled across the room and stopped beside Flora. Several people gave him disapproving looks. Frances Reynolds glared at him. "I believe I'm off the hook," he said.

"I should say so. At the risk of your reputation for being agreeable."

"Ah." He looked around the room. "Well, couldn't be helped. I'll have to retrieve it through, er, social good works."

"Social… What would those entail?" When his blue eyes laughed down into hers, it was hard to see anything else. She simply wanted to fall into them.

"Oh, teaching a few young sprigs how to tie a neckcloth. Dancing with one or two neglected young ladies. Ingratiating myself with the dowagers."

"And you are very good at that."

"When I want to be."

He kept looking at her. All impediments had been removed, his expression seemed to suggest. Life now opened up to them, a spacious playground. "Will Lady Victoria forgive you so easily?" Flora asked.

"Not for a while." He shook his head. "Youngsters can become so attached to a wrongheaded idea. I know I did. Of course I had three older brothers only too ready to administer a salutary dose of reality. But Trevellyn is right there to, ah, catch her."

"He's clearly eager to do so," Flora replied.

"So, a relief all 'round then."

Not quite all, Flora thought. Her father had taught her to divide a question into its important components, examine each one, and formulate a solution from the results. But she hadn't been able to apply his method lately. Bits of information kept slipping away from her and then rushing back like a storm surge at the seashore, tipping her into a froth of confusion.

"I'll offer her my apologies," Robert said. "Once she's settled, ah, elsewhere."

The play had diverted energies that should have been devoted to deciphering her situation, Flora acknowledged. In two days, it would be over. She'd figure it all out then. "I promised Frances I'd look at her costumes with her," she said, and moved away.

Flora had thought the tableaux caused a buzz of activity, but that was nothing to the frantic action in the last hours before the performance.

A team of local seamstresses had been recruited to alter old clothes for costumes. A stream of housemaids went in and out of their room, fetching people for fittings and trays of tea and cakes to fuel the good ladies in a crescendo of stitching. Estate workmen came to install a curtain across one end of the ballroom. Footmen carried in chairs from around the house and arranged them in rows. Carrick grew ever more wild-eyed and dictatorial, even quarreling with his friend Wrentham.

Two hours before the performance was to begin,

the ballroom was a chaos of last-minute alterations, muttering of lines, and shrieks of dismay at some lost bit of adornment. In his gray-wigged guise as father of the hero, Robert began to think they were facing a debacle. But somehow, at the last possible moment, the helpers drew back, the actors in the opening scene took their places, and the footmen pulled the curtains back on *The Rivals*.

The result was mixed, Robert decided, as the action unfolded before the other guests. Some of them, like Frances Reynolds and Flora as Mrs. Malaprop, did splendidly. The audience clearly enjoyed their appearances. Others made a decent showing, speaking their parts and managing their entrances and exits without obvious mistakes. Robert included himself in this second category. And then there were those who had to resort to the prompter, a young lady who'd volunteered to give up her few scenes as a servant to follow along and feed lines to those who required them.

Lady Victoria was the chief culprit. She limped through her speeches, with frequent pauses for a reminder. It became more painful as the play went on, because she grew more self-conscious, and thus stumbled more often. Finally, about halfway through, during a scene she shared with Carrick, she seemed to lose her way entirely. Robert—observing from the side as he waited to go on again—couldn't restrain a wince. Carrick's ferocious scowl certainly wasn't helping matters.

"'So, while I fondly imagined we were'…uh." Victoria made a fluttering gesture. Then she gave up all pretense, asking, "Oh, what comes next?"

The prompter provided the next word.

"Yes. '…deceiving my relations, and flattered myself that I should…should…'"

The murmured aid from the prompter came again. Clearly the audience could hear it, Robert thought, peeking around the edge of the curtain. Lydia Fotheringay had begun to smirk and roll her eyes. The Salbridges looked pained. Harriet Runyon gazed about as if wondering what she could do to save the situation.

Victoria forged on. "'…outwit and incense them all. Behold my hopes are to be crushed at once, by my aunt's consent and…and…'"

The young lady behind the curtain provided another boost.

"Yes," said Lady Victoria. "'Approbation. And I am myself the only dupe at last! But here, sir, here is the picture—Beverley's picture!'" She groped in a pocket especially sewn into her gown. "Oh, where is the wretched thing?" she exclaimed impatiently.

Robert turned at a scrabbling sound from the corner behind him. A table had been set up there to hold objects needed for the play. Trevellyn pawed through them, found what he was looking for, and hurried to toss a square of pasteboard onto the stage. It landed at Victoria's feet. She picked it up. "'Beverley's picture,'" she said triumphantly, then stalled again. "Oh lud, what's next?"

The prompter gave her the words.

"Yes, '…which I have worn, night and day, in spite of threats and entreaties! There, sir.'" She threw the pasteboard at Carrick, with quite convincing relish. "'And be assured I throw…the…the original…'"

Robert could see that she was truly distressed by this time. It was difficult to resist the impulse to help. But there was nothing he could do. The young lady with the pages of the play before her whispered the next line.

"'…the original from my heart as easily,'" Victoria said. And stopped again. "Um."

Carrick snapped. "You stupid girl!" he cried. Anger and frustration etched his face. "You've completely ruined the play."

Victoria shrank back. The imperious queen of their revels disappeared, and she looked very young and thoroughly humiliated.

Robert heard the audience draw a collective breath. Whether from sympathy or anticipation, he couldn't tell. Just as he concluded that he had to intervene somehow, Edward Trevellyn strode from behind him onto the stage, even though his character wasn't part of the current scene. "You are offensive, sir," he said to Carrick. "Quite beyond the line."

Moving to Victoria's side, Trevellyn took her hand. A surprising dignity cloaked his stocky frame. He gazed down at Victoria, heart in his eyes, then heedless of all those around him, dropped to one knee. "Who the devil cares about the play?" he said. "Or a bunch of silly speeches. You are wonderful in every way. I beg you to make me the happiest man on Earth by becoming my wife."

Victoria flushed. She swallowed the obvious beginning of tears and drew a shaky breath. The slump in her shoulders gradually disappeared. She clutched Trevellyn's fingers. "Yes," she said. "Yes, I would like to."

The man sprang up, grinning, and put an arm around her. The audience broke into applause.

"This is a travesty of a performance," exclaimed Carrick.

"Oh, who cares?" said Victoria, her imperious manner restored. "We're not going on." She smiled up at Trevellyn.

The other actors poured onto the stage, laughing and offering congratulations. Robert joined them as Carrick pulled off his hat and wig, threw them on the floor, and stomped them to pieces.

The audience left its seats and added their felicitations to the happy couple. The earl sent for champagne, and a round of toasts to his daughter's happiness began. Everyone except Carrick seemed to be having a fine time. Robert sipped from his glass and congratulated himself. He judged that Victoria was well settled with Trevellyn, though he wouldn't have said so even a week ago. He thought the fellow would be a fine husband for her.

A movement at floor level caught Robert's eye. Plato sat there, gazing up at him. Robert bent to pat his head. He'd brought the little dog down for the performance because he felt he'd neglected him lately, and he'd had no fears of misbehavior. Indeed, Plato had sat at Mrs. Runyon's feet while the play was going on, and now, when any other dog would have been running about and barking in the excitement, he remained philosophical.

"So, we've done the thing, Plato," Robert murmured. "You've heard the phrase 'as good as a play'? This was miles better than our mediocre efforts."

The dog emitted one of his odd curmudgeonly sounds.

"Yes, but it is one obstacle removed," Robert pointed out.

"I beg your pardon," said Sir Liam Malloy, standing nearby. "Did you speak?"

"Just wishing them every happiness," answered Robert, raising his glass.

"Ah." Sir Liam nodded, and drank.

Twelve

"THE DRAMA OF LIFE IS MORE VIVID THAN ANY PLAY," Randolph said later that night. The two brothers sat on either side of the library fire, glasses of brandy in hand. Plato lay at their feet with his dark head resting on crossed paws. Most of the household had gone to bed, and the place was very quiet.

It occurred to Robert that Randolph had seen a great variety of life by this time, in his profession. Parishioners no doubt came to him for guidance, and he was undoubtedly good at giving it.

Robert remembered an incident from the summer when he was eight and Randolph ten. They'd joined a mob of estate children playing king of the hill, a scrum of boys shouting and jostling and exulting in the July heat. Some of them began mocking the son of the local miller, who had a stutter and declared himself k-k-k-king. Robert was chagrined to realize that he'd forgotten the lad's name.

He and Randolph had both objected to the teasing, and it had stopped. And that had been that for Robert. He learned later that Randolph visited the boy during subsequent school vacations and helped him overcome the stutter, without telling anyone that he was doing it. Robert had thought ever since that Randolph was the kindest of his brothers.

Still, he hesitated. Robert Gresham wasn't accustomed to asking for advice. He wasn't accustomed to needing it. He glanced down and noticed that Plato was staring at him, almost as if urging him on. "I wonder…" he said.

Randolph's head came up as if he'd heard some unusual sound. He turned and met Robert's eyes. There was no sign of the amusement that so often danced in his blue gaze.

Robert considered a moment longer, then plunged ahead. "I suppose, as a clergyman, you hear about all sorts of problems."

"People sometimes bring their concerns to me," Randolph agreed.

"Have any of them been plagued by bad memories? So strongly that they can't shake them off? That they…intrude against the person's will?"

Robert endured a long silent assessment. Finally, seeming satisfied, Randolph said, "A man or a woman?"

"Does it matter?"

His brother shrugged. "The approach might be different. If you're speaking of a man, the cause is often battle. If it's a woman, usually a more personal attack."

"Nothing like that," Robert said. And then he wondered. Flora had been overpowered and imprisoned. "A woman," he said.

"Miss Jennings?"

"Why would you say so?" Robert was wary of revealing confidences.

"First, because there is something…dimmed about her, at bottom," replied his brother. "And second because of the way you care for her."

"There are times when I find our family entirely too talkative," Robert complained.

"Gossip was hardly necessary," Randolph said. "It's obvious, seeing the two of you together. Quite lovely, in fact. I envy you. And it must be very strong, for you to go so far as asking for help."

"I ask for help when necessary."

"No, you don't."

"Nonsense."

"What about that time at Eton, when you rowed across the Thames alone to retrieve those cricket bats?"

"That was fifteen years ago, Randolph!"

"I'd have gone with you. I was playing, too. But you had to be seen as the nonpareil."

"I beg your pardon?"

Randolph nodded. "Yes, that trick of raising one eyebrow and looking down your nose is marvelously effective. How old were you when you learned to do that? Fourteen? I always wondered if you practiced in the mirror."

In fact, he had, Robert thought, when he was a callow youth. But there was really no need to discuss that now.

"There's no harm in it," added Randolph cordially. "We all set out to distinguish ourselves in our own ways."

"Perhaps we could return to my question?"

Randolph's eyes twinkled. "Certainly. I can tell you what I've observed, and gathered from colleagues. In such cases, the reaction often eases with time. Like grief. Or despair."

Robert found these uncomfortable comparisons.

"It does no good to push a person so...afflicted to 'get over it.' Most are already ashamed that they cannot. Far more helpful to tell them they're not wrong to feel as they do. And to believe it."

"Of course they're not wrong. Why would anyone think so?"

"I've noticed that many people judge themselves far more harshly than they do others."

Robert remembered what Flora had said about weakness. When, in fact, she was one of the strongest people he'd ever encountered.

"And society expects people to make light of their difficulties," Randolph added.

Robert nodded. He waited. His brother said nothing more. "None of that seems like *doing* anything," he finally said.

"Ah." Randolph looked sympathetic. "When all one can offer is compassion, it's a hard lesson."

"There must be something more."

His brother considered. "Some people find ways to...correct the experience that haunts them."

"Correct?"

"That's not the right word," Randolph said. "It gives the wrong impression. Say rather that life sometimes shows these individuals that they can cope with what haunts them."

"How would that be arranged?" Robert asked.

"I'm afraid it's more serendipity than planning," his brother replied.

This was frustrating. Robert wanted to make all right for Flora. For his own sake, yes, but even more for hers. He *hated* to see her bowed by this unfair burden. He longed to take decisive action, and he'd hoped his brother would know how that might be done. Still, Randolph had offered his best. "Thank you."

"My dear Robert, of course." Randolph smiled at him.

It was odd. The handsomest of his brothers looked less perfect when he smiled. He also looked unutterably charming. "Do you remember the son of the miller at Langford?" Robert said. "The one with the stutter?"

"Edward Farley."

"That's the name."

"Of course," said Randolph. "He runs the mill now, though his father is still there every day. Putting his oar in, as Edward says. He married the prettiest girl in the village. His words, again. They have four children."

Of course Randolph would know all this, Robert thought.

"His eldest son won a scholarship to Winchester. Edward's so proud he could burst."

"Someone must have given him a sterling reference."

Randolph looked self-conscious.

Robert raised his glass to him.

❦

In the aftermath of the play, several of the party's younger guests declared life to be wretchedly flat and boring. They talked of other events they might plan to match the excitement of preparation and performance, but Flora didn't think any would actually occur. Lord Carrick had departed, still sulking, and Lady Victoria was wholly occupied with her fiancé and wedding plans.

The latter was a great relief. In the course of a day, Lady Victoria had shifted from a disapproving shadow dogging Flora's steps into a distant presence who seemed barely aware of Flora's existence. It was a measure of the younger girl's focus on herself, Flora thought. Flora no longer had a place in her personal universe. "I've regained the freedom of obscurity," she told Harriet the following afternoon, as they settled in one of Salbridges' cozy parlors to write letters.

"Not completely," said her companion. "Your performance as Mrs. Malaprop was much admired. You could build on that notice."

Flora laughed and quoted. "'O fy! It would be very inelegant in us. We should only participate things.'"

Harriet smiled. "I couldn't make out what her speeches meant half the time."

"Just to cause laughter, I think. And perhaps the satisfaction of feeling clever—to hear *precipitate* in a similar word, for example."

"I prefer to work less hard for my jokes," Harriet replied.

The door opened. At first, it seemed there was no one there. Then a small black-furred creature trotted in from the hallway, stopped, and surveyed the chamber and its occupants with solemn care.

"Hello, Plato," said Flora.

The dog came closer, sat, and fixed his unnerving

gaze upon her. It was so hard to dismiss that piercing regard as mere animal habit.

"How did he reach the latch, I wonder?" said Harriet.

"I helped with that," answered Robert Gresham, coming in and shutting the door behind him. "He wanted to come in here."

"Your dog did?" Harriet was clearly amused. "How does he convey his wishes to you?"

"Sometimes I believe he has the power to plant ideas in my mind." Robert appeared to be only half jesting. "I'll be thinking of something else entirely, and then suddenly, there it is—take Plato for a walk, or order up a bowl of scraps."

Harriet laughed. "Would you—and Plato, of course—care to join us?"

"Delighted, thank you." He walked over to sit on the sofa beside Flora.

He was not so very near her, but all Flora's senses came alert. He was the picture of masculine beauty in his immaculate blue coat and pale pantaloons.

"I must attend to my letters," Harriet added. She looked around, then rose. "A writing desk. Just what I want."

Her expression was simply pleasant, with none of the arch consciousness of a chaperone allowing her charge some leeway. She crossed the spacious room and settled in a straight chair before the small desk. It faced a window, Flora saw, looking out over the autumn gardens. Harriet would be properly present, but with her back to them and unlikely to overhear a quiet conversation. They could talk about anything. Uncharacteristically, Flora's mind went blank.

"I hope your mother is well," said Lord Robert.
Flora nodded.

"Is she pleased at the way your visit is going?"

Meeting his sparkling blue eyes, she saw something new there. She couldn't quite pin it down. His look was at once quieter, deeper, more penetrating, as if he could see right through her. It was almost as if he knew how difficult it had been to write her mother just now. She hadn't told Mama about her most recent conversation with Lydia Fotheringay, because she couldn't decide whether Mama would rather know she'd been mistaken about being snubbed, or not.

"The parts you've told her about," Robert added.

A short laugh escaped her. "How did you know I haven't included every detail?"

He smiled and shrugged. "Family correspondence is a delicate art. How best to share the details of your life without…overdoing? And still be certain to get in your side of the story, in self-defense."

"What story?"

"Any of them." He gestured gracefully. "With five brothers, there's always something."

"Scrapes? Pranks? Didn't I hear something about a wolfskin at your eldest brother's wedding?"

"Exactly what I mean. You jump in first to, er, set the tone of the discussion."

What had he been like as a small boy, a stripling? Flora wondered. Her memories from her few visits to his home long ago were fragmentary, and mainly concerned her mother's anxiety at being back among her noble kin. "Your family are all active letter writers?"

"Excessively so. Our correspondence will fill

several shelves in the library at Langford, when it's all collected."

"Would anyone do that?"

"Tradition." He gave her a charmingly rueful smile. Flora's pulse speeded up. "I could show you three volumes of appallingly tedious letters chronicling a great-uncle's grand tour in 1754. And two slender, leather-bound sheaves from my great-grandmother at the royal court, waxing silly and syrupy about James the Second. How I could have a forebear with such poor taste? Charles the Second, yes. Famously captivating. But his boorish brother?"

"I suppose you make do with the king you have," said Flora with a laugh.

"In terms of loyalty and obedience." He shrugged agreement. "But you do not describe a...a sow's hairy ear as a shiny silk purse. I can't understand why she didn't chuck the letters after they threw him out in 1688."

"Perhaps someone else kept them."

"There you are," said Robert with a nod. "I discovered a few years ago that my mother keeps all our letters, along with copies of her own, in some secret drawer somewhere."

"Secret?"

"Well, I don't know where it is." He considered. "Must be a fairly large drawer. Six of us, from the time we were barely literate. You can imagine the pile."

Flora could imagine some fascinating reading.

"She wanted us to add our letters to each other. And Nathaniel said he just might, the rogue."

"Shouldn't he?" Flora liked his manner when

talking of his family. It was full of warmth and affection under his careless charm.

"He's the one who got us—some of us—out of those long-ago scrapes. Mama doesn't know about half of them. My father, even less."

"Would they be so shocked?" Flora knew that young noblemen engaged in all sorts of idiotic, even shameful, high jinks.

"Not shocked," Robert said. "More likely to laugh themselves sick." He paused as if reviewing a mental list. "Maybe a bit disappointed, here and there. One hates to disappoint Papa."

His expression had gone neutral, but Flora heard the depth of respect and admiration in it, the determination to be worthy. It was a sentiment she thoroughly understood. She'd felt the same about her father. She'd met the Duke and Duchess of Langford briefly in Oxford. They'd been cordial and sensible and open-minded, not at all the judgmental figures her mother had led her to expect in the leaders of society. But they'd also been…formidable. "I hope your parents are both well," she said.

"Splendid, as ever. They're in Scotland."

"It's going to be more and more letters from now on," Robert added pensively. "I'm about to be an uncle twice over. Nathaniel's wife is expecting, as well as Alan's. Everyone's delighted that Violet's to produce an heir for the line."

He said *the line* as if it was a perfectly ordinary notion. Flora felt an echo of her old scorn for the *haut ton*. "And I suppose they'll be proportionally unhappy if it's a daughter?"

"Not at all. Nathaniel will worship at her feet." Robert made an airy gesture. "And from what I've seen, they'll be only too happy to keep trying."

Flora flushed and looked away. A wave of heat rolled down her body—face, neck, chest—and pooled in her lower regions as she recalled his hands on her as he carefully detached barbed thorns.

"I'm clearly going to have a coachload of nieces and nephews, all of whom will be expected to produce letters."

"You'll make a wonderful uncle. I'm sure they'll adore you."

Her penultimate word seemed to hang in the air between them.

There was an odd, guttural noise. At first Flora thought that Robert had cleared his throat. Then she realized that it had come from Plato. She looked down at the dog.

"He doesn't bark or whine or growl," Robert said, shaking his head. "Not once since I pulled him from a roadside thicket. He just does *that*."

Plato was staring at her, as he also habitually did. "Do you think there's something wrong with his throat?" Flora asked.

The dog cocked his head without breaking eye contact. Flora would have sworn that he looked reproachful. She nearly begged his pardon.

"He seems healthy, more so every day." Harriet Runyon shifted in her chair on the other side of the room, and the rustle of her silk gown reminded Robert that they weren't alone. He'd nearly forgotten the older woman was there. And that he didn't have unlimited time. How he wanted unlimited time with Flora! For the rest of their lives. But he had a plan for their next meeting. "Thank you for bringing that article," he said. "The one by Stanfield. On the similarities between Akkadian and Aramaic. I read it with great interest."

"Oh. Yes." Their shared scholarship seemed like an echo from a different world.

"Quite an astonishing level of detail."

"Stanfield has devoted his life to comparative study of the two languages," said Flora.

"And to looking at every scrap of clay tablet in existence, it seemed to me."

"He claims as much." Flora smiled.

"I was impressed," Robert continued, pleased with the way things were going. "Also rather amused. Stanfield seems unable to resist sniping at Aramaic. He treats it like an invader, or usurper, crowding in and taking the place of the far-more-admirable Akkadian language."

"I think he saw it exactly that way."

"That passage in the middle about the Assyrian scribe pressing his stylus into wet clay under a dusty sky orange with sunset—quite poetic, eh? And the later one contrasting our small single lives with the countless ranks of people behind us." His expression encouraged her to enjoy the phrases with him.

"Father always said that one's personal feelings had no place in rigorous study, but I wonder if it's that simple?" The thought was disorienting, as if some inner compass had flipped over, or turned inside out.

Robert cocked his head, waiting.

"Because they're *there*, aren't they?" Flora went

on. "We can pretend otherwise, but it doesn't change the reality."

"They?"

"The feelings. They don't go away just because we declare them inappropriate. They…sneak around the edges and push their way in." Robert had shown her this.

"No escaping them," he agreed.

Flustered by the warmth in his eyes, Flora rushed on. "For example, Papa despised the Sumerians. He positively…squirmed over their hymns to Inanna. One of their goddesses. He went out of his way to discredit anyone who wrote about them, no matter how meticulous their research. Because he felt that way." It was as if she'd betrayed a secret and said something perfectly absurd, both at the same time.

"It can be difficult to admit our prejudices," said Robert.

Flora stared at him. Sometimes it seemed he could actually read her mind. "They look so foolish when we hold them up to the light," she agreed, dropping her eyes. "We'd… I'd rather pretend they never existed."

"Like a cat who leaps at some imagined danger, then starts grooming to convince the world that nothing happened."

Flora laughed. "Unlike a cat, I will own my discovery that the *haut ton* is not made up of worthless fribbles." She shook her head as she remembered all the sweeping, intemperate judgments she'd uttered about society. "Or monsters of snobbishness. Or any one thing. They're…just people, with strengths as well as flaws. Some likable, some not."

Robert said nothing, but she was hyperaware of his presence at her side.

"Look at those involved in the play," she went on. "They worked so hard, and some showed real talents, not to mention Mr. Trevellyn's unsuspected compassion."

"What about our charm?" said Robert. His voice was light but perhaps just a touch unsteady.

"Trust you to remind me of *that*," said Flora. "The thing is, I could live happily among them, sometimes." She met his eyes, offering up her gaze wholeheartedly. "Just as you found a place in Russell Square."

It was foolish to imagine that doors could open in a person's expression, she thought. Yet it felt like that. And she suspected something similar showed on her own face.

An indefinable interval ticked by. They reached a silent understanding, though Flora wouldn't have been able to voice the details. The process was too nebulous, unlike the facts and proofs she'd been taught to trust. And yet she knew it was just as true.

The sound of a chair scooting over the floorboards jolted them back. Harriet added a small cough of warning as she rose, before she turned from the writing desk. "We must go," she said. "I promised Anne I would walk with her before luncheon, and I fear I cannot leave you here alone. A cozy parlor is rather different from a garden bench."

Flora let out a long breath.

"Please don't do that," Harriet added. "You will tear the cloth. Stop at once!"

Robert turned and saw that Plato had moved, in the silent way he had. The little dog stood by Mrs.

Runyon. He'd taken a bit of her skirt in his teeth and was tugging on it, as if to keep her from leaving. "Plato! Come away from there."

Mouth full of cloth, his eccentric little pet looked at him. He must give up imagining he saw some urgent message in those brown eyes, Robert thought. "Now," he said. "Drop it, sir."

A dog's shoulders could not slump, Robert told himself. It wasn't possible. Though he could not have said what else to call Plato's movement as the dog opened his jaws and let Mrs. Runyon's skirt drop.

"Come over here like a proper dog," he said. "And behave yourself."

Slowly, like a creature trying to demonstrate, with limited resources, the wisdom of his own schemes compared with the debacle before his eyes, Plato complied. He went to sit on the hearthrug.

The two ladies took their leave. Robert gave them a bow and a smiling farewell, very satisfied with his morning's work. "That lacked finesse," he said to Plato when they were gone. "Not up to your usual standards."

Plato grumbled. He rose and trotted over to the door.

"Yes, you want to go for a walk outside." Robert followed the dog into the corridor. "I beg pardon for delaying you with my petty concerns. About the rest of my life, and so on."

Plato turned toward the front door.

"We will go upstairs for my coat and hat," Robert informed him, moving in the opposite direction.

The small animal rumbled a response.

"There's a sharp wind. You may find yourself

chilled even with all that fur." Robert paused at the foot of the staircase. "And I've just spoken as if you complained to me. Really, it's past time for me to set up my household and have a more…responsive companion to chat with. We'll get you a couple of cats for company."

Plato stopped on the landing above him and stared.

"What are cats, you ask?" Robert started up the steps. "I'm surprised you haven't come across one or two on the property here. Lovely creatures. You have quite a bit in common with the average cat. Enigmatic. Stealthy. A shade tyrannical." Feeling buoyant, Robert savored the taste of the words. "I'm sure you'll be enchanted," he told Plato.

Thirteen

ROBERT GAVE PLATO ALL THE WALK ANY DOG COULD desire. In his current mood, he would have thrown sticks for him, if Plato had been the sort of animal who deigned to fetch sticks. Instead, they made a great circle through the grounds, leaning into the wind and ignoring innumerable squirrels. Robert's thoughts were exuberant, and the experience was pleasant until the very end, when they came upon Anthony Durand smoking on the terrace.

"Our hostess doesn't allow cigars indoors," the man commented when they came near. "Except in a little hole-in-the-corner room miles from anywhere. Wretched stuffy place. And damned inconvenient." The tip of his cigar glowed red in the wind; smoke swirled away above his head.

One of the advantages of being in the play had been not seeing much of Durand, Robert thought, as he prepared to pass by with a nod.

"So you're after the Jennings chit, are you? Seems rather spiky to me, but no accounting for tastes."

It took all of Robert's self-control not to react.

"Of course, you're known for impeccable taste, aren't you? I'll have to look into her…appeal." Durand's dark eyes glinted, taunting.

Rising to this sort of bait only encouraged more of the same. Robert knew this. He still came within an inch of reaching out and throttling the man. "Where did you pick up such a curious idea?" he replied, employing his blandest tone.

"Observation. People like your father taught me to notice things. In my own defense."

He would write Papa about this fellow after all, Robert decided. It seemed he was going to have to do something about Durand, and one couldn't have too much information about an adversary.

"Do you think she's so eager to worm her way into the *ton* that she'll…accommodate you?"

This was so far off the mark that Robert laughed. "Haven't you anything better to do than gossip like a fishwife?"

Durand scowled, clearly furious. Prodding him might not be wise, but it was satisfying.

With a careless wave, Robert walked on. He was certain he appeared bored and dismissive—in every sense the opposite of his seething thoughts. A man like Anthony Durand shouldn't be at this house party. He shouldn't be anywhere near Flora. He would have to be eliminated.

"If you should ever wish to bite anyone, that fellow would be my first choice," he told Plato as they walked up the stairs.

He found Randolph waiting in the hall outside his bedchamber. "I've been looking for you," his brother said. "I have to get back to Hexham. Something's come up."

Robert nodded and walked into his room.

Randolph followed him in. "What's wrong?"

"What should be?"

"Well, I don't know, but you look just like Papa does when he's discovered something intolerable. And is about to loose bolts of annihilation. Should I seek shelter?"

A short laugh escaped Robert. "Nothing like a duke for retribution?"

"Only well deserved."

"Yes." He wasn't much concerned about Durand's just deserts, Robert thought. He simply wanted him gone.

"You missed my classical reference," Randolph said.

Robert eyed him. "No, I rejected it. I don't care for my choices if our father is Zeus."

"Ah." Randolph smiled. "That does get rather awkward, doesn't it? You might be Apollo and Sebastian, Ares, I suppose. But then—"

"Do you want Hermes?" Robert asked. The game was silly, but it lightened his mood. "Are you going to dub Alan Hephaestus for his inventive skills? That still leaves Nathaniel and James. I can't see either of them as Dionysus."

Randolph snorted at the idea. "It's so often a case of too many brothers, isn't it?" he complained.

Robert laughed.

Randolph stepped closer and put a hand on his arm. "Seriously, Robert. I don't know what vexed you, and you needn't say. But if I can help, send for me."

"And you'll plunge in, no questions asked?"

"Of course."

He had just the right number of brothers, Robert thought, or just the right sort, perhaps. "I might take you up on that."

Randolph looked surprised, then touched. "I hope you will."

&

Flora went down to dinner that evening happier than she'd been in... Well, if she was honest, happier than she could remember being in years. She didn't give a snap of her fingers for the fact that she'd worn her blue evening dress three times during this visit or that she had no jewels or, particularly, that Lady Victoria didn't spare her a glance. Indeed, she reveled in being ignored by the daughter of the house.

It was strange to go from being the bane of someone's existence to a nonentity in a day, but it was delightful to know that when Robert came in, he could walk right over and speak to her without pouts and glares. She hugged the memory of their recent talk to her like a warm coat on a winter day. She was down rather early, but soon he would appear.

Other guests trickled in. The room began to fill. Flora watched Edward Trevellyn bend his head to listen to his fiancée make some remark and thought, All's well that ends well.

Movement in the corner of her eye made Flora turn. Her smile died when she saw the dark, stocky figure of Anthony Durand approaching. He stopped beside her, a bit too close for comfort. Though he was only a few inches taller, he managed to loom. And to give the impression that he was cutting her off from the other guests.

"Miss Jennings," he said. "I've been learning the most fascinating things about you."

"Indeed." Flora tried to say it as Harriet might have, a great lady accosted by someone she barely knew. But this man, and the associations he brought, roused her anxiety.

"One thing about Lydia…" he continued. "She picks up information like a hen snatching grain. So you needn't dissemble." Clearly, he viewed irony as his forte.

Flora offered raised eyebrows and silence. She checked the immediate vicinity, searching for someone who might be invited to join them. But Durand had chosen his moment well. She found only richly clad backs.

"Your charitable works are extensive, I understand." He made it sound ridiculous.

This cut too close to the past. Where was the call to dinner? Flora wondered. "Are you interested in helping the unfortunate?" she managed. "Perhaps you would like to make a contribution?"

Durand snorted. "I have better uses for my money."

"Better than aiding your fellow man?"

He sneered. The expression did not flatter his harsh features. "People who are willing to work, who are not shiftless and greedy, have no need for my assistance."

Anger dissipated some of Flora's uneasiness. "Greedy? Do you know what wages are paid in the shops and mills? Or the price of bread?"

He shrugged. "Workers who know the value of frugality—and avoid drinking themselves insensible at every opportunity—can get on very well."

"On the contrary, they can barely feed themselves. And what about their children? I suppose *they* are to be grateful for backbreaking jobs in the factories as well?"

"The poor have far too many children," her companion declared. "They have no self-control. And then neither they nor society have any use for the packs of brats they produce."

Flora was too angry to speak.

Durand smiled. It was an unsettling expression. "You're quite lovely when you're furious, by the way."

She couldn't throttle him. It would be a scandal, and she didn't know precisely how to go about it. A gap in her extensive education, Flora thought darkly.

"And so their urchins infest the streets of London, begging, picking the pockets of honest folk, and moving on to worse, some of them. Like the bit of scum who killed my friend Royalton. I suppose you heard about that?"

A cold thread of fear snaked through Flora's indignation.

"And you would have me subsidize them? I think not."

"Good evening." Sir Liam Malloy stepped up beside her.

Durand gave him an ironic bow. "Here is your gallant defender once again. We will talk another time, Miss Jennings. Such a pleasure." He strolled off. Lydia Fotheringay had been lying in wait for him, Flora noticed. She gripped his arm and peered up into his saturnine face.

"What did that fellow want?" asked Sir Liam.

"Nothing."

"He's not the sort of…friend you should cultivate."

"I am certainly not doing so!"

"It's just that…a gentleman does not speak to a lady without encouragement."

Flora turned on him. "Encouragement? Do you think that sort of…creature waits for encouragement? He and his friends take whatever they please without a thought. And no one does anything about it!"

Sir Liam rocked back as if she'd slapped him. She'd spoken loud enough to attract a few curious glances as well.

"Shall we go in to dinner?" said Countess Salbridge. She was on the other side of the room, but she had a penetrating voice for such occasions.

Wordlessly, Sir Liam offered his arm. Flora took it. "I didn't mean—" he began.

"Please do not speak!" As they moved with the flow of guests toward the dining room, Flora spotted Robert at last. He was just coming in, nearly late for dinner. He'd missed her conversation with Durand.

She didn't want or need to be rescued, Flora insisted silently, fighting the dark tide of emotion rising in her. She could take care of herself, certainly.

"Miss Jennings," said Sir Liam.

"I'm sorry I snapped at you," she said. "I was annoyed about something else."

"Anthony Durand," he concluded. "Understandable."

Flora turned her head away. She couldn't explain it to him, a virtual stranger.

"If I can be of any assistance, I should be very happy," he said.

Was this it then? Must men see her as a wilting
flower in perpetual need of help? She did not require
his aid, or Robert's, or anyone's. She allowed Sir Liam
to hold her chair and seat her only because that was
the custom and objections would be rude.

Robert took his place in the dining room. He
did not sit gazing at Flora, much as he would have
enjoyed the sight. Any exchange between them in
such a public place could only be anticlimactic. He'd
wanted to savor the memory of her lovely open
expression, the look in her eyes this morning. If he
could have his way, he would find her in the library
tonight, offer for her with his heart in his hand, and
hear her say that she would be his wife. Followed by
a thoroughly delightful interlude of celebration. It was
such a compelling picture that he was lost in it for a
bit. Until reality intruded.

Would she say it? He wanted a joyous, unreserved
yes. But their situation was complicated. It always
was with Flora. And he wouldn't have it any other
way. He required a plan. His mind was just laying out
alternatives when a determined voice intruded.

"The table has turned," said Frances Reynolds at his
left side. "Miss Shaw may not care whether you speak
or not, but I am quite *bored*."

She said the last word loudly, provoking a startled
glance from Charles Wrentham on her other side. Miss
Reynolds appeared to be miffed or unhappy. Robert
couldn't tell which. For his part, he'd sat through half
of dinner without making any attempt at conversation,
which was utterly unlike him. "I beg your pardon," he
replied, offering his most charming smile.

"Well, you don't need to beg *mine*. Because I insist that you talk to me."

"I should be delighted."

"As long as you don't speak of shooting. I am heartily sick of the subject."

Once again she spoke quite loudly, and attracted Wrentham's attention. Robert concluded that she'd meant to do so. "That shouldn't be difficult," said Wrentham, briefly abandoning etiquette. "Lord Robert has hardly been shooting. Too busy walking that odd dog of yours, Gresham?"

Robert found the brush of male mockery in Wrentham's tone amusing. Robert was a crack shot, and most here knew it. And clearly the remark was part of a quarrel with the young lady at his side and didn't really involve him at all.

"Lord Robert saved Plato from starvation and…and destitution," said Miss Reynolds.

Robert suppressed a smile. He hadn't thought in terms of canine poverty.

"So the ladies are always saying," answered Wrentham, as if kindness to dogs was an affectation calculated to show him up.

Miss Reynolds sniffed like an outraged dowager. "We will talk of something *interesting*. The play perhaps." When Wrentham shrugged and turned back to the girl on his other side, Miss Reynolds looked both triumphant and forlorn.

❦

It was amazing how one's mood could go from elation to despondence in a few moments, Flora thought.

Oddly, it was worse when Anthony Durand wasn't standing before her. Her memory and imagination got to work, recalling the anguished stories of pain and terror she'd heard from street children. That such cruelty and indifference existed in the world!

She'd meant to escape to her room when the ladies left the dinner table, but Frances Reynolds cornered her and begged for a bit of conversation. She seemed so distressed that Flora hadn't the heart to refuse. It turned out that she wished to discuss Mr. Wrentham, at great length.

"Of course I know that most gentlemen come here for the hunting," said the younger girl, drooping at Flora's side on one of the drawing room sofas. "So it is no wonder they talk of it. All the time."

Flora nodded. She was trying to pay attention, but her own concerns kept intruding.

"It is just that when we were together, practicing our roles for the play, he seemed so different. And then it all came to an end."

She waited for a reply. Flora nodded.

"And I understand that the play is finished," Frances said. "But we might still talk of something besides the day's take of birds. Dead birds. Don't you think?"

Flora nodded again.

"Sometimes it seems that he doesn't wish to... further our acquaintance. The way he spoke to me at dinner...as if we were strangers. When we had said such things to each other just a few days ago." She sighed.

"Those were speeches written by someone else," Flora pointed out. She didn't add that the sentiments might be beyond anything Mr. Wrentham could voice, or indeed felt.

"I know, but they seemed so sincere."

"Frances."

"I'm not a fool," the younger girl interrupted. "It wasn't just the words. He looked as if he truly meant them. And I don't believe he is that skilled an actor."

This sounded a bit more sensible. "You could just ask him," said Flora.

Frances turned to stare at her, aghast. "Oh, I couldn't!"

Life would be so much simpler if people just said what they meant, straight out, Flora thought. Then she remembered Durand. It would be lovely if people like him were constrained by the rules of politeness, while those like Frances and her wished-for beau were free to speak openly. But one couldn't pick and choose. Unfortunately.

"I wouldn't dare," Frances added. "What if he gave me a setdown? Or told the others what I'd said so that they all laughed at me?" She looked anxious, and mournful, and very young. "I'm here alone. I have no mother or other chaperone to…give him a hint."

"Alone?" That was unusual for a girl of seventeen, as Flora knew Frances to be. She hadn't seen her with any older female, she realized. But she hadn't thought about it, or asked why. Was she becoming horridly self-centered?

Frances shrugged. "My mother was a cousin of Earl Salbridge. So I'm part of the family, in a way. Not exactly alone, but…it feels as if I am. I only met them when I came here."

"Your mother?" replied Flora gently.

"She died three years ago," answered Frances in a flat voice. "She was ill a long time before that. As long as I can remember, really."

"I'm sorry."

"It was rather…odd. Mama was always bedridden. She never came downstairs. Our housekeeper managed everything. But when she was gone, it left a…a great hole somehow."

Flora was moved by the mixture of grief and mystification in the girl's tone. "I'm sure it did."

"I used to read to her for hours each day," Frances added. "And sometimes—often—I wished that I needn't…take quite so much time. But then when it stopped, I felt so empty." She blinked and visibly gathered herself. "We got through a great many books together. I learned a lot. Mama was curious about so many subjects, even though she was ill."

Flora nodded, offering her full attention and sympathy now.

"So last summer Papa…sort of woke up and noticed… That is, he declared that my future needed to be settled. Unless I am to live with my brother when he inherits, which I would rather not do." Frances glanced anxiously at Flora. "We get along well enough. It's just that we don't have a great deal in common. And he will have a family of his own eventually. Of course."

It was a story told in many places, and yet each instance was unique, Flora thought. She was fortunate, and unusual, in that her home would be hers when Mama died, along with a small income. Very small, but workable for a careful woman, she had always thought.

"Papa wrote to the Salbridges, and they kindly invited me," Frances continued. "Lady Salbridge has promised to include me in London next season as well, though I'll be staying with another cousin." She ducked her head. "Not nearly so grand. I'm, uh, being handed about a bit, from one to another of our family connections." She made a wry face. "Rather like a parcel no one wishes to keep too long."

"I'm sure they're glad to have you," Flora said. She hoped it was true. Or, if not, that it was comforting to be told so.

"People have been very kind," Frances acknowledged. "But I would like it to be...over." She seemed to realize that she'd been leaning close to Flora. She sat back. "I thought Mr. Wrentham might share my interest in reading, you see, because he seemed to enjoy doing the play. And perhaps other things as well. If I am mistaken, then of course, I shall..." She trailed off and took a breath. "In any case, I wondered if you might play the part—so to speak—of my chaperone?"

"What?"

"You were so good at acting," said Frances with a rueful smile.

"But I..." Flora didn't know what to say.

"That was a joke. But couldn't you sound out Mr. Wrentham? Try to discover his...sentiments?"

"It should be Lady Salbridge," Flora said, mildly horrified at the idea.

"I've scarcely spoken to her," Frances said. "But you and I are friends. I hope we are. And you are older." She made a quick gesture. "I don't mean that like Lady Victoria did. You're just so self-assured and knowledgeable."

Flora might have laughed at this description, but she could see that Frances was not only serious, but positively yearning for an ally. Yet she remained reluctant. "You exaggerate my...capacities."

"Oh no."

What could one do in the face of such confidence and hope and faith? "I will...try," Flora said.

"Oh, thank you. That is such a relief." Frances looked as if the weight of the world had been lifted from her shoulders. Flora tried not to sigh. "There he is," the younger girl added.

Flora looked. Wrentham had come through the door with a group of gentlemen, including Durand. When she turned back, she found Frances gazing eagerly at her. "I'll need some time to think what to say to him," Flora said desperately.

"Oh. Yes, of course." The younger girl rose. "I can't tell you what a comfort it is to know that you'll help me. It is so difficult to be all alone."

As Frances left her, Flora noticed that Sir Liam was trying to catch her eye. She'd been quite rude to him. She smiled now, and he came to sit beside her.

"You gentlemen haven't spent long over your port," Flora said.

"Trevellyn practically snatched the glasses out of our hands," the Irishman replied. "I've never seen a man more eager to abandon his wine. Couldn't wait to get back to his inamorata."

They looked over at the engaged couple, cozily ensconced on a small sofa.

"It warms one's heart to see him," Sir Liam continued. "If ever there was a man who'd attained his heart's desire, there he is."

"It certainly seems so," said Flora. Lady Victoria looked equally happy.

"He makes one long to emulate him, assuming one could find a similar ideal."

"That is the difficulty, isn't it?"

"And yet it happens."

Something in his tone made Flora examine him. What she found in his eyes startled and unsettled her.

"Quite unexpectedly," he added. "A marvel of... serendipity."

"Sir Liam—"

He held up a hand. "Not the moment... Anyone can see that. Trust me."

Having either too much or too little to say in response to that request, Flora remained silent.

Fourteen

FLORA OFTEN FELT FRANCES REYNOLDS'S EYES UPON her after their conversation, a thread of anxious hope. And when the ladies reached the drawing room the following evening, the girl pounced, wondering if Flora had spoken to Mr. Wrentham and what he had said. "It hasn't been long since you asked me," Flora pointed out.

"It seems like forever," Frances replied. "I think he's avoiding me. But I can't see why he would." She looked distressed.

When Mr. Wrentham entered the drawing room later, near the end of the cluster of gentlemen joining the ladies, Flora thought he looked rather glum. Surely he'd been bright and lively earlier in this visit? During the play, for example? Yes, she remembered him that way.

He went to sit at the edge of a chattering group. Flora observed him for a short while, and saw that he wasn't really joining their conversation. Harriet would have called his demeanor brooding, she thought.

Resigned to her fate, Flora went over and, without

speaking or allowing him time to stand, sat down beside him. Mr. Wrentham looked a bit startled. Flora was acutely aware of Frances, staring at them from the other side of the room, hands clasped in hope. Well, there was nothing to do but dive in. "Good evening, Mr. Wrentham," she said.

"Miss Jennings."

How did one discover the romantic intentions of a man one barely knew? Flora wondered. Why would he confide in her? "Are you missing the excitement of the play?" she asked. "We were all so busy then, and…united."

"I suppose," he said.

He gazed out over the room rather than at her. She'd considered him a handsome enough young man, Flora thought. But the glum cast of his features tonight rendered him much less appealing. "You were quite good in it," she added.

"That was due to Miss Reynolds," he answered. "She made it all easy."

Flora tried to gauge his tone. He sounded regretful, she decided. "You don't give yourself enough credit. You looked very natural, playing the lover, with all those pretty speeches."

He shrugged. He really was a most unhelpful young man, Flora thought. Or perhaps he was a bit dense. She abandoned subtlety. "So I suppose it is natural that an inexperienced young girl, like Miss Reynolds, might mistake playacting for reality. And believe you cared for her."

Now she had his attention. He stared at her as if she'd poked him with a hatpin.

"You will say that is foolish."

"I would never call Miss Reynolds foolish!"

"Well, good." Flora waited. He said no more. "So you are fond of her? In reality?"

"I have no right to any such feelings." Mr. Wrentham struck a pose—head back, shoulders stiff, expression grim. "You mustn't ask me."

Flora ignored this. "Why don't you have any right?" she asked.

"Circumstances," he answered through clenched teeth. "Of which I may not speak."

"Why? Are you already married?"

"What?" He was startled out of his performance. "No."

"Engaged to another lady? Promised to your family's choice of mates? Or perhaps you are joining a religious order?" She threw in the last to unsettle him. And succeeded. Wrentham goggled at her. "Yes?" Flora added.

"I said I couldn't speak of it." He looked aggrieved.

"But gave no good reason. Unless you just enjoy being mysterious."

"You are not supposed to ask after that," he complained.

"And yet I have." Flora waited expectantly.

Wrentham seemed at a loss. There was still a mulish cast to his features, however.

"Miss Reynolds has been distressed by your behavior. I think she deserves an explanation." Flora used the tone her father had employed when she hadn't prepared very well for a lesson. It had always worked on her.

It did not fail in this instance. Wrentham suddenly

looked younger and far less sure of himself. He turned in his chair, toward Flora, away from the crowd. "I would die rather than give Miss Reynolds a moment's pain," he declared.

"Too late for that," replied Flora caustically.

Wrentham blinked, rather like an owl disturbed at noontime.

She could see why Harriet had no patience with brooding young men, Flora thought. They were an intolerable drag on conversation. "Just tell me," she commanded, out of patience.

He jerked slightly at her tone. At first it seemed he wouldn't answer, then he slumped in his chair. "It is as well that she knows. I shouldn't hide the truth from one I…" He gritted his teeth. "I've lost some money. A great deal of money, actually. I've run up debts that will take me a year or more to pay off. If indeed I can." He bent his head. "I'm leaving here tomorrow, going home to arrange my affairs. I'm certainly in no position to consider…an attachment of any kind."

Flora frowned. "Do you frequent gaming hells?" If he did, Frances was better off without him.

"No! I'm not a flat." Wrentham scowled. "Or I didn't think I… It was here at Salbridge that I lost—" He stopped short. He took a breath, sat straighter. "My situation is nothing to you." He frowned. "Indeed, I don't see what right you have to ask me about Miss Reynolds. You are not related to her." His jaw hardened. "This is barefaced prying." He rose, sketched a bow, and walked away.

Flora let him go. It was clear he wouldn't say more. But she sat on, bits of information she'd heard shifting and realigning in her mind. Mr. Wrentham had been a lighthearted young man when he arrived, and now he was oppressed. He'd lost a lot of money here at Salbridge Great Hall. Anthony Durand had won a large sum in a card game on his first night here. Not from Mr. Wrentham; it had been a neighbor. And then the earl had forbidden deep play.

Durand was rumored to make much of his money at cards. He cared nothing for others' scruples or desires. Was it not possible, even likely, that he'd organized some secret gaming sessions and lured in susceptible male guests? Flora nodded to herself.

It would be late at night, she thought, after most people had gone to bed. But some of the servants must know. The players would want a fire in the hearth, drink. Wouldn't they stop an activity that the master of the house had forbidden? Perhaps some could be bribed, Flora thought. Or they might not know about the ban. They would see no harm in a bit of gambling. It was a common amusement for those they served.

Flora looked across the room. Anthony Durand was sitting with a group of older gentlemen, looking deeply bored. Papa would say that her ideas were all speculation, tinged by self-interest and prejudice. He would insist she verify a mere theory. Well, she would do so. And she would best the blackguard. Flora felt a thrill of satisfaction.

A hand closed on her arm. Frances Reynolds tugged to turn her a little. "What did he say?" she asked.

"Not a great deal," Flora replied. "He has some problems to deal with. They are preoccupying him."

"What problems?" Frances demanded.

"Financial…issues that prevent him from making any plans for his future just now." If her suspicions about what was going on at Salbridge could have helped Frances, she'd have told her, Flora thought. But they wouldn't. "He's leaving tomorrow," she added.

"What?" Frances looked appalled.

"I'm sure you'll see him again. In London in the spring." Perhaps she could make sure they met, Flora thought. "Circumstances may be quite different by then."

"The spring!" Frances made it sound like eons.

"That's not so very long."

"Oh, you can say so. It's nothing to you." Frances surveyed the room, spotted Mr. Wrentham. "I have to talk to him."

"Frances, don't do anything you might—"

The younger girl rushed off.

Flora watched her march up to Mr. Wrentham and interrupt a conversation with one of his cronies. She watched Wrentham brush Frances off, and Frances then broadcast her hurt to the room. Flora was sure everyone could see it. Here was something else for Durand to answer for.

"That clearly didn't go well," said Harriet Runyon, sitting down beside Flora. Her eyes were on Frances.

"I'm sure she'll regret it," Flora agreed.

"I'm sure she already does."

Frances nearly ran from the room.

"I tried to stop her, but she wouldn't listen."

"There's little one can do when people are bent on making fools of themselves," Harriet replied. "And those two are just the age for it."

"I wanted to help. Frances sees me as a kind of

older sister, I think. She asked me to discover Mr. Wrentham's intentions toward her."

"You?" Harriet looked amused.

"She's here alone." Flora shared some of the younger girl's story.

"Poor child," said Harriet when she was done. "I had no idea. Her family is not known to me."

"Or to anyone, apparently."

"I take it Mr. Wrentham's answers were not satisfactory?"

Clearly Harriet had missed nothing of the earlier scene. Flora shook her head.

"Odd, I would have said he was smitten with Miss Reynolds."

"He has money worries."

"Ah." Harriet waited. When Flora said nothing more she added. "I saw Anthony Durand speak to you last night. I couldn't break away to interrupt."

"It was nothing," Flora replied, not quite truthfully. But it didn't matter anymore. She was going to solve the problem of Anthony Durand herself.

※

The very next day, Flora discovered an opportunity. Anthony Durand had for once joined the hunting party, instead of sleeping through the morning as he usually did. Lydia Fotheringay had attached herself to a group of ladies who intended to take advantage of the sunny weather and go for a drive. With both of them out of the way, Flora decided to test out her theories with a look around Durand's room.

She knew the single gentlemen occupied chambers

along a corridor on the eastern side of the house, separated from the young ladies on the other side by the quarters of married couples. Guests' names were written on small placards in brass frames on the doors, so it would be a simple matter to find the right room.

When she judged that the servants had finished their morning tasks, Flora set off. She didn't sneak. She walked like a woman with a purpose, ready to veer off, should she encounter anyone. The upper floors were deserted, however, and she reached Durand's door without seeing anybody.

Flora stood outside it for a moment, listening. Nothing. Gathering her resolve, she turned the knob, opened the door, and slipped inside.

The room was empty.

Letting out a breath, Flora looked around. There was nothing unusual about the bedchamber. It was neat and comfortable, like her own. Two long glass doors in the outer wall gave onto a decorative balustrade. The furniture and hangings showed the Salbridges' characteristic mixture of taste and tradition. Feeling underhanded but determined, she began to search.

She found only clothing in the wardrobe, with no convenient revelations of wrongdoing in the pockets. There were shaving things and a scatter of personal items on a side table. An open book lay facedown on the cushion of the armchair by the hearth. Checking the spine, Flora found it was a history of Russia. She found this piece of information oddly disconcerting. She wouldn't have imagined that Durand read. Which was silly. Books didn't guarantee virtue.

Uncertain where else to look, Flora stood in the middle of the room and turned in a slow circle, examining it foot by foot. She walked the perimeter, but there was nothing out of the ordinary to find. She looked under the bed.

There, concealed behind a ruffle of coverlet, sat a small wooden chest, about the length of her forearm and half as wide. Flora might have thought it belonged to the house, but Durand's initials were inlaid into the top. She knelt, slid it out, and tried the lid. It was securely locked. Here, then, were any secrets he wished to keep. She pulled at the lid again, but the chest was sturdily constructed, and the mechanism didn't appear simple.

Flora gazed at the small box. If this were a boys' adventure story, she thought, she would pluck a pin from her hair and pick the lock with a few deft movements. Shrugging, she tried it. Her hairpin rattled ineffectually in the keyhole. It didn't catch on anything. Papa had neglected to include any such skills in her education. Flora looked around. She'd seen no keys in the room. Undoubtedly Durand kept this one with him. For now, his hidden possessions were out of her reach.

The door handle rattled and started to turn.

Heart suddenly pounding, Flora shoved the chest back into place, sprang up, and ran to the glass doors. She stepped behind the long drapery at the side, making certain the fall of cloth concealed her skirts. The curtain stopped a half inch above the floor. Her feet would be visible in the shadows if anyone looked closely.

The door opened. Someone came in. The door

shut. The hunting party couldn't have returned so soon. Perhaps it was Durand's valet, Flora thought with a sinking heart. Who knew how long he might linger at his duties?

And then she heard the distinctive sound of the wooden chest sliding along the floor.

Pulse racing, Flora risked a peek through a chink in the draperies. Lydia Fotheringay knelt as she herself had a moment ago, with the chest before her. Lydia was trying a key in the lock. When it didn't turn, she muttered a curse and set the key aside. From a small cloth bag at her side, she took another. Clearly, she'd come prepared. She tried the second key, without success, laid it by the first, and repeated the action. By the fifth attempt, she was obviously frustrated. She threw that key down. Metal rang against the wood of the floor.

Mrs. Fotheringay went very still. She waited. When nothing happened, she sighed. She started to reach into the bag, then hesitated and looked around the room. "Is someone there?"

Flora shifted very slightly behind the curtain. Often, people could tell they were being watched. If she stopped looking, would Mrs. Fotheringay's suspicions subside? It was agony not to be able to see what was happening. The older woman might be walking softly toward her right now.

The sound of another key rattling in the lock reassured Flora. But she still fervently wished herself elsewhere. How many keys had the woman brought?

Flora's gaze lit on the bolt that secured the glass doors.

Beyond the drapery, Lydia Fotheringay cursed colorfully.

Flora dared a quick look. Her fellow intruder was glaring at the chest, muttering. She snatched another key from her bag.

Under cover of the metallic sound as she rattled it in the lock, Flora pushed at the bolt. It slid back easily. Before she could change her mind, she opened the outer door, slid through, and closed it silently behind her. She blessed the efficient caretakers of Salbridge Great Hall, who saw to it that hinges did not creak. With nowhere to hide, she waited with pulse pounding and fingers crossed. The door remained closed. Lydia Fotheringay did not rush out and discover her.

Flora breathed again. She stood in a narrow space behind the ornate stone balustrade. It was purely decorative, not a proper balcony, but a narrow ledge extending along the side of the house past several rooms. There was barely room to stand between the coping and the wall of the house.

A cold wind tugged at Flora's skirts. Her gown was no protection at all. The weather had worsened since early morning and would probably cut the hunting short. Flora debated whether to wait where she was—surely Mrs. Fotheringay would be on her way soon—or to risk entry through one of the other bedchambers. Neither option was very appealing.

Three rooms down from where she stood, another set of glass doors clicked and opened a crack. A familiar small dog emerged. Plato turned and looked directly at her, as if he'd fully expected to find a young lady huddled against the house. He trotted toward her.

"Plato," came a familiar voice from inside. "Where do you think you're going?" Robert leaned out of the open door. "Come in at once, sir," he commanded. He saw Flora.

One problem solved by another, Flora thought as she moved quickly along the narrow passage. At least she didn't have to pass Durand's window. She didn't look to see if any of the other rooms were occupied. Best to move by very fast; an observer might think he'd imagined her. Flora reached Robert and slipped past him into his room, Plato at her heels.

Robert followed. He closed the glass door and shot the bolt. "What on Earth are you doing?"

"Getting in out of the cold." Flora rubbed the goose bumps on her arms and went to stand near the fire. "I should have brought a shawl, but I didn't think I'd…"

"Yes?" he said when she broke off. "Didn't think you'd what?"

Robert wore only a shirt, half unbuttoned, and breeches. His feet were bare. Flora couldn't take her eyes off him. He looked so unlike his customary polished self. Disheveled, she thought, or tousled or disarrayed. Delectable.

"Whatever were you doing out there?" he asked again.

A surge of elation went through Flora. She'd taken a risk and gotten away with it. By herself, without needing help or rescue. Well, Plato had helped. But he was only a dog. Her spirits soared.

"Flora? Is something wrong?"

His auburn hair was mussed. Flora had never seen him this way. He looked so very…touchable. Flora met his vivid blue eyes, and felt as if she'd been dipped in fire.

He went still. "You…shouldn't be here," he said, his voice suddenly thick.

She barely heard through the pulse drumming in her ears. A kiss now would far surpass the ones in the garden; she was sure of that. Her gaze traced the strong column of his neck down to the muscles of his chest.

"Are you listening to me?" He went to the door, then stopped at sounds of people in the corridor outside. "Everyone's changing after the hunt. The halls are full of servants."

As if this was a cue, there was a brisk knock on the door. The knob turned.

In an instant, Robert was beside her. "It's Bailey," he murmured in her ear. "I rang for him earlier." The door opened. He pushed her behind it and blocked the panels from moving farther. "Ah, there you are," he said.

"My lord," replied an emotionless voice.

"You know, I believe I'll lie down for a bit of a rest, Bailey. Freezing out there today."

"Of course, my lord. Shall I bring tea? Or some hot broth, perhaps?"

"No, no. Just give me an hour or so. I'll change later."

"Very well, my lord. I'll leave these neckcloths in the—"

"I'll take them."

"But, my lord."

There was a rustling, as of cloth being tugged, then Robert said, "Plato, where are you going?"

Flora could see nothing but the door panels inches from her face.

"The animal is sitting at the end of the corridor, my lord. Staring." The valet's tone made his distaste for the dog very clear.

"Take him down to the kitchen," Robert said. "Cook loves to cosset him."

"We had established that the creature was not my responsibility" came the icy reply.

"He isn't. Just leave him in the kitchen. Thank you, Bailey." Robert shut the door. Flora could easily imagine the valet's outrage.

Robert let out his breath. He had no key to the door's lock. He'd have to trust Bailey to do as he'd asked, which he would. Robert turned to Flora. She had her arms wrapped around her body. "You're still cold." He threw the stack of neckcloths on a chair and fetched his dressing gown. "Here." He went to put it around her.

His hands lingered on her shoulders. He couldn't make himself remove them. It wasn't only desire that throbbed in him. Seeing to her comfort was such an intimate gesture. Being married would be full of such small caresses, as well as passion, he realized. It would offer a thousand new sensations. The idea was as seductive as her lovely face and form.

Flora turned under his hands. She didn't move away from him. She leaned in and raised her face to his. He could do nothing but kiss her.

Her arms slid around him. Her fingers left trails of heat on his skin, palpable through the thin cloth of his shirt. She pressed close, and he pulled her closer. They kissed for an eternity, paused, and kept on kissing. Before he knew what he was doing, he had her backed up against the bed.

"When you kiss me, I just…melt," she whispered.

Robert would have said that he couldn't be more aroused, but that did it.

She'd gotten her hands under his shirt. They slid across his back, down his sides, over the taut muscles of his belly. Robert shivered. Without consulting him, his arms lifted her onto the bed. She urged him to another kiss, her knees parting to let him move closer. When she relaxed as if to fall back on the coverlet, Robert held her upright. "Flora…this isn't… I don't want you to think that I—"

"I'm not thinking," she murmured. "And it's absolutely delightful."

She pulled him down with her, and Robert's scruples flamed to ash in a welter of tenderness and desire. He touched her the way he'd been dreaming of doing—forever, it seemed. Fingertips to silken skin, lips trailing kisses, he did everything he knew to make certain her pleasure was as incandescent as his. He took it as a triumph when she cried out in release and entered her with every bit of care and control he could muster. She hesitated only briefly. Then their bodies' rhythm caught and meshed and mounted in tandem. Release took him by a storm.

Afterward, they lay tangled together with discarded clothing and the twisted coverlet while breath and pulses slowed. "Are you all right?" Robert murmured.

"It was my choice, and I'm happy—very happy— with it." Flora smiled and kissed him. She stretched luxuriously. Her body wanted nothing more than to nestle in his arms for the rest of the day. She rested her head on his shoulder.

He smoothed her hair with gentle fingers, savored the sight of her at his side. "You never said what you were doing on my, er, doorstep."

"I was searching Anthony Durand's room. Lydia Fotheringay came in, so I had to sneak out onto the parapet."

Robert went very still against her. "I cannot have heard that correctly."

"I've discovered something, you see, which will—"

"Durand might have walked in on you!"

"I got away. I wonder if he caught Mrs. Fotheringay with her bag of keys." That would not have been a happy meeting.

"What?"

"She came in to snoop. Also." It was rather pitiable, Flora thought, remembering the older woman crouched over Durand's wooden chest with her hoarded keys. "She's made a poor choice of lovers." The last word reverberated in Flora's brain, in the very air of the room. It held vivid echoes of his kisses, the touch of his hands.

"But what the deuce were *you* doing?" Robert said.

"Looking for validation of a theory."

Robert rose on one elbow and looked down into her face. "A theory. About Durand. Flora, you—"

"About his activities here at Salbridge," she interrupted. "Mr. Wrentham told me something that gave me an idea." Before he could speak again, Flora quickly explained her reasoning. Robert grasped the details at once. The combination of a fine mind and such a handsome form was all one could ask for in a man, she thought.

"It makes sense," Robert said. "Durand would enjoy defying Salbridge in that underhanded way. And there are young men here who would revel in illicit card games." They'd find it less appealing if they knew they were being systemically fleeced, he thought. He had no doubt Durand was cheating.

"I thought there might be evidence among his things," Flora said. "It was only one idea. I have others."

Robert suppressed a shudder at the pictures this conjured up. "If there's anything to find, Durand hasn't left it lying about. The man is clever, Flora. And dangerous."

"I know," she answered fiercely. "He must be stopped."

She was obviously thinking of more than gambling. He didn't want Flora anywhere near Durand, Robert thought. They could simply share her suspicions with Salbridge and let their host handle the matter. "We could go, you know," he said. "Leave for London tomorrow. Get a special license and marry in Russell Square. Your mother would like that, wouldn't she?"

Flora pulled a little away from him, her eyes wide and wary.

"But it's not that simple," Robert added.

She stared at him. "How do you know what I'm thinking?"

"Tell me why it isn't." He wanted to understand everything about her.

Flora let out a breath. After a moment, she said, "That's what people do—walk away, look away. Retreat into their comfortable lives. And so no one stops men like Durand and Lord Royalton. No one stands up to them." Her hands closed into fists. "When I set up my refuge for the street children, I was so proud at first. Smug, really, about sheltering and feeding them—which it is imperative to do, of course. But gradually I learned that physical comforts don't erase what's been done to many of them." She shook her head.

Robert hated to see the sadness in her face.

"Telling their stories—and hearing the injustices condemned—can help, a bit. So I listened. To such dreadful tales, full of helplessness and futility."

She shivered. Robert drew her closer.

"But that's not enough either. We must stop the villains before the harm has been done!"

Robert saw that it was no use saying this was just about a card game. Because in her mind, it wasn't. She'd connected this incident to the past, and Durand now stood for much more. Deservedly, Robert supposed. The man obviously had few scruples. He'd admitted he was looking for opportunities to do the Greshams a bad turn. No, Robert didn't want Durand out there either, ready to target any member of his family at any time. He had to be neutralized. "I can take care of this," he said without thinking.

Flora sat up. "I am not tossing all my woes on you. Like some...damsel in distress." She reached for her petticoat and held it to her chest. "*I* can take care of it myself."

There was a final factor, Robert realized. A very delicate balance. Could they find their way to the sort of restorative experience Randolph had described? "But isn't that the thing about love? That you don't always have to?"

Flora's pulse jumped at the easy, certain way he said *love*. She'd earned her father's love through years of study. He'd despised laziness and shirking; he'd been quite cold when she'd failed to master all he asked. With her mother, it always felt as if the whole world trembled in the balance when Flora faltered. "You don't feel that it's weak to need help?" she said slowly.

Robert smiled up at her. It struck Flora, again, that they were in bed. Together. Oddly, this eased some of the tension that had begun to tighten her shoulders.

"Would you call my father weak?" he asked.

"The duke?" If Flora had been asked to name a person without weaknesses, she might well have chosen the Duke of Langford. She shook her head.

"Well, he has asked me for help."

She tried to imagine the rather awe-inspiring figure she'd met in Oxford doing such a thing.

"A few years ago, this silly chit of a deb got the notion that Papa was her 'destined mate.' Didn't matter that he was married. And that he adores Mama. Or that he gave her no encouragement. She was convinced he was going to throw his life out the window for her."

"But he told her he wasn't interested?" Flora suspected that Robert was using this story to lighten the mood. She found she didn't mind.

"Oh yes. Nicely. And then firmly. And finally quite sharply. She ignored it all. Papa said she didn't appear to hear his actual words when he talked to her. She went all dewy-eyed, and some kind of epic story seemed to run in her head instead. He was worried she'd put herself in a compromising position."

"Not him?"

"Well, yes, but that wouldn't be quite the same."

"No." Men, particularly noblemen, could brush through most scandals unscathed, Flora thought.

"She was increasingly rude to Mama as well, so Papa asked me for help."

"Because you're known for your social address," Flora responded.

"Precisely." He smiled at her again.

Without really noticing, Flora let her petticoat drop. "It sounds like a situation that would require more than polite bows and compliments."

"Well, it did. I went to her younger sister—"

"Not her parents?" It seemed natural to lie down beside him once again.

"No, they were…rather a nightmare. Made one see where some of the girl's problems came from. But the sister had…has a good head on her shoulders. Trouble was, she was still in the schoolroom."

"You appealed to a schoolgirl?" Flora smiled. "How did you even get to her?"

"I had to lurk about a circulating library for several days."

Flora laughed.

"Exactly. But I did it, and spoke to the sister, and got her to see the problem. She managed to wangle a trip to Harrowgate to visit their grandmother. Now there was an exceedingly sensible woman. Once the matter was explained to her, she set the chit straight. Found her a very suitable husband, too. They're quite fond of each other."

"How do you know?" Flora wondered.

"I made it my business to know. I wasn't going to fob her off to a life of misery."

Flora gazed at him with tender admiration, and not only for the merits his story revealed. She felt vastly better.

"Promised I wouldn't spread that story," Robert added. "So you mustn't mention it."

"I won't."

"The point is, we stand together. I've helped out my brothers as well. And they've done the same for me. Weakness doesn't even come into it."

Just a few months ago, she'd seen the Greshams as snobbish and trivial, Flora thought. It was disorienting to substitute this very different picture, and to see herself as part of it.

"So we're in this together, eh?"

Flora nodded. "I'll…do my best," she said. Even as the words left her lips, she remembered her father's characteristic response to this phrase. "Those who excel aren't limited by some preconceived definition of their *best*."

Robert pulled her into his arms. He held her as if he wanted to be a bulwark against every ill. Then he drew back, muttering, "Bailey will be back in a few minutes. Why didn't I tell him *two* hours?"

Flora had to laugh, though she saw her frustration mirrored in his face. She picked up the petticoat and slipped off the bed to dress. It was a little unsettling to do so in front of him, even though he was busy pulling on his own clothes. She used his brush to tidy her hair, a curiously intimate act.

When she was ready, Robert checked the corridor. "All clear," he murmured. Flora stepped out and hurried away, before she was seen in this part of the house.

Robert went back to the bed to straighten the covers. Her scent lingered in them, and he breathed it in. He loved his family. He'd imagined himself in love a time or two in his youth and enjoyed some tender connections with willing ladies later on. But he'd never felt anything like this. His love for Flora made his life feel larger.

Fifteen

FLORA REACHED BACK TO FASTEN HER SMALL STRING OF pearls around her neck. She couldn't get the clasp closed. It occurred to her that if Robert was here, he could do it for her. Although that might lead to taking off more than pearls. Which would make her late for dinner. Which wouldn't do.

When Flora looked up into the mirror above the dressing table, she found that she was smiling a smug, secret smile. The memory of his fingers on her skin was delicious. The mere thought of his kisses made her sigh with longing. She'd taught Robert how to read cuneiform tablets, but he had shown her that the body had as much to offer as the mind. More perhaps. And she would have the chance to study this new subject thoroughly in years to come, because Robert had asked her to marry him. Tacitly. It had been more of an assumption than a proposal, but Flora didn't mind. She wasn't a stickler for social formalities. Or…perhaps she'd make him do it over in proper form. She imagined the grand Lord Robert Gresham down on one knee before her. Yes. She might tease him a little before she confirmed that she would marry him.

She would marry him! The knowledge sang in her veins. Their months of studying and sparring had come down to this. He hadn't been dissembling last spring as he bent with her over her father's lifework. He truly cared for her. She had the answer she'd come here to find. She loved him. It had taken quite a time to see it, but she surely did.

Flora's pulse accelerated at the thought of being his wife. Together, they would explore the delights of desire, as conscientiously as she had cuneiform or Akkadian or any other arcane subject. And when they'd plumbed the depths of passion, they would also have the congruence of their minds. They'd always have something to say to each other. Not that they would always agree.

Flora smiled at the thought. But the sparks that flew in a good argument could be as exciting as a caress. Robert was a partner to match her at every point. Flora lost herself in a dream of the future, until the sound of people passing outside the door recalled her. She needed to hurry, or she'd be late for dinner.

Flora was not a good house-party guest that evening. She barely made it downstairs in time to follow the others into the dining room. Despite occasional prodding from the young men on either side of her, she said very little during the meal. She couldn't keep her mind on the food, or the filthy weather that had cut short the shooting that day, or the exciting plans that had been announced for Guy Fawkes Day next week. Her thoughts inevitably drifted off again, and she lost the thread of the conversation. She kept falling into a reverie, hugging the interlude with Robert to her in silent delight. She could almost see the appeal of an illicit love affair. There was a thrill to sitting among an oblivious crowd with a delicious secret.

Her distraction persisted when the ladies went through to the drawing room after dinner. Frances Reynolds commented on it more than once, and finally left her to talk with some of the other young ladies. Flora felt a touch of guilt. She was so happy, while Frances was dispirited about Mr. Wrentham's snub and later departure. She vowed she'd find a way to help her younger friend. In London, next season, as Robert's wife, Flora would be in a perfect position to do so. This idea sent Flora back into a lovely day-dream, which lasted until Sir Liam Malloy sat down beside her. "Luck is with me for a change, to find you alone," he said.

Flora gave him a smile and nod in greeting.

"This isn't a very private setting, but on the other hand, no one is listening. And I really can't wait any longer."

"Sir Liam—" Flora began, afraid she knew what was coming.

"I had memorized several pretty speeches," he interrupted. "But they started to sound more like the play than life. So I will be plain and direct. Miss Jennings, I admire and love you. Will you be my wife?"

Flora wanted to be both firm and kind. "I'm very sensible of the honor you do me, but I must refuse."

"Why must you?"

"I don't wish to marry you," she replied gently.

His shoulders slumped. "It's to be Gresham then?"

Flora could hardly share her intentions with Sir Liam when she hadn't even told her mother. "I'm not sure why you say…"

"He's made it rather obvious—to a rival."

Flora said nothing.

"Or perhaps there is still hope?"

"Sir Liam," she said again.

He rushed on. "I'm not one of those insufferable fellows who thinks that a lady means yes when she says no. But perhaps you haven't absolutely made up your mind? I'm very rich, you know. It is a silly cliché that all Irish estates are ruins. Mine is not. It's a fine old place."

"I'm sure it's lovely."

"You'd like Ireland, although we would come to London as often as you wished."

Flora shook her head.

"Ah…well." He let out a sigh and ran a hand through his black hair. "It's too bad. I insist upon a sensible, intelligent wife, and you fit the bill more than any other woman I've met." He tried a winning smile. "As well as being beautiful and charming and elegant, of course."

Flora was relieved that he didn't seem crushed, or speak of a grand passion. "I'm sure there are many such women in England, and Ireland too."

"You'd be surprised. Your species is, in fact, quite rare."

"Not rare but hidden," Flora said. "Because women are encouraged not to reveal their intellect, to be decorative, and not to outshine the men."

"*You* speak your mind."

And the result has sometimes been complicated, Flora thought.

"Hidden," Sir Liam repeated. "How does one flush them out?"

"By treating them like reasoning human beings," replied Flora a bit tartly. "We are not speaking of a hunting expedition."

He smiled. "It would be a deal easier if I could use beaters and dogs."

Flora stifled a laugh at the outrageous picture.

"So many women natter on as if reason had no place in their existence," Sir Liam complained. "You're sure you won't change your mind?"

Flora frowned at him.

"Sorry. I won't plague you. I'm just heartbroken, you know."

"I don't know anything of the kind," she said. "Let us be done with this and part friends."

"Ah, the death knell, when a lady you admire wishes to be friends." But he was smiling.

"Better than enemies surely?"

"Ah, but one avoids enemies, reducing the possibility of pining away."

"I don't think you're in danger of that."

"I could pine, if it would help." He assumed a woebegone expression.

"Sir Liam, I wish you very well and hope you find the sort of wife you want, but please do stop."

He bowed his head, then turned the movement into a nod.

Who would have imagined it, Flora thought when Sir Liam left her. At the age of twenty-five, practically on the shelf, an acknowledged bluestocking, she'd received two extremely eligible offers of marriage. It was surprising and, admittedly, gratifying. Harriet would be proud of her. Mama would be... Well, this would be another amazement for her mother to absorb.

Flora looked for Robert, and found him deep in conversation with their host. They looked as if they'd be involved for a while. She would go to the library, she decided. She'd had enough company, and he would know to find her there.

The corridors were empty of guests. Flora saw only a footman on some errand. She reached her familiar refuge without incident. Lighting several branches of candles from the library fire, she settled before it. As always, some part of her spirit relaxed in solitude. She'd spent her life in rooms like this. Papa's books had spread through their home. She'd been taught to love them.

When the door opened, she looked around with a welcoming smile, expecting Robert. The smile died when she discovered Anthony Durand in the doorway. His penetrating gaze and sardonic expression were like a slap in the face.

"So this is where you hide when you slip away. I followed along to see." He looked around. "A pleasant private place. Ideal for an assignation. Perhaps you have one."

"No." He stood blocking the door. Flora felt a wave of despair at this ruin of her refuge. She'd never be able to feel safe here again. And then, as always, Durand's presence evoked dark memories that threatened to rise.

He strode over and sat down beside her.

She started to rise. "If you will excuse me, I must—"

"But I won't." He grasped her wrist with crushing force and pulled her back down. "You will sit."

"Let go of me!" Flora tugged. His fingers felt like steel bands.

"You will speak to me," the man said, "one way or another."

Flora looked at the door. Robert would be coming.

"Salbridge has recruited some of the younger men to help with his Guy Fawkes scheme," he told her. "They're huddled with him in his study. Likely to be there for some time. So no rescue coming, I fear."

Galled by the word, repressing her fears, Flora repeated, "Let go of me."

This time he did so. She started to rise.

"Lydia has been telling me that your mother was involved in a scandal years ago," Durand said as if they were simply conversing.

Anger cut through Flora's desolation. "There was no scandal," she said.

"Well, Lydia must have had some reason to cut her."

"Oh, she's finally remembered that, has she?" As soon as she said it, Flora wished she hadn't. Durand had been goading her to get more information, she realized. And she'd fallen into his trap.

"With a bit of prodding. She is extremely stupid."

"You speak so of your—?"

"Lover? I don't choose my bedmates for intelligence." His tone was matter-of-fact, not at all salacious. "If I tell her to, Lydia will spread the story about. She'll enjoy it actually. She likes the excitement."

"There is no story to spread," Flora replied through clenched teeth.

"Can you be so naive? I'll lead her on to recall something that suits my purposes." He smiled at her. "We will make it up, Miss Jennings."

Flora's heart thumped painfully. "Mrs. Fotheringay has professed undying friendship for my mother."

Durand shrugged. "She'll do as I say. That is one of her attractions. And she doesn't like me paying attention to other women, you know, particularly younger, prettier ones. It's the one area where she's quite acute. She's growing wary of my questions about you."

Indeed, Mrs. Fotheringay had been shooting Flora venomous glances now and then. These were now explained.

"Any number of people will do as I ask, Miss Jennings. I can rouse a storm of gossip with very little effort."

"Why would you wish to?"

"Ah, now we come to it." He spoke like a man who had won all his battles and was settling down to negotiate the surrender. "I have a use for you."

The phrase and the tone were equally insulting.

"I should very much like to see Lord Robert Gresham humiliated. Or, at the least…discomfited. You are a perfect instrument for my purposes."

"I? What have I to do with—"

Durand held up a hand. "Please. Don't pretend stupidity. You fool no one."

Flora said nothing. Her mind was racing.

"That's better." He looked disgustingly compla-cent. "You and I are about to begin an intense and public flirtation, Miss Jennings. You will show this *exclusive* house party that you are utterly taken with me, and that you've quite gone off Gresham." He sounded calm and reasonable, as if they were talking of commonplace things.

"Don't be ridiculous." It would have been laughable, if the idea hadn't been so distasteful.

"You will join me in entertaining our fellow guests in this way—with not a word of explanation to Gresham, mind—or Lydia and I will amuse them with tales of your mother's transgressions."

"There were no transgressions!"

Durand looked amused. "You cling to the idea of truth. As if it made a difference. People prefer a juicy story to mundane reality, Miss Jennings. They would always rather hear the salacious, and it's what they remember when all is said and done. Even if it's been proved false."

"You are despicable," she said.

He laughed. "I've been called worse. And endured worse. I've had whispers spread about me by Gresham's holier-than-thou father."

"I'm sure they were completely accurate."

Durand's expression hardened. "Go along, and your mother won't have to endure humiliation."

"Mama lives quite out of society." Flora's voice sounded weaker than she liked.

"And why does she do so? Because she can't endure sniping?" Flora knew her face had betrayed her when he added, "I thought as much."

Flora could imagine her mother's bewilderment and pain. It was wretched to think of. Even so, she couldn't join in his bizarre charade. Her mother wouldn't want her to. "No."

"You prefer promoting your own chances to your dear mama's feelings? I certainly understand that. But you weren't thinking that the son of a duke would marry you?" Durand's voice dripped with feigned pity. "A mere nobody?"

Flora almost rose to his bait again to set him straight. She stopped herself in time.

"You might even enjoy our little flirtation. Find you wish to make it more than that. I have certain skills." He slid an arm along the sofa back as if to pull her close. Flora jerked away and jumped up. "It is very dangerous to thwart me," Durand added softly. "I can ruin your family. I can make certain no gentleman will associate with you, in public." His dark eyes drilled into hers. "Disgrace is very isolating, Miss Jennings."

He looked so smug, so certain she'd give in. They were all like that, the people who thought they had the right to take whatever they wanted, who felt no remorse. Durand thought he could destroy people—over and over, with impunity—because so many others fell into line and let him get away with it. She hated the idea and system.

The locks Flora had set in her mind rattled and tossed and fell open. A storm of terror and anguish came roaring out, stronger for having been pent up so long. The girl of eight, with a wild mane of red hair, whose small body had endured a savage beating. The small boy curled into a ball of perpetual fear, unresponsive. Children who only cried at night, alone; those who fought like feral cats. But instead of drowning her, this time the stories merged into a pulse of fury. Flora couldn't change the whole world, but she could fight the battle at hand. She would defeat this man, who brought injustice right to her door and crowed about it.

Some of this must have shown in her face because Durand actually pulled back. But he immediately stood and stepped close to her, too close. "You'd be a fool to oppose me. Stronger people than you have tried and been sorry."

He had no notion of her strength or her capabilities. But Flora didn't say so. She'd learned her lesson about being goaded into speech. She didn't bare her teeth either, much as part of her wanted to snarl.

Durand grabbed her around the waist and yanked her against him. "You do know that young ladies who lurk alone in dim rooms invite a man's attentions?"

Flora kicked at his shins. She twisted violently in his grip. She raked her nails down his cheek.

Durand shoved her away so hard that she stumbled and fell, hitting the side of an armchair with bruising force. "You really are a vixen, aren't you?"

She did snarl this time.

Durand backed away. "You may have a few days to consider my demands. Till Guy Fawkes, shall we say? And then all…explodes." He turned and walked swiftly out.

She'd defeated him, Flora thought as she pulled herself up. Temporarily. She didn't think he'd be back here any time soon. Still, her refuge was ruined, and she felt battered. She'd won a battle but not the war. In solitude, with no one to see, she huddled in the chair to recover.

When Robert entered the library half an hour later, he found his love sitting stiffly in an armchair beside the hearth, staring at the wall of books as if she saw none of them. The fire was nearly out. One of the candles was guttering. Her face was in shadow. "What's wrong?"

"Anthony Durand was here."

"What?" Robert started forward.

"He had some demands."

Flora's voice was an unsettling monotone. Her blue eyes burned with a different sort of fire than the zeal he was accustomed to. He wanted to sweep her into his arms and comfort her, but he could see this was not the moment. "Tell me."

She did. As she spoke, Robert's rage built until it was nearly intolerable. Though she mentioned no physical attack, he saw marks on her wrist. "I'll kill him," he said when she was done.

"No."

"Flora."

At last, she held his gaze. "We must take away what he values most—his power. We must leave him with nothing. That's what he does to others, and that's what he deserves."

Robert was transfixed by her intensity.

"Some might say that this plot over a flirtation is a petty thing. Silly, really. To be shrugged off," she continued.

"I do not."

"But it's all of a piece with worse things," she went on as if she hadn't heard. "He thinks nothing of hurting my mother. Or anyone else. He doesn't regard them as people like himself. They…we are mere pawns. You see?"

"Absolutely."

The conviction in his tone appeared to reach her. Flora sat back; she took a deep breath. "Do you know what your father did to him?"

"Quietly let it be known that he was a cheat, I believe. Papa certainly told me never to play cards with Durand. But there was no proof."

"Then that is what we must find," she replied. "The proof. Exposing his secret card games was never going to have much effect."

"No."

"But if he's shown to cheat, society will reject him."

"He'll be ruined," Robert said.

"We can't help what he might go on to do after that, but he'll have much less power to harm." She looked up at him.

"Then that is what we will do."

Flora jumped up and ran to him. Robert caught her and held her. She was shaking. Not with fear, he thought. Or not mostly fear. She was also angry and determined and fierce. She was everything that he'd admired in her from the beginning and everything that he'd come to love.

Sixteen

ROBERT WAS ON HIS WAY TO BREAKFAST THE FOLLOWING morning when Philip Moreton rounded a corner ahead and hailed him. "There you are! I've been looking all over. I've had some great news." He waved a densely written letter before Robert's face.

"Have you? Splendid."

Robert had been touched and encouraged when he learned that Flora had sent Philip to him for help with the lad's studies. He'd done his best with an extremely reluctant student. He'd written his brother Alan in Oxford to arrange a welcome. Philip's main response was a growing hero worship that occasionally became burdensome.

"It's from an old school friend of mine," Philip went on, pacing alongside Robert toward the breakfast parlor.

Philip was of an age to be completely absorbed in his own affairs, Robert thought. But he was always so eager and confiding that one couldn't snub him. Robert did continue walking, however.

"He is heading up to Oxford next term as well,"

Philip said. "He wasn't going to bother, but he's changed his mind."

"So you'll have a…ready-made acquaintance," Robert said. Lack of friends had been a concern of Philip's.

"Exactly! And Samuel's full of schemes. He always was." Philip laughed. "I remember one time at Harrow, there was this new assistant cook who was serving us the most dreadful porridge. Full of disgusting lumps, and it tasted odd. I don't mean just unpleasant. Truly inedible. Well, Samuel got hold of some brown dye. I can't think where he found such a thing. And he sneaked it into the great pot of porridge at the serving table. Made it look exactly like… Well, you can imagine. With the lumps."

Revoltingly, Robert could imagine.

"And he played the best prank on the Latin master! Latin is bad enough, of course, but old Sproul would cane you as soon as look at you. Found a hundred excuses to beat us boys. You could tell he enjoyed it, too. So Sam spread some really strong glue on the chair behind his desk. If you could have seen Sproul's face when he tried to get up and his trousers stuck to the seat!" Philip waited, clearly expecting admiration.

"Your friend should make a lively companion at college," Robert said. There would be little scholarship involved, he suspected.

"Absolutely." Philip grinned at him like a much younger lad. "Look here, he says we should share the cost of a carriage in Oxford." He pointed to lines in the letter, smiling. It was too far away for Robert to read.

"There you are."

Philip nodded. His smile faded. "I'm still worried about my Greek though."

"Let's have a look later." Robert didn't specify a time because he was impatient to find Flora.

"Right." As they continued along the corridor, Philip's expression shifted from enthusiasm to self-consciousness. "I rather went on and on about that porridge."

"It was an amusing story," Robert assured him. He remembered how easy it was for a youth to veer into embarrassment and self-doubt.

"Like some annoying small boy. What you must think of me!"

Robert caught Philip's eye and gave him a direct look. "I'm very glad you'll have a good friend in place in Oxford. He sounds like a capital fellow. Have you eaten breakfast?"

"What? No."

"Then let us do so." Robert gave him a comradely smile and ushered him into the parlor. Thankfully, several others were at the table to divert Philip's attention.

"I've been supervising the men gathering wood for the bonfire," Philip said to Robert and Edward Trevellyn as they ate a bit later. "It's going to be a tremendous Guy Fawkes celebration."

Robert was thinking of Flora. An exceedingly common occurrence these days.

"Perhaps I should lend a hand," said Trevellyn.

"You're thinking of the mess with the balls and mallets." Philip shook his head. "It won't be like that. I have everything under control."

Encountering his eager look, Robert realized he was looking for an ally. "There'll be fireworks," he replied, rather at random.

Young Philip seemed to take this as a criticism.

"They'll go off without a hitch," he declared. "Papa has engaged an expert to manage them. He's supervised displays for the *king*."

Robert's interest was caught. "Not the one that went wrong in St. James's Park a few years ago, I trust?"

"Did you see the pagoda burn?" asked Philip eagerly. Robert nodded.

"I read about that," said Trevellyn. "Recreating the battle of the Nile, weren't they?"

"They put a fleet of rowboats on the canal to represent Nelson's ships," Robert answered. "Celebrating a hundred years of Hanoverian rule as well. But the gaslights in the pagoda flared, and it went up like oil-soaked paper."

Philip nodded with ghoulish enthusiasm. "I heard the crowd thought it was all part of the show."

"There was wild applause," Robert agreed. "A couple of men were killed putting it out."

Philip subsided. "We'll do nothing like that. Our display will be much smaller, out by the lake where there's plenty of water. It'll still be some jolly good fireworks though. After we burn the Guy." He leaned in. "Don't tell, but we're dressing him as Napoleon."

"Is that proper, now that he's safely exiled?" said Trevellyn. "And anyway, isn't the straw man supposed to be Fawkes? *Gunpowder, treason, and plot* and all that?"

"People use different costumes," said Philip defensively. He looked to Robert again.

"I'm sure it will be splendid," replied Robert, only half attending. Flora had come in, along with two other young ladies. She wore a rose-pink gown, the color as vibrant as her lips, and her eyes warmed when she noticed him.

Philip leaned close. "I'm to inspect the bonfire pile this morning, and I was just thinking. Perhaps you'd come with me?" He continued before Robert could reply. "I'll be conferring with the fellow in charge of the fireworks, too."

Robert was conscious of a spark of curiosity. But he had more important things to do. He intended to spend the day with Flora. "I don't think—"

"Oh, Miss Jennings, you must come with us," said a young lady across the table.

It was Victoria's opinionated friend, Olivia, Robert saw.

"We're walking into the village, and we need you to explain about the scents the herbal woman concocts."

"I'm sure she would be much better able to tell you—"

"Oh no, you would be far superior!" Olivia turned to the girl at her side. "Miss Jennings knows everything."

"I'd thought to write some letters," Flora replied.

"You can do that any time," scoffed Olivia. "I *insist* you come."

"Very well." Flora met Robert's eyes as she gave in. She didn't quite shrug, but he shared her rueful regret.

"Actually, I was hoping you'd help me," said Philip at his side. "Or just lend your support, really. You needn't do anything but look...older. He acts as if I'm a mere schoolboy."

Which, in essence, he was. "I thought matters were well in hand."

"Well, yes." Philip shifted restlessly in his chair. "But I was thinking the display would look so much better against a dark stand of evergreens, you see. And that means moving it to the far side of the lake. However, I can't get them to listen to me."

"I suppose your fireworks man wants to save work."

"Probably." Philip looked glum. "It would be farther from the house that way, though. Remember the pagoda."

"You think there's a danger of Salbridge burning down?"

"No," Philip conceded. "But...I wager he'd at least let me show him the spot if you were with me. It won't take long." He threw out another lure. "They're going to be preparing their fuses and so on."

He looked so hopeful that Robert couldn't refuse. It would have been like leaving Plato by the side of the road. And the ladies were leaving. If he got this over with, he would be free later, when Flora had returned from her forced expedition. Finishing his breakfast, Robert resented the effort required to manage a bit of private time with her. He couldn't wait to be married.

The thought brought a smile. He could hear Sebastian's teasing voice, reminding him that he'd once vowed he'd only marry when he was forty or so and had dwindled into a dull country squire, which he'd called "as good as dead." He shook his head, amused.

"Will you come?" asked Philip anxiously.

"Very well. I'll bring my dog. He doesn't get outside as much as he'd like."

The younger man leaped up in elation. "Splendid. I'll meet you at the back door in ten minutes."

"Twenty," answered Robert as Philip hurried out.

Upstairs, Robert put on his coat and picked up his hat and gloves. When he turned to inform Plato that they were going for a walk, he found the little dog already by the door, poised to set off.

At the back entry, Philip was practically dancing from foot to foot. He wore a voluminous greatcoat and a low-crowned beaver hat. "There you are," he said. He was out the door before Robert could reply.

The November day was overcast and chilly, clouds streaming across the sky like a great gray river. Philip marched him to a flat, open space beyond the kitchen garden and proudly pointed out the logs piled up for the Guy Fawkes bonfire. The stack was huge, well above their heads. It was going to make a towering blaze, Robert thought, happy to see that it was well away from any buildings or trees. The grass right around it might catch, but the flames could be easily stamped out. The grass wasn't dry; they rarely had a problem with that in England. Plato walked around the pile, taking an occasional sniff.

Philip proudly pulled back a sheet of oilcloth and showed Robert the Guy lying on the ground. The straw man wore an improvised French military uniform and a crested hat. "We made it short in stature, like Napoleon," Philip said.

Robert didn't understand why the lad was so eager for approval. His father was a pleasant person. Then Robert remembered things Philip had said about his sister and brother. He knew what it was to have very competent siblings, and to be compared to them. Compliments from outsiders had been quite important to him at one point in his youth. And so he smiled and admired and generally did his bit to give Philip that kind of reassurance.

Plato came over and put his nose to the Guy's straw face. "Don't let him chew it," said Philip.

"I don't think he will."

Indeed, the dog merely gave one of his characteristic harrumphs and turned away.

The Guy was covered again, and they walked on to a small outbuilding to meet the fellow in charge of the fireworks. Robert was glad to see that they hadn't put him too near the stables. Horses and pyrotechnics did not mix well.

There were actually two men bent over a huddle of wooden crates inside, both stocky and strong looking, with sandy hair and sharp hazel eyes. Robert pegged them as father and son and thought that they looked smart and capable. "This is Mr. Andrew Phelps and his son Donald," Philip said, confirming it. "Lord Robert Gresham."

The place smelled of gunpowder. There were no lit lanterns or candles about, Robert noticed, which seemed sensible but left the shed dim, with deeply shadowed corners.

"Your lordships," said Phelps. He had the air of a skilled professional, more like a doctor or solicitor than a laboring man.

"Lord Robert is interested in our display," Philip added.

The elder Phelps seemed amused by the *our*, but glad to show off the paper tubes of the individual fireworks with their fuses. "We use a slow match to light 'em up," he said, pointing out coils of cord. "Same as the navy does for their cannons. The rope's treated with chemicals so it burns slow, see."

He appeared to see Robert as a sort of inspector. His curiosity roused, Robert accepted the role. There was no harm in a double check, after all. "You don't worry about being so close when the things go off?" he asked.

"We'll be wearing these." The man gestured, and his son slipped on a heavy canvas coat that covered him from neck to ankle and wrist. "There's clay rubbed into the fabric so it don't catch."

"That's clever." His brother Alan would be fascinated by the coat's composition, Robert thought. Sebastian would be angling to set off a few of the fireworks himself. Randolph would revel in the spectacle. He'd have to make certain Randolph got an invitation.

"We'll be taking all this out to the lakeshore on the afternoon of the day," Phelps went on, indicating the crates with a sweep of his arm.

"What if it rains?" Robert asked. That was always likely at this time of year.

"There'll be an awning set up on the spot, and we've plenty of oilcloth. Have no fears, my lord. We'll be able to set them off whatever the weather." He paused and acknowledged, "The effect is less striking when it's wet."

"You seem well up on your subject," Robert observed.

"Dad's read every bit of that Frenchy's *Treatise on Fireworks*," said the younger Phelps proudly.

At Robert's inquiring look, his father said, "It's a book put out more than a hundred years ago, my lord. By Amédée-François Frézier."

His accent was not at all bad, Robert noticed.

"I had a translation," Phelps added modestly. "It's about the uses of fireworks outside the military."

"So, Lord Robert agrees that we should move things to the other side of the lake," Philip blurted out.

This was more than he'd promised, Robert thought. He suspected his expression showed as much, from the look Phelps gave him.

"Just come, and I will show you how splendid it would be," Philip urged.

In the end, he persuaded them, even though the wind had risen. They came out of the shed to find Plato waiting on the path that led back to the house. "We're going this way," Robert told him, indicating the opposite direction.

The little dog stared at him.

"He don't think much of the idea," said the younger Phelps with a grin.

"He is a creature of strong opinions," Robert answered, earning amused looks from the Phelpses.

In the end, Plato conceded, and the group marched out to the small lake in the western part of the park and around its edge, Philip constantly assuring them that it "wasn't much farther." It couldn't be, Robert concluded. They had to be more than halfway around the small body of water.

Finally, Philip came to a stop. The grass was sparse on this bit of shoreline, tufts interspersed with smooth mud and an occasional rock.

"You see how the fireworks would show against those trees," the younger man said. He directed their attention to a line of evergreens. They looked almost black under the clouded sky. "And there's plenty of space to set up," he went on, striding closer to the water. "It would be—" Abruptly, as if he'd stepped into a hole, Philip sank to his knees in sticky mud.

With a startled exclamation, he threw up his arms. Mud squelched as he jerked and struggled. Then he seemed to slide a little sideways, and sank up to his waist. The skirts of his coat bunched up around him on the ground.

The mud quivered like a blancmange for several feet in all directions. There must be an underground spring here, Robert thought, saturating the lower levels. "Don't flounder," he said. "You'll just go deeper."

Philip didn't seem to hear him. He lunged and clawed at the mud, cursing. The Phelpses moved as if to go to him. "Stay back or you'll be mired too," said Robert. "You too, Plato."

The dog had climbed onto one of the small rocks and was surveying the situation. He looked over his shoulder at Robert as if to say he wasn't such a dunce.

It started to rain.

"Philip!" said Robert. "Stay still a moment."

"This beastly stuff has got one of my boots." He bent and plunged a hand into the mud. "Pulled it off like a bootjack."

"Leave it," commanded Robert.

"They're brand-new boots. From Hoby. They cost a mint. Papa will be angry if I lose it." He groped in the mud. One of his shoulders went under.

"He'll be angrier if you're smothered by mud."

Philip ignored him.

"We have to lend a hand, my lord," said the elder Phelps.

"And so we shall," Robert replied. One advantage to having five brothers was an encyclopedic knowledge of how to get out of scrapes. Just about any misfortune that could befall a person outdoors had happened to one or the other of them at some point. "Philip, you must stop flailing about and try to move as if you were swimming."

The young man was still groping for his missing boot. He'd gotten mud on one cheek and into his hair. Now he paused. "What?"

"Lean a little forward and try to spread yourself over the mud. Imagine your legs are floating." Robert turned to the Phelpses. Rain spattered his face. "You two find a stout branch." He pointed to a cluster of ornamental trees nearby. "Break one off there. The longer, the better."

The older man hesitated. "The earl won't like us tearing up his garden."

"Just do it!" Robert could rap out a command nearly as well as his father.

The Phelpses snapped to attention and went to attack the nearest tree.

"Do as I say, Philip."

"But my boot."

"To hell with your boot. I'll buy you a new pair. If you haven't sunk completely away, that is."

Finally, the younger man listened. He stopped struggling and leaned over the mud, trying to float atop it, with mixed success. Robert could see that he was shuddering with cold.

The Phelpses returned with a branch as thick as Robert's arm and as long as he was tall. They'd stripped off any twigs. He took it and moved very carefully forward, testing the ground at each step, stopping when his boots went in to the ankle. Bailey was going to be livid.

Robert bent and slid the branch toward Philip. Mercifully, it reached. Philip grabbed, nearly snatching it from Robert's grip. "Easy! Slowly. Just relax and hang on." Robert pulled. Philip shifted in the mud.

Robert gestured, and the Phelpses came up on either side. Each put a hand to the branch. "Steady pressure," Robert ordered. His boots had sunk a bit deeper, he noted. "Move back slowly."

They pulled, stepped backward, pulled some more. Rain soaked them. Gradually, with liquid squelching sounds, Philip came free. When his feet popped out of the mud, one bare, he made as if to stand. "Stay as you are," Robert said, "Let us draw you along."

Philip subsided. They slid him closer. At last, Robert judged he was well out of it. "You can get up now," he said. The young man surged upright. He stumbled, staggered a few steps, and caught hold of Robert to keep from falling flat again. Robert supported him— and was slathered with mud from chest to knee for his pains. The sodden skirts of Philip's greatcoat slapped the tops of Robert's boots with still more mire. Rain pelted his face and ran down the inside of his collar.

The four of them stood like a tableau while Philip recovered. At last, the young man stepped back. He scraped at the mud caking him with shaking hands. Plato came over and sniffed at his bare foot.

"We'll stick with the original spot for the display then?" said the younger Phelps.

Robert choked on a laugh.

"This is not funny!" said Philip.

"Not at all."

The older Phelps snorted. He turned his back. His shoulders shook as he picked up the branch and carried it over to the trees.

"Let's get back to the house," Robert said.

"My boot." Philip looked at the roiled mud. His left foot was white and mottled with cold. The mire had taken his stocking as well.

"Perhaps some of your gardeners will know of a way to search for it," Robert suggested. "Come."

They set off, Philip limping. The walk seemed even farther on the return journey. The Phelpses slipped away as they neared the stables; Robert supposed they'd been given a room there.

He slogged along at Philip's side until they reached the back door and entered. There was no hope of avoiding notice. They were spotted at once by a kitchen maid and soon surrounded by exclaiming servants. These included Bailey, whose eyes bulged at the state of Robert's boots and coat. "I know," said Robert. He slipped out of the mud-slathered garment and handed it to his valet, who held it well away from his own immaculate clothing. "We'd best leave what we can down here," Robert said to Philip.

The younger man seemed stunned now that they were back. He simply stood and shivered.

"Help him off with his things," Robert told a footman. "Just leave his shirt and breeches. We'll sneak up the back stairs to our rooms."

"That is most improper, my lord," said Bailey.

It was lucky the valet hadn't been with him as a boy, Robert thought as he sat on a bench by the door to shed his mud-caked boots. He'd have seen worse than this. "I don't care. Could you organize a bath?" He looked at the footman. "For Lord Philip, too."

"I'm knackered," Philip said. "And starving. I wonder if they'll give me some sandwiches." Robert looked at the footman and got a nod of acknowledgment.

When they'd removed all the clothing they decently could, Robert took Philip's arm to urge him up the back stairs. Plato climbed at their heels, stepping around the bits of mud they left on the treads.

Their bad luck held. When they emerged from the stairwell on the upper floor, they came upon Victoria and two other young ladies moving along the hall in a phalanx.

"Philip!" cried Victoria. "What have you done this time?"

"I didn't do anything! How was I to know there was a mudhole in that spot? I've walked around the lake a thousand times."

"But where are your *clothes*? Why are you parading around the house half naked? Mama will have a spasm."

Philip looked anxious, but he mumbled, "I am not half naked."

"We meant to slip unseen from the back stairs into our rooms," Robert said. "Which we will do now." He put a hand on Philip's elbow.

"But what have you been *doing*?" Victoria demanded. She was blocking the way to the bedchambers and showed no sign of moving.

"I stepped into a quagmire on the other side of the

lake," Philip replied. "Which was *not* there before, I would swear. Lord Robert got me out. He saved my life!"

The eyes of all the ladies shifted to Robert.

"An exaggeration," he murmured.

"No, it isn't," Philip said. He seemed to be recovering his customary spirit. "You knew just what to do. Except for my boot. You don't think if we go back—"

"No," said Robert firmly.

"You lost your boots?" cried Victoria. "The new ones? But you promised Papa that your feet weren't going to grow anymore."

Philip blushed crimson. "Just one of them." He looked woebegone.

"If you will excuse us," Robert said. "We are wet through." He moved forward, and the ladies parted before him, drawing their skirts away from the threat of mud. Robert made sure Philip got to his room before slipping into his own.

Plato was right behind him. Robert had nearly forgotten about him in the fuss. The little dog trotted over to his cushion by the hearth and flopped down with a sigh.

"Indeed," said Robert. By the time a bath was brought and he'd set himself to rights, the day would be well along. And he hadn't seen Flora, properly, for any of it, which he counted as a day lost.

Seventeen

"Did you explain the herbal scents to Miss... Olivia and her friends?" Robert asked Flora that evening. "I don't seem to know her last name."

"Townsend," Flora replied. "And as I knew very well, the woman who concocted them was far more expert. My presence was quite superfluous." Her tone was tart, but she couldn't help it. She was feeling frustrated. Everything about the day had conspired to keep them apart. Now, sitting on a sofa in the drawing room, they were surrounded by chattering fellow guests. Including Anthony Durand, planted like a storm cloud in one corner. "How are we to plot properly in this crowd?" she complained. "We might as well be onstage again."

"People are always plotting onstage," Robert replied. "Look at Iago. Hamlet, too."

"Are you suggesting that I step forward and address the audience?" She gestured at their surroundings. "Inform them of our plans in a dramatic soliloquy perhaps?"

"Your acting was much admired," he replied.

"Mrs. Malaprop does not seem relevant. Quite *mal à propos* in fact."

"Had you missed the French reference? All this time?"

"Are you *trying* to start an argument with me?" Flora was half amused, half exasperated.

"I do miss them."

"You miss bickering over every second word?"

"A bit." His smile was heart-stopping.

"I can dispute anything you care to say. I'm very good at it."

"That's it. You are. It's like watching a virtuoso play a fine instrument."

He said it so simply. He looked so admiring. "Me?"

"Of course, you. There's no one but you."

A woman couldn't ask for more than that sentiment, and the look that accompanied it, Flora thought. He couldn't know, because she was certain she'd never mentioned it to him, but every piece of clay tablet Flora had ever deciphered, every historical insight she'd drawn from the fragments, had been disseminated under her father's name. In publications, lectures, symposia, her significant contribution to his scholarship had never been mentioned.

Papa had praised her intellect to his friends. But he literally didn't see the difference she made to his work. When she'd tried to show him, once or twice, it was as if she used a language far more foreign than Akkadian. He'd been mystified. Even now, some years after his death, if she submitted a piece to a learned journal, it was presented as an extension or leftover of her father's work. As if she was only a conduit.

"What is it?" Robert had been trying to keep the

conversation light, in front of all these people. Her emotions had been so raw the last time they spoke, not the sort of thing to be exposed to the sharp tongues of society.

"Papa taught me everything I know," Flora said slowly.

"No, he didn't."

"What?" This was a fundamental tenet of her existence, accepted by all those around her.

"You've learned more since he's been gone, for one thing." Robert's tone was astonishingly matter-of-fact. "And I'm sure you had any number of original thoughts before that. I've seen how you work, remember."

In that moment, Flora understood that her desire for respect went right to the depths of her soul. Perhaps it had been planted by Papa's struggle for recognition, or Mama's wounded sensibilities. Whatever the source, it was a fundamental part of her. She would sacrifice a great deal to get and keep respect. And here it was, looking at her from a pair of beguiling blue eyes. Her throat grew tight.

"I miss our talks, and our studies," Robert added. "I see us back in Russell Square, never at a loss for things to discuss." He leaned closer. "Or do. It's maddening being near you and not allowed to touch you, Flora."

Breathless, she nodded. He was practically murmuring in her ear, in front of everyone. And Flora only wanted him closer still.

"All right," called Lady Victoria from the center of the room. She clapped her hands to get people's attention. "We're going to have a game of charades. Everyone must play."

It was so ironically appropriate that Flora laughed.

"So much of life in the *ton* seems like a charade." Before Robert could reply, she added, "I don't mean that as I used to. I feel a great deal of sympathy for them. So many people trying to communicate, yet forbidden to simply say what they mean. Instead they must imply and gesture and hope."

Robert gave her a raised eyebrow. Before she could respond Lady Victoria marched up to stand before them. "You are on my team, Miss Jennings," she declared. "I daresay you'll be quickest at getting the clues."

"Without a doubt," Robert said.

Lady Victoria looked from one of them to the other. "I knew you two were going to get together," she crowed then. "I spotted it long before anyone else." She gave Flora a smug smile. "You *were* my rival. Back then. Before I came to my senses. Edward says I am extraordinarily intuitive."

"He's clearly besotted," Robert murmured.

"Oh, do be quiet. Your famous social address is useless if people say what they truly think."

"If they're willing to be rude, you mean?"

"Forthright," said the daughter of the house. "I learned how to do it from Miss Jennings. Edward thinks plain speaking is better, too."

"Not if it's vulgar," Robert said.

"I don't know what I ever saw in you." Lady Victoria looked at Flora. "Are you quite sure you're not making a mistake? He's the most irritating man. How could I not have noticed that?"

Flora was saved from replying by Edward Trevellyn's arrival. "All's ready," he told his fiancée.

Lady Victoria turned away. "Charades!" she called.

"Let us meet later in the library," Robert said to Flora under cover of the noisy beginnings of the game.

"Durand knows about it now."

"Let him come," he replied. "I'd be only too happy to throw him out on his ear." He hesitated, then added, "Leave after me. I'll wait for you there."

The charades seemed to stretch on forever. Even admiring Flora's brilliance at decoding the mimed clues didn't reconcile Robert to the wait. And when at last the game was finished, many wanted to sit about rehashing the details. Victoria's team had of course triumphed, chiefly due to Flora. It was nearly midnight before Robert was finally able to slip away to the library. It seemed another eon before Flora arrived.

Her cheeks still glowed from the praises of the other guests. Her eyes sparkled. She looked happy and so very beautiful. Robert imagined the two of them running hand in hand, laughing, up to his bedchamber and repeating all they'd done yesterday, and more. He wanted her eager and carefree. He wanted her in every possible way. For now, however, his vision was not possible. "So, we plot," he said instead. It was not second best, or even fourth best, but it would have to suffice.

Flora came to sit beside him, bringing the heady scent she always wore and an entrancing smile. "Papa always said that any problem will yield to a combination of care and diligence," she said. "The first step is to amass as much information as possible."

"Right."

"It's vital to have all the facts. Then one orders

them, through analysis, allowing the solution to slowly emerge."

"Indeed."

"It's much more pleasant to ignore Durand," she went on. "One wants to think of him as little as possible. Never, really. But we must treat him as an obscure bit of cuneiform, to be broken down into specifics in order to be deciphered. And, in this case, defeated. Why are you looking at me that way?"

"What way?"

"With a sort of half smile, and an odd glint in your eyes."

"Because you are utterly adorable."

A remark that might have offended her from another man seemed perfectly acceptable from Robert— admiring rather than dismissive. Flora indulged in a long shared glance. It would be so easy to be diverted. Into kisses, for example. His expert, melting kisses that led so naturally to caresses and embraces and absolutely delicious sensations. That made her wild to study with him as he'd learned from her. The idea left her breathless. And then her annoyingly practical mind offered up the thought that Anthony Durand was a spiteful man. Even if he didn't return here himself, he might send others to plague them. Lydia Fotheringay, or some even worse gossip. She couldn't trust the safety of this room any longer. "So," she managed. "What facts do we possess?"

Robert gazed at her as if he'd followed each step of her reasoning. "What do I know about Durand?" he replied. "Let's see. He has an estate in…Shropshire? But rarely goes there. He is a creature of London, always to be found in one gaming hell or another. An inveterate gambler, from need and from love, it seems. His fortune is unknown, but suspected to be small."

"What about his family? The name sounds Norman."

"I've never heard of any other Durands. Thankfully."

"One presumes they wouldn't all be like him."

"*One* is being charitable," he answered with a smile.

Flora dithered briefly under the warmth of his gaze. "He is…connected with Lydia Fotheringay."

"Demonstrating a deficiency of taste."

"In friends, too," said Flora in a more subdued tone. "He chooses them from among men like Lord Royalton, who live lives of idleness and debauchery."

Robert merely nodded.

"I don't see how any of that helps us," she said.

"He is not much liked, so he has no allies to call on here."

"Except Mrs. Fotheringay."

"A slender reed," Robert said.

"No one likes her very much either," Flora acknowledged. She sighed. "Papa's methods don't seem to apply when the problem is people rather than artifacts. What are we going to do? How are we to catch him cheating?"

"I could probably spot it," Robert replied. "But trying to get myself into the games won't work. I've told him I won't play with him. Durand wouldn't go for it. And even if I managed the thing, he wouldn't cheat if I was there."

"No."

"I can't even ask where the games are being held without a risk of rousing his suspicions."

Flora nodded. She began to fear that she was better with dusty old tablets than human beings, too. "Perhaps Lord Philip could? Ask, not play. You did save his life." She'd heard the full story of the mud by this time.

"An exaggeration. But, no. Durand wouldn't want to include Salbridge's son. Too much chance he'd let something slip to his father."

"Right."

Hating to see her dejected, Robert considered other helpers. Randolph had volunteered, but as another Gresham, he couldn't be sent into the games either. And he was a terrible gambler. Notoriously incapable of a bluff. Mrs. Runyon was a resource, if he found just the proper application for her skills.

"You know," said Flora then. "We might be able to spot the place if we look around the house. The gamesters probably leave some signs of occupation in a room where there should be none. I doubt they pay much attention to housekeeping."

"A good point."

Flora half rose, eager for action. "Let's look."

"Not now. The card game will be starting, and we might be seen. Tip our hand, so to speak."

"Oh." She sank back. "Yes, of course. We should explore in the daytime. After breakfast tomorrow?"

He nodded. "Men who gamble half the night away are rarely up and about in the morning." He could probably pick out some of the players that way, Robert noted. The ones who weren't young idiots who cared nothing for sleep.

"Good." Flora smiled at him.

Their plan made, silence fell over the room. The dying fire popped and crackled.

"I should go to bed," Flora said.

The phrase seemed to hang in the air between them. Her cheeks reddened.

"I can't escort you to your door," said Robert. He didn't like thinking of her walking the maze of dark corridors alone. Yet, the most reckless male guests were most likely seated around Durand's gaming table by this time.

"Nor I, you," Flora replied.

He laughed, and the building tension dissipated. "We'll reconvene tomorrow."

She nodded, rising. "Good night."

He stood and bowed. "Good night." He didn't add *my love*, but he thought they both heard it nonetheless.

It wasn't fair that she couldn't be getting into bed with Robert right now, Flora thought a little later, as she pulled up her coverlet. People were sneaking into bedchambers all over the house party, or so she'd been told. Not the unmarried women, though. They... she...were in a special, separate category where all was denied.

Flora punched down her pillows. She was so very ready to be a married woman instead. She wanted all the delights of love, an epic and fiery passion. She wondered if Robert was thinking of her, as she was of him. She was practically certain he was. It was ridiculous—the two of them, lying in their segregated beds, aching for each other.

She remembered his suggestion that they return to London, get a special license, and marry in Russell

Square. She could be his wife in a week. Perhaps less. Why not just do that? He'd said her mother would like it, and she would.

Until Durand started spewing his venom about Mama's supposed transgressions.

Flora sat up and punched her pillows again, this time imagining that they were Anthony Durand. He was despicable. He spent his life hurting people, and enjoying it. It wasn't only Mama. How could Flora return to her children's refuge and face them if she hadn't lifted a finger to stop Durand?

She lay down again, but it was some time before she fell asleep.

∽✦∾

Despite the short night, Flora woke early, washed and dressed, and went down to breakfast. She found Robert already there, along with a few others. They exchanged a secret glance over their meal; there was no need for more. Ten minutes after he had left the table, she met him in the library.

Flora was surprised to see Plato sitting at his feet. "Mightn't he bark and attract attention to us?"

"Never." Robert looked down at the dog. "He is the soul of discretion."

Flora remembered how Plato had left Robert's bedchamber after ushering her through the glass doors, leaving them alone. At the moment, the little animal was staring into the dimmest corner of the room as if some fascinating drama was unfolding there.

"He also has rather uncanny insights, now and then. Shall we begin?"

They left the library and moved along the hallway outside, quietly but not furtively. Flora realized that having Plato along lent their expedition an appearance of innocence. Who took a pet on an assignation? The thought made her smile. "Durand wouldn't use any of the familiar public rooms for his card games," she said.

"No, even late at the night someone might wander in," Robert agreed. "He'd want to be far from sleeping guests, too."

Flora had gotten a general sense of the geography of the house during her visit. There were two long wings, on opposite sides, both older than the central block. Which was odd, suggesting that the center had been rebuilt between them at some point in the past. "The rooms in the wings don't seem much used."

"No. The Salbridges are barely settled in here."

They began with the east wing, for no particular reason, walking through a series of parlors that opened into each other. Early sunlight filtered through the windows, revealing disused furniture and, as they got farther from the central block, worn carpets and draperies.

Plato sniffed at the wainscoting here and there. "Yes, undoubtedly there are mice," Robert said to him on the fourth such occasion. "But they are not our affair."

"You talk to him as if he was a person," Flora noted.

"It is an increasing concern to me," Robert replied with a wry smile.

Though they stepped softly, their feet seemed loud in the empty rooms. Movement on the left made Flora jump, only to face her own indistinct form in a large mirror. Many old houses were said to be haunted.

Flora half wondered if they would encounter a ghost. But they reached to the end of the wing without finding anything worse than a creaking floorboard.

They retraced their steps to the more inhabited part of the house. Flora rubbed her arms. The rooms without fires were chilly on this late-autumn day. "Get a shawl from your room," Robert suggested.

"I'm all right."

"You're cold. I'd offer you my coat, but that would look odd, should we encounter anyone."

"I don't need—"

"When I said I missed our disputes, it was not this kind," he observed. "Where you argue against your own interests just to disagree with me."

"I am not doing that."

"You *want* to be cold?"

"Our search is more important."

"Granted. But we have time for you to fetch a shawl."

Flora started to pose another objection, and then conceded that he was right. A few minutes would do no harm, even if the interruption was irritating. She turned.

"Plato and I will lurk in the library."

Flora choked, well aware that he'd used the word to make her laugh. Then she let the laugh out. "I'll be quick."

"You always are," Robert answered.

She tried to rush without appearing to do so. Fortunately, it was still early, and she met only two other guests in the corridors. A simple nod and greeting was enough for both. Quite soon she was back in the library, fortified with warm cashmere.

At first, the west wing was much like the east—disused

chambers, not dusty but somehow forlorn, their colors faded by time. They'd passed through several parlors, and Flora was getting worried when they found what they'd been looking for.

A room near the end of the wing was much as the cardplayers must have left it. Chairs were shoved carelessly back from two card tables that had been pushed together. A deck of cards lay untidily upon them. Empty glasses were scattered about. A sideboard held an array of decanters. The scent of stale cigars from the stubs left in ashtrays filled the air. Robert was reminded of Durand's complaints about the cramped smoking room. Clearly, he was ignoring his hostess's wishes as cavalierly as his host's.

It didn't take long to search the plain, shabby little room. There was no other furniture; there were no convenient secret closets. Robert was examining individual playing cards when they heard footsteps approaching.

Moving quickly, Robert pulled Flora into the next room along the wing, leaving the door open a crack. Unlike others they'd seen, this chamber was cluttered. It seemed to be a storeroom for unused pieces of furniture too fine for the attics.

Someone entered the card room. Glasses clinked, and chairs scraped across the floorboards. This person was taking no particular care to be silent. Robert leaned sideways and took a quick look. It was one of the Salbridge footmen, clearing up. He'd undoubtedly been bribed to take care of this room on top of his other duties.

Flora jostled Robert in order to peek through the crack herself. Plato was staring into the card room at his feet, Robert noticed. A neat little trio of spies. He smiled at the thought.

Silently, they waited for the servant to finish. He didn't approach their hiding place. Robert hadn't expected that he would. Durand and his cohorts would have no use for this cluttered room. There was barely space to move among the crowded furniture.

The footman shifted the chairs away from the card tables and separated them. Picking up his tray, now laden with glasses, he went out. They waited a while longer to make sure he wasn't going to return.

"We could hide in here and watch the game tonight," Flora said then. "You could see how Durand is cheating. There are plenty of places to duck out of sight if anyone should suspect."

Robert surveyed the room—a tangled pile of straight chairs, many broken; a tattered sofa; a large wardrobe; and several small tables. Flora opened the wardrobe, releasing an overpowering scent of camphor; it was packed solid with clothing. She squeezed around it to a large cupboard shoved against the wall. When she turned the wooden catch, a broad door sagged open, revealing a long dusty space with a litter of broken shelves at the bottom. Flora stepped up and in, pulling the door closed behind her. "You see?" she said from behind the panels.

Robert didn't laugh aloud. He wasn't foolhardy. He kept his expression bland as Flora emerged from the cupboard, shaking dust from her skirts. His mind was busy with arguments proving that he should take over their efforts from here. He was not sanguine about their reception. "The door to this room was shut when we arrived," he pointed out. "Durand would expect it to remain so." The other players might not notice a change, but he was certain Durand would.

Plato starting scratching at the door in question. The pressure of his paws pushed it closed. "Stop that," said Robert. This wasn't like his phlegmatic dog.

Flora came to stand beside them. "Look." She pointed at the spot Plato had been addressing. "The panels are old and dry. They've shrunk back from the joins." Flora knelt and peered through the biggest crack. "I can see quite well. Good dog, Plato!"

Disgruntled, Robert joined her on the floor. It was true. The warp in the door gave him a wide horizontal view of the room. If he put his eye right up to it, he could see up and down as well.

"Splendid." Flora rose and brushed away more dust. "We should bring cushions for our knees. We will have to be in place well before the gambling begins, and then who knows how long we'll have to watch."

"Very tedious, no doubt," Robert said. "And physically taxing. Perhaps I should take on the task."

"You can't be trying to exclude me." Flora's fiery blue eyes drilled into his.

"Not at all. Though I am the more experienced cardplayer, and more likely to spot whatever methods Durand is using to cheat."

"I shall be here," she declared. "You can't stop me."

And it would be a mistake to try, Robert concluded. He thought he could see a flicker of fear in her gaze, along with annoyance and defiance. This had been her plan, and she needed to act on it, not sit by and wait for someone else to step in. He gave up the idea. The spying wasn't physically dangerous, after all. Just taxing, as he'd said. Faintly ridiculous, perhaps. Potentially embarrassing. If they were discovered, Sebastian would laugh himself sick at the story. Perhaps, in that event, Robert would be making use of Flora's cupboard after all.

They walked side by side back through the west wing to the central block. They were about to part at the staircase when Harriet Runyon came down it. "Wherever have you been?" she said. "I've been looking everywhere for you." She eyed the dust still clinging to the hem of Flora's gown. When Plato came from behind them to gaze up at her, she blinked in bewilderment. "Victoria has been asking for you. Your absence has been noticed."

"We were just looking around the house," said Flora.

"There's a magnificent eighteenth-century clock in the east wing," Robert offered.

Mrs. Runyon gave him a sardonic glance. "I am your chaperone," she said to Flora. "I have a reputation to maintain, too, you know. If you keep haring off together to parts unknown, tongues will wag. Or perhaps you have some news for me?"

"News?" said Flora.

"Don't play games with me." Harriet's tone was amused.

Flora could see that Robert wanted to speak. It had developed somehow over the last few months, this ability to understand his feelings without words. Flora had had an intellectual bond with her father, and she felt an emotional connection to her mother. But she'd never experienced this kind of deep link, which encompassed both of those and a great deal more. It promised so much for the future. "We're engaged to be married," she said. She felt rather than saw Robert's slow smile.

"Ah." Harriett looked delighted. "Splendid."

"But we're not announcing it just yet," Flora added.

"Why not?"

"There are one or two things to be settled first. I must write to Mama." Harriet would certainly agree that Flora's mother must be told before any public announcement was made.

"Well, do so," the older woman replied. "And settle these…things. Because after a while, if there is no announcement when all the signs point to one, there will be talk."

"I am so very tired of thinking about gossip," said Flora.

"There you are then. Put an end to it by announcing your intentions." The older woman turned around on the stairs. "And now come with me and join the other young ladies in the drawing room."

"Must—"

"Yes, you must."

Eighteen

FLORA PLEADED A HEADACHE THAT EVENING AND WENT up to her room not long after dinner, before the gentlemen had left their wine. In her bedchamber, she changed into her drabbest gown and then set herself to wait. She and Robert had snatched a few minutes earlier to make plans for the evening. They'd agreed that nine would be a good time to take up their posts. Durand was always in the drawing room till at least that hour.

The waiting was difficult, but it was easier here alone than downstairs, trying to make conversation. Flora sat in the armchair before the hearth and told herself to be patient. She put her head back, closed her eyes, and set her thoughts adrift. Inevitably, they fixed on Robert, like a boat carried on a steady current. She so wanted all to be well for their future. Surely when they had bested Durand, she'd be able to put the past behind her. Robert deserved her whole heart, without old fears rising to plague them both.

Just before nine, Flora rose, went to listen at her door, and heard nothing. She bundled a small cushion into her shawl and slipped out. If she met anyone, she planned to say she was going down for a book. Most guests would still be in the drawing room. Those who weren't probably had affairs of their own in mind.

In fact, she met no one. She reached the library without incident and found Robert waiting for her there. No sign of Plato this time. "Here I am," she said.

"Right on time."

"You're not going to try again to dissuade me from coming?" She found that a bit surprising.

"Not at all. On the contrary, I hope you will maintain a general view of the game as it progresses. All the players. I intend to focus my attention on Durand's hands."

"Of course."

"Shall we go?"

"You have nothing to kneel upon," Flora pointed out. She showed him her cushion.

"Ah. I forgot. Well, never mind."

"Nonsense. The floor will be terribly painful after just a few minutes."

"We haven't time."

"A moment won't hurt." Flora began a quick search of the library. At last she found a miniature pillow tucked into the seat of one of the armchairs. "Here. This will do." She strode over and handed it to Robert.

"I'm not quite sure how I will explain this, if I am called upon to do so," he said, tucking the item under his arm.

"Didn't you once tell me that one secret of social success is never to explain?"

"Did I?"

"Yes. One night in Russell Square. You said that people would label odd behavior as a charming eccentricity, unless one showed uncertainty by trying to justify it." Flora gave him a sidelong glance. She rather enjoyed teasing him with his own words.

"How, ah, wise of me," he murmured with a smile.

They made their way carefully down the west wing, ready to step out of sight if necessary. They saw no one, but the parlor was once again set up for gambling—the two tables pushed together, the fire crackling, branches of fresh candles ready to be lit. They'd timed it well. The footman was gone, but none of the players had arrived.

They moved across the parlor to the far door, went through, and closed it quietly behind them. Flora placed her cushion on the floor and knelt to check the view. She could see the table quite well. "I wonder where Durand will sit?" she said very quietly.

"Facing the entry door, I imagine. He wouldn't care for people coming in behind him."

A sound from the other side of the door ended their conversation. Flora looked through the crack. Anthony Durand had arrived and was puttering about the room. She pulled her shawl around her shoulders and set herself to watch in silence.

And then Robert was right beside her, his shoulder pressed against hers. He had to stoop a bit to look through the crack. He surveyed the scene, then turned his head to look at her, his face only inches away. He gave a little nod, as if to say, "Here we go."

Durand circled the card room. He poured himself a glass of brandy from a decanter on the side table and carried it to the chair nearly directly in front of them. Their vantage point was perfect, Flora thought with some relief. She could see his hands on the table, a three-quarters profile, and his full figure in the chair.

Durand sat very still, as if listening. Flora held her breath. Against her side, Robert was unmoving. Apparently satisfied, Durand picked up the fresh deck of cards lying on the table and very carefully unwrapped it, picking at the paper so that it didn't tear. Taking another deck from his coat pocket, he proceeded to trade the two. Then he wrapped the second deck in the discarded wrapping, fixing it closed with lick of his tongue so that it looked unused.

Robert hissed very softly at this blatant act. The sound was right in her ear. Flora shivered at the feel of his breath on her skin, his upper arm and thigh pressed to hers.

After a while, two young men came in, laughing over a shared joke. They poured brandies and sat at the table. Over the next few minutes, five others arrived. Flora recognized them all from various parts of her visit. She'd sat beside one at dinner. None had taken a role in the play or engaged her in any prolonged conversation. They were not the sort of gentlemen who bothered with an impecunious female.

Anthony Durand "unwrapped" the cards and offered them to the player opposite him. That man cut, the one next to him shuffled and dealt, and the play began.

Flora's left side, pressed up against Robert, was warm. The other grew chilled despite her shawl. Her knees started to ache a bit. Flora suddenly remembered reading that medieval knights had knelt in vigil for a whole night before their elevation. She wondered if they had worn their armor when doing so, and whether that would have been more or less uncomfortable than her current position.

In the next room, hand succeeded hand. Durand didn't win every one, but the clutter of banknotes before him steadily increased. Robert had no doubt, from the way the man handled his cards, that those he'd substituted were subtly marked.

Durand kept the brandy decanter circulating, too. Each time it reached him, he seemed to refill his glass. But in reality the level remained much the same. Robert had seen that trick before, too. The other men grew befuddled; Durand did not.

It was tedious to watch people play cards, Flora thought. There was none of the excitement or strategy of managing one's own hand. She glanced at Robert. His gaze was riveted on Anthony Durand.

Night deepened. Flora grew tired. She shifted on her sore knees. In response, Robert put his arm around her and drew her closer. She let herself lean a little. He was solid as a rock but far more comfortable.

Abruptly, Robert's grip on her tightened. One of the young men in the next room had begun to rail at Durand's run of luck, suggesting that it wasn't natural. He was drunk and growing belligerent. The others were glancing at Durand and one another. Some looked uneasy; others appeared to be giving the accusation serious consideration.

Anthony Durand sat carelessly in his chair, left hand shoved into his coat pocket. The pocket where the original cards rested, Flora noted. The substituted cards were stacked in front of him. "You've overindulged, Trask, and you're growing offensive," Durand said.

"I can hold my liquor, damn you," exclaimed Trask. He surged out of his chair, knocking it over in the process. He swayed and had to lean on the table to catch himself. It wobbled under the impact. All of the others looked at him.

In the instant when every eye was diverted, Durand picked up the deck before him. With his other hand, he casually slipped the original deck out of his pocket. Coolly, in one careless movement, he switched them, slipping his marked deck into the opposite pocket. Flora and Robert saw him do it from their hidden vantage point, but it was clear that none of the other players caught on.

Even if they'd been looking, they might not have noticed, Flora thought. The shift of Durand's body had seemed so natural, the drop of one hand to his lap and simultaneous rise of the other to the table so quick and deft. If she hadn't been staring right at him, from the back, she might not have been certain.

Durand took a sip of brandy. "Do take a damper, Trask," he said. His voice was perfectly steady. Indeed, he sounded amused.

Trask lurched forward and snatched the cards from in front of Durand. "I'm taking these," he declared. Turning with some difficulty, he staggered out of the room.

There was a brief hush. Some of the players gave Durand furtive looks. "Shall we call it a night, gentlemen?" the latter said with cordial disregard. "Or have a final hand to…clear our palates, so to speak?" Shamelessly, he opened a small drawer in the card table and extracted a fresh, wrapped deck.

With murmurs and some shifting in chairs, they resumed play. Flora examined the other men. None showed the least sign of suspicion. Some were too drunk. Others were feverishly focused on their cards, obviously driven by a nearly irresistible compulsion.

Durand lost the hand, along with a number of the banknotes he held. The winner was jubilant, and the game broke up with only a bit of grumbling about losses. Durand gathered up his spoils, finished off his brandy, and went out as if he hadn't a care in the world.

It seemed an eternity before the room was empty. The players milled about, had a final drink, fumbled with candles to light their way to their rooms. Finally, though, the last one departed, snuffing the remaining tapers, leaving Flora and Robert in darkness.

They waited a little while longer to make certain no one was coming back, then Robert rose and helped Flora to her feet. She stumbled a little on her aching knees, and he steadied her. When she was stable, Robert opened the door, went through, and lit a single candle at the coals of the fire. Flora picked up their cushions and followed him.

Robert was flicking through the cards on the table. "He begins the night with his marked deck, wrapped to divert suspicion, then substitutes if need be, or in any case at the end of play. So that he can leave the cards for anyone to examine." He turned over the king of spades.

"It's so brazen," Flora said.

"I daresay he enjoys the risk. He's also chosen

some of the dullest young men here for his games. I'm surprised Trask objected. But then he's not quite as well-heeled as the others who were here tonight." Robert flipped over another card. "The odd thing is, Durand's quite a skilled player. I daresay he'd do well without cheating."

"Not well enough for him, apparently," Flora said.

"No."

"We must tell Lord Salbridge."

Robert nodded absently. "He must have gotten hold of some of the cards they keep here ahead of time. It's a common type, but you saw that the decks matched exactly."

"That footman?"

"Yes, that would explain it."

Flora's mind had been busy. "We'll need some proof beyond our word, won't we? If we want to be rid of him for good."

"Yes. I suppose I'll have to burst in on them tomorrow night. Bring Salbridge along, give him a look at the fuzzed deck."

"But what if Durand isn't using the marked cards?" Not only would Robert be humiliated, but they'd lose their chance of exposing the man.

"Likely to be," Robert replied.

"We can't be absolutely certain." As she frowned over this dilemma, she remembered the locked chest in Durand's bedchamber. "Ah."

"What is it?"

Flora met his eyes in the flickering candlelight. "Mr. Durand wouldn't want to leave marked cards lying about. Or carry them with him all the time."

"No. That would be foolish."

"Which he certainly is not. I'd bet anything they're in the small locked chest under his bed. I told you about it."

"That's right. You were in there." Robert frowned at the memory. "The right size for a few decks of cards?"

"Well, quite a few. But there was nowhere else to hide anything. It's not as if he could count on finding a hollow behind the paneling or under the floorboards in a strange house."

Robert nodded. "A good idea."

"Unless I'm wrong," Flora replied with a sudden qualm.

"You so seldom are. I'll take Salbridge up there first thing in the morning, and we'll find out."

"I won't be pushed aside," Flora objected. "I figured out what was going on. You wouldn't know about the chest if not for me."

"This is a matter of honor, Flora."

Or to translate, Flora thought bitterly, the men would draw together and decide what was to be done. Nothing to do with "the ladies." Anthony Durand would be ostracized from the gentlemen's clubs. He would simply disappear from the lives of their wives and daughters. Most of them would never be told why. Because what did a woman need to know?

"I don't discount your part in this," Robert said. "Far from it. But it will be easier for me to deal with Salbridge."

Flora would have liked to deny it, but she couldn't. Her presence would make the earl uneasy. "So my efforts were for nothing," she said. "I might as well have…sat back and embroidered handkerchiefs."

"*I* am well aware of them," he said. "And I'll tell Salbridge how cleverly you reasoned it out."

"So unusual for a female," Flora burst out. "But I'm never to actually *do* anything."

"You know I don't believe that," he said.

Flora moved toward the doorway. Suddenly, she was worn out. "It's late."

He started to light another candle.

"We should leave those," Flora said. "We're more likely to be seen if we carry a light." One more thing that was different for her. The cardplayers could stumble about the dark house half drunk, waving their candles like signal flares, and they'd merely be mocked. If she was discovered, particularly in the company of a man, scandal would engulf her. "The moon is only a little past full," she added.

Robert snuffed his candle. They moved slowly into the breathing darkness, creeping silently through the sleeping house to the upper floor. When they parted at the intersection of two corridors, Robert pressed Flora's hand and whispered, "I won't fail you."

She said nothing. She trusted and admired and loved him. But at this new turn of affairs, an old melancholy had risen to overwhelm her.

❧

Robert was in the breakfast room when the earl came down the next morning. He knew their host was an early riser, so he'd been up betimes to await him. "I must speak to you," he told his friend's father when the older man walked in. Fortunately, no one else was about at this hour.

"You look very serious," was the reply.

Robert simply wanted to get it over. "Anthony Durand is holding late-night card games in one of your parlors," he said.

"What?" said Salbridge.

"Deep play. And he's cheating."

The anger in the other man's face shifted into calculation. "That is a serious accusation. And it's been made before. Unsuccessfully."

Robert nodded an acknowledgment of this truth. "I was observing last night. From, ah, hiding. I saw him switch decks. He has fuzzed cards, and I'm pretty sure I can prove it."

"How?"

"By confronting him in his room and finding them. Now."

Salbridge exhibited the natural hesitation of a host asked to flout the rules of hospitality. "Pretty sure, you say?"

"He has marked cards. I believe I know where he keeps them. So it will not be simply one man's word against another's." This was where he was supposed to credit Flora's reasoning processes, Robert thought. But he realized that Salbridge was more likely to be shocked at her intervention than admiring.

The earl had been considering. Finally, he nodded agreement. "I'll trust you on this, Robert," he said.

As they walked together up the stairs, Robert had a moment's concern. What if Durand wasn't there? But even if he'd been in Lydia Fotheringay's room for part of the night, he'd be back now. That was how people maintained the fiction of propriety.

They reached the man's room. Robert opened the door without knocking. The key to victory, as Sebastian would say, was surprise and speed.

Durand was in bed, still sleeping. When the door shut with a snap, he stirred, stared blearily at them, and sat up. "What the devil?"

Ignoring him, Robert went to the foot of the bed and looked underneath. As Flora had said, the chest was there. He pulled it out, tried the lid. Locked. "Open this," he said.

Durand threw back the covers and stood before them, feet bare under his flowing nightshirt. "The hell I will. What sort of household are you running here, Salbridge? Get out of my room."

The earl faltered a little. Robert forged ahead before he could speak. "You cheat at cards," he said to Durand. He caught a flicker in the man's dark eyes before they went opaque. "I saw you. Open the chest."

Durand took a step closer. He looked grimly belligerent, formidable even in his disheveled state. "And if I refuse?"

"I'll break it open." Robert strode over to the hearth, got the poker, and returned.

Fury twisted Durand's face and visibly vibrated in his body. Violence hovered in the air. Robert tensed to fend off an attack. For a very long moment, it seemed inevitable. Then Durand made a contemptuous sound. He pulled a thin gold chain from beneath his nightshirt and over his head. A small key dangled from it. He knelt and used it to open the wooden chest, then stood back like a showman unveiling some marvel.

The interior of the box was divided into small

compartments, each of which held a deck of cards. Robert let their host examine them while he kept an eye on Durand. "This is the sort of deck we use here!" the earl said, picking one up and fingering it. He traded it for another deck. "He has all the most common brands here." Salbridge lifted out a shallow tray and revealed a lower level of the chest with more decks. "Good God! These are cards from White's. And here's one from Boodle's. You switched decks at the clubs?" He seemed more outraged by this thought than by the covert games in his own house.

Durand shrugged. "Only now and then, when I had an irresistible opportunity."

Robert looked over the array of cards. Many places had their own individual types. He recognized some from Brooks's as well. Others were distinctive but unfamiliar. He imagined they matched those from some of the gaming hells. It was outrageous. Looking up, he found Durand gazing at him with what seemed to be amused contempt.

"You will leave my house at once," said Salbridge. "As soon as you can pack up. Please leave behind whatever amounts you have won here, and any notes of hand, of course. I shall see to it that you do not play at any gentlemen's club again."

Durand made a languid gesture, as if their reaction was simply tedious.

"I don't expect to see you again," said Robert. "But if I hear that you're trying to make trouble for anyone—at all—your cheating will become common knowledge."

Durand's examined him closely. "Ah." He nodded as if he'd solved a puzzle. "That's it, is it? She's behind this."

"There's nothing to blame but your own dishonesty," Robert replied sharply. "You've been cheating for years. As my father said."

Durand bared his teeth. "It adds a bit of spice to the game. A whiff of daring in a dull age. And it's so easy. Some men seem to beg to be gulled."

"Have you no sense of shame, man?" said the earl. "You are dishonored."

Suddenly, Durand looked weary. "Your quaint ideas of honor are not always affordable for a man without your wealth and broad acres, Salbridge. Or the damned Duke of Langford, either." He shook his head as if they, and not he, were guilty of some stupidity. "I'll try the Continent now that it's open to Englishmen again. Full of opportunities, I understand."

Robert closed the chest. The key was still in the lock. He turned it and picked up the box.

"Do you mean to take away the…tools of my trade?" Durand asked. He seemed about half serious.

"Regrettably, I'm certain you can replace them," Robert replied. "We'll retain this in case any…questions should arise."

"I didn't realize you had quite so much of your father in you," Durand answered.

He didn't sound complimentary, but the idea warmed Robert. He offered an ironic bow.

"I'll order a carriage to take you to the village," Salbridge said. "I shall expect you to be in it within the hour. You can make your own arrangements from there."

Durand nodded. If he felt any regret, for his cheating or its exposure, the emotion didn't show on his face. They left him ringing for his valet.

Nineteen

As Flora sat in the drawing room, awaiting word of the confrontation with Durand, Sir Liam Malloy sank down beside her. "I've come to say farewell," he said. "I'm leaving first thing tomorrow."

"Before the bonfire and celebration?"

"Well, Guy Fawkes is not a particular holiday for an Irishman. Some of my countrymen wouldn't mind seeing the English parliament blown sky high." He smiled to show he was joking. "Not I, of course."

"Of course."

"So, I wanted to take my leave of you. And just to inquire."

"Yes?" Flora asked when he hesitated.

"Well, there's been no...announcement. I wondered if, in fact, there might be a chance for me after all." He leaned forward. "I could stay on."

"No. My sentiments are the same."

"Ah. Too bad." He gazed at her. "So there *will* be news of your engagement soon?"

Flora felt she owed him the truth. She nodded. "I've written my mother."

"Ah," he repeated. "And you are very happy?"

"I am."

He examined her. Flora shifted under his gaze. "You're quite certain?" he asked.

"Sir Liam." She was, Flora insisted to herself. It was just that so much had happened in the last few days. Soon she would feel the elation she'd seen in others. Lady Victoria, for example, her brain wryly suggested.

"None of my business. Yes, I know. Would that it were."

"I hope you have a pleasant journey," said Flora firmly.

"More likely a cold one." He rose and stood before her. "If you should change your mind, you need only send one word."

"I shan't." She wanted to be kind, but not encourage false hopes.

Sir Liam shrugged. "Well, perhaps I shall see you in the spring in London. I plan to be there for the season this year."

At this moment, that seemed a long way off. Flora simply smiled.

"Good-bye," said the Irishman.

"I wish you well."

"And I, you." He offered her a bow and a smile before walking away.

Frances Reynolds came around the back of the sofa and plumped down on it. "Is Sir Liam going away, too?" she asked.

"Yes. In the morning."

"Everyone's leaving." The younger girl let out a long sigh. "It's quite flat here now, isn't it?"

She'd been making this observation often since Mr. Wrentham's departure.

"The fireworks are coming up."

"I daresay they'll be disappointing. It will probably pour rain." Seeming unable to sit still, Frances rose again and wandered off.

Lydia Fotheringay swept through the drawing room doorway and rushed over to their hostess, who was talking with several of her friends, Harriet Runyon among them. Ignoring the others, Mrs. Fotheringay grasped the countess's arm and pulled her away, launching into what was clearly a tirade, even from a distance. It must be finished then, Flora thought. Anthony Durand had been thrown out. Offstage, as it were, from her perspective. She felt a little like a bit player observing the main action from the wings of the theater.

Harriet hesitated in the center of the room, looking as if she wanted to intervene. But in the end she couldn't match Mrs. Fotheringay's effrontery. She came to sit with Flora instead. "I wonder what's gotten into her?" she said.

There could be no doubt who she meant. "Mr. Durand was caught cheating at cards and thrown out," Flora replied. She didn't know if she was supposed to keep this fact a secret. No one had bothered to tell her. She wasn't going to. She'd tell whomever she pleased. Or, just Harriet, perhaps.

"Lord Robert managed to prove it?" The older woman sounded impressed. "There have been rumors for years."

Flora looked at her. Even Harriet, who liked and

respected her, didn't think that Flora might have had a hand in Durand's downfall.

"And of course it doesn't occur to Lydia Fotheringay that public protests will merely increase the gossip about him."

"Quite oblivious," said Flora.

Harriet frowned at her. "That's very good news, isn't it?"

"Very."

"And yet you seem downcast."

"No, I'm not."

"Not downcast," Harriet agreed. "Resentful? Impatient?"

"Why would I be?"

"Why indeed?" Harriet examined her face for a long moment. "I would expect to be joining you in celebrating a happy conclusion to our visit, my dear. You are engaged. A despicable man has received his just deserts. I know how you value justice. I don't understand what's wrong."

"Nothing's wrong." Nothing should be. Harriet was right. And if a dispiriting sense of powerlessness still hung over Flora, well, she was being ridiculous. Yet that inner voice nagged. Would it be like this for the rest of her life? Would Robert always want to act for her? Capably. Lovingly.

"Flora?" said Harriet. She looked concerned.

"I've written Mama, and we'll tell everyone once she's had a chance to receive my letter."

Harriet kept gazing at her.

"Do you think you should help the countess?" It was a diversion, but their hostess did look as if she could use an ally. Lydia Fotheringay had backed her into a corner and was berating her from inches away.

"Oh dear," said Harriet. She rose and went to the rescue.

❧

Robert had meant to go directly to Flora and let her know the matter was settled. But Salbridge had wanted to discuss all that had happened and decide what to say to whom. There was also the matter of securing the incriminating chest. Who was to keep it? And where? Thus, it was nearly eleven before he found her in the drawing room and drew her aside for a private conversation. "Durand is gone," he said quietly. He told her the story of their confrontation. "And he won't trouble you again. I made sure of that."

"Thank you," said Flora.

"So all's well," Robert added.

"Yes." She nodded. "Thank you," she repeated.

"And yet, you sound as if I've given you an ugly birthday gift. Well-meant but tasteless."

"No, I don't."

"In fact, you do."

Words seemed to pop out of her. "I wanted to save myself, you see."

"And despite all you did, you don't feel that you—"

"I'm being idiotic," Flora interrupted. "Of course I'm glad that he's gone and won't make trouble for anyone else. You managed everything with your usual finesse."

This sounded oddly like criticism. He waited; she said no more. "So, we will announce our engagement and get married."

Flora nodded.

"You don't seem overwhelmed with joy." The hurt was startlingly sharp.

"I am! I want to marry you. Of course. It's just… You never actually *asked* me, you know." Perhaps *that* was behind this feeling of anticlimax—another occasion when important matters had been taken out of her hands and settled when she wasn't even there. "You just assumed—"

"I was under the impression that we both assumed."

Flora made a throwaway gesture.

"You did tell Mrs. Runyon…" Robert began. Then he broke off. This was not an occasion for argument. Emphatically not. On top of all else, in his current emotional state, he was likely to say something cutting. "Clearly a situation to be remedied as soon as possible." He sketched a bow and walked away.

Watching him go, Flora was flooded with regret. What was wrong with her? Was she the most foolish, persnickety creature on Earth? She had everything she wanted. Why not simply reach out both hands and take it?

❧

Robert strode along a path in the Salbridge grounds, hands thrust deep into his coat pockets. The leafless trees and biting wind matched his mood. He'd thought to spend the afternoon writing letters with news of his engagement—to his parents first, and then possibly to a brother or two. He hadn't even cared that he'd be teased over his earlier protests that he was *not* in love with Flora. But after their latest conversation, the letters had seemed premature. "Sebastian was positively buzzing with joy at his wedding," he said aloud.

Plato, trotting along beside him as swiftly as his short legs could manage, fixed Robert with his penetrating, liquid gaze.

"Nathaniel and Alan…radiated contentment. No, that's too dull a word. They were…smug…glowing." Robert smiled to think how that label would revolt his eldest and youngest brothers.

Plato kept pace without breaking his stare.

"James, now… He was at his wit's end for a bit. But not in a…sort of anticlimactic way. It was all storm and shoals with him." Robert met his dog's steady brown eyes. "I use an oceanic comparison for the navy man, you see. I am an acknowledged wit."

Plato gave one of his curmudgeonly harrumphs.

"You might help keep my spirits up," Robert complained.

The little animal responded with a grumble that could only be interpreted as a stern admonition.

"You know, Plato, sometimes you sound uncannily like my old mathematics master at Eton. That Indian fellow at Sebastian's wedding—what was his name? Mitra. He'd say you might very well be old Cranston reborn."

Plato snorted.

Robert walked faster. Movement was good, even in this gray November landscape. "Cranston always used to say, 'You're a smart lad. Figure it out for yourself.' He wouldn't hear excuses."

A gust of wind rattled bare branches. Otherwise, the scene was silent. Any sensible bird had taken cover, Robert thought. "Flora is not a mathematics problem, however. If I can't reach her…" He refused to finish this sentence.

Plato seemed to clear his throat, even as his small legs labored on.

"Of course I'm not giving up. No question of that." Robert noticed that the dog was panting, his tongue lolling out. "I've set you a blistering pace, haven't I? I beg your pardon." He turned back toward the house, walking more slowly.

As they neared Salbridge Great Hall, a man emerged, waved, and hurried toward them. "They told me you were out walking," Randolph said when he got closer. "Dashed cold for it!"

"We're headed back inside." Sebastian had once remarked that being joined by a brother always felt like reinforcements. Robert decided that he'd described the feeling precisely. "Here for the fireworks, are you?"

"I am. And full of anticipation. You're well, I hope?"

Robert surprised himself by saying, "I'm pondering how best to offer for a lady in a manner that, ah, dazzles her."

"*You* are?" Randolph looked amazed.

"Yes, I know I used to say I wouldn't marry till I was forty and buried in the country. One's opinions can change."

"It's not that." Randolph shook his head. "You always know exactly what to say. I've admired your savoir faire for years. Never seen you falter."

"Somehow, in this case, my, er, powers have deserted me."

"May I ask who—"

"Flora Jennings. And yes, the family was right about that. Too."

Randolph nodded, unsurprised. "A beautiful and accomplished young lady."

"She is, isn't she?" Robert enjoyed hearing his brother say it.

"I wonder if I could help? I write a sermon every week, you know."

"A…sermon."

"Not the same thing at all, of course," Randolph hurried to add. "But they are words designed to move people's spirits, you see."

Robert was impressed, and touched. He never would have thought of it, but… "I'd appreciate your help," he said.

"Really?" Randolph looked astonished.

"Yes." What was the point of brothers if one didn't accept their support, Robert thought.

"Splendid. We'll sit down for a planning session at once!" Randolph rushed ahead.

A bit bemused at the flood of enthusiasm he'd unleashed, Robert followed him inside.

Twenty

"Now then, we can get to it." Randolph rubbed his hands together like a man anticipating a good meal. He sat at the writing desk in Robert's bed-chamber. Robert watched him draw a notepad and a small pencil from his coat pocket and lay them out before him. "First, a list of the things you need. Some flowers, I think. I'll take care of those." He jotted it down.

"You think flowers are necessary?"

"Women love flowers, don't they? And then privacy. This is a large house. We'll find a spot."

Robert thought of the library, then wondered if a fresh place might be better.

"So, what do young ladies expect from a proposal?" Randolph asked. "You have more experience with society. You must know."

"I've never actually offered for anyone before." Which had been Flora's point, Robert noted. He hadn't offered for *her*.

"Nor I." Randolph frowned, then brightened. "Literature is full of famous love stories. Let me see.

We never hear precisely what Paris says to Helen to lure her away from Greece, do we?"

Robert gazed at his handsome brother with budding fascination. "He started a war."

"True. Not a good example. There are problems with Romeo and Juliet. Hmm, Troilus and Cressida. A remarkable number of great lovers end up betrayed or dead, don't they?"

"More than I realized," replied Robert dryly.

"Tristan and Isolde. No, the Guinevere triangle problem. Heloise and Abelard—oh, definitely no! *Quite* inappropriate."

Robert gazed at him. "Because?"

"Heloise's uncle had Abelard castrated."

"Good God!"

Plato added an emphatic harrumph. Randolph gave the dog on the hearthrug a startled glance. Robert pursed his lips. He tried to avoid addressing Plato in anyone else's hearing.

"Perhaps we shouldn't look to literature," Randolph concluded.

"I think not."

"Writers seem to sacrifice verisimilitude for drama." Randolph considered. "I've performed many weddings of course and spoken with the couples beforehand. Though not about the proposals."

"Your dedication to my cause is flattering, Randolph. But…why *are* you so interested?"

"Well, I intend to make an offer myself next season."

"I didn't realize you had a bride in mind."

"I don't, yet. I'm determined to find one, however, and…ah. Oh. That's it."

"What?" Robert was increasingly rapt.

"Never mind."

"No, no, you must tell me what has made you go white."

Randolph grimaced. "Mama took me along to a *ton* party a few years ago when I was visiting London. I sloped off to a quiet corner, because I knew very few people there, you see. A group of *very* fashionable young ladies congregated on the other side of this…arrangement of greenery and began dissecting their acknowledged and hoped-for beaus in, really, daunting detail. You can't imagine."

"Ah, they compare notes. I've heard a bit of that." It had been educational.

"They might have been touts handicapping a horse race, or placing bets on a cricket match," Randolph said. "Only more graphic and…ruthless. Also, they knew things that I had thought hidden from gently reared females. What they'd said about Colefax! And then cackled like a bunch of hens." Randolph shuddered. "I thanked God that none of us were mentioned. If I'm to face girls like that next spring…well, as Sebastian would say, I need more ammunition."

Robert hid a smile.

His brother let out a breath. "So, then. All young ladies like to be told they're wonderful."

"Don't we all?" Robert murmured.

"And unique. That's important, I believe. We… you should say there's no one else like her."

Flora certainly fit the bill in that regard, Robert thought.

Randolph scribbled on his notepad. "Mention that she's changed your life, can't live without her."

Also perfectly true, Robert acknowledged.

"What else?" his brother wondered.

"Actually ask her to marry me?"

"That goes without saying."

"And yet, it doesn't," Robert murmured. "Which is the point of this rather odd exercise."

"I'm sure you can find the words for that. You're a veritable tulip of fashion, aren't you? Acknowledged wit and all that?" Randolph's smile softened the comment.

"I once thought so."

Randolph consulted his pad. "I think that covers it. So tomorrow then?"

Robert discovered a thread of anxiety deep in his consciousness. He banished it and nodded.

"Morning or afternoon?"

"The latter. Everyone is awake and alert."

"But people are often scattered on various expeditions," Randolph objected. "Harder to pin down."

From the hearthrug Plato responded with a characteristic grumble.

Robert weighed options. "The hour before it is time to change for dinner, I think. There's an...atmosphere of expectation. And yet nothing much to do."

The dog's curmudgeonly gurgle included a snort at the end, rather like an exclamation point. Robert nearly answered him.

"Good," said Randolph. "I will begin the arrangements at once." He stood. "Roses, I think. Yes, must find some roses." He hurried out of the room.

Robert looked down. Plato's brown eyes were not twinkling with amusement. It was merely a healthy shine.

⁂

On the following day, in the slack time before people went upstairs to change for dinner, Robert stood in his bedchamber once again, snipping the thorns off a single red rose with a pair of nail scissors.

"Good notion," Randolph said. He shifted from one foot to the other, seeming more nervous than Robert. "Better than a great armload of flowers," he said, not for the first time.

"Much better."

"The gardener in the greenhouse thought so."

Robert suspected the fellow was more interested in conserving his stock than a random guest's wishes, but he didn't say so. And if Flora chanced to throw her arms around his neck, accepting him, there would be no awkwardness about where to put a bouquet. There would be no bloody fingertips either, he thought as he finished his task, much as they might evoke his and Flora's encounter in the brambles.

"I considered ordering up a bottle of champagne," Randolph said. "But I decided that looked like overconfidence."

"That seems wise."

"I'll go and herd her then, shall I?"

"Yes." They—mostly Randolph—had chosen a small parlor on the south side of Salbridge Great Hall as the...Robert found himself thinking...*stage*. The room was little used but pretty, papered in a narrow green-and-white stripe and cozily furnished. He'd asked for a fire to be lit.

Randolph departed. As Robert waited the prescribed quarter hour, he thought of his married brothers. James had bungled his first proposal, as he told it, blurting out, "If you want a proper husband, take me." He'd come right in the end, however. Nathaniel had made a stilted offer in form, with Violet's parents right there looking on. Smiling, Robert wondered what Alan had said to Ariel. Had he given her a scientific argument about why she should favor him? Sebastian had no doubt flailed in a morass of words. They tended to get the best of him. Georgina had probably had to offer for herself. They all would have expected him to show them how it was done, Robert thought. But summoning smooth phrases was rather different when one's entire future was at stake.

It was time. "Come, Plato," he said.

In the drawing room, Flora hid a yawn. She'd played a longish game of cards with Frances Reynolds and some of the other young ladies. It had broken up, and now she was sitting with a group including Harriet. She didn't know where Robert was, and she felt a bit anxious about that. They'd hardly spoken five words since her impulsive request for a proper proposal. He hadn't seemed annoyed. But then... where was he?

Lord Randolph came in, surveyed the room, and came up to her with a polite bow. "Would you care to take a turn about the room?" he asked. "I think we're all feeling rather cooped up on this wet day."

"The rain has certainly worsened," she said, rising to take his proffered arm.

"It was just a drizzle this morning when I was hunting down gardeners."

"You were—"

"But it's really pelting down now," Randolph interrupted.

Indeed, water ran down the long windows overlooking the gardens. The patter of raindrops masked the conversations taking place around the drawing room.

They strolled along the outer wall, turned, and walked up the side of the chamber. "Very large room," Randolph remarked. "Big enough to provide a decent walk on a filthy day. If you go 'round a few times."

Flora agreed, wondering what had come over Robert's scholarly brother. These were the remarks of a witless rattle.

"Shall we continue along the corridor?" he suggested as they neared the doorway.

Increasingly mystified, Flora agreed. They walked. Randolph began a rambling story about the artifacts he'd found hiking along Hadrian's Wall. When he repeated one of his sentences, she started to ask him what was wrong. But at that moment he drew her into a pretty little parlor. "Just remembered something I have to do," he said. He rushed out leaving her alone. She stood there, astonished. Had he been taken ill?

The door opened. Flora looked around, expecting Lord Randolph's return. But no one came in. Then she caught a movement near her feet. Plato stood there. He had the stem of a red rose in his teeth, like a gypsy dancer.

"What in the world?" said Flora.

Plato sat. He stared up at her, solemn as a judge.

Flora reached for the bloom. As she grasped it, the dog opened his jaws and set it free. "Thank you?"

"I do hope you like red," said a dearly familiar voice from the doorway.

Robert stood there, in an immaculate coat and pantaloons, the picture of a polished man of fashion. He came in, smiled at her in a way that made her pulse accelerate, and went down on one knee.

"Aren't your knees sore? Mine are." Flora nearly added to herself—*idiot*. Why had she said something so silly?

"We are not going to discuss my knees, or yours. Lovely as they are."

Flora's fingers tightened on the rose. There were no thorns, she realized. The implications of that fact nearly made her cry.

"We are not going to *discuss* at all," Robert continued. "Or argue. I hope. I am simply going to tell you that I love you with all my heart."

Flora swallowed the threatened, and unwanted, tears.

"And why is that?" he said, as if in one of her father's Socratic sessions. "You are lovely, of course. The determination and compassion with which you fight for justice inspire me. You ravished my mind, which no one ever did before. Having met you, I can't imagine any other wife. Indeed, I won't have one."

"Oh, Robert."

"You will want to know about my fortune," he said.

"No, I don't ca—"

"It's nothing like a duke's, but I inherited a

comfortable competence from a great aunt. I believe you have an income as well."

Flora blinked in surprise.

"We would be a joint enterprise, would we not? You'd want a hand in the, er, direction of things? If, that is, you consent." For the first time, his confidence seemed to falter.

"Yes," said Flora. "Yes!"

"Is that a general yes? Or a yes limited to my financial question?"

"It is a wholehearted, unqualified yes." She held out her hands. "Do get up. Your knee must hurt, whatever you say."

"A bit." He rose gracefully and started to pull her up into his arms.

The parlor door swung, and Lady Victoria surged in. "You've settled it at last. Bravo! I knew you would. I told Edward so." Her fiancé followed her in. "We didn't mean to listen at the door, but you left it a little open." Her tone indicated that the interruption was demonstrably their fault. "Good, I can speak to you both at once."

"Perhaps this is not the time?" Trevellyn suggested.

"It's perfect."

Trevellyn subsided in a manner that Robert deplored, in this instance. It also boded ill for the man's future. Meeting Victoria's eyes, Robert saw an iron will gazing back at him. The cat's foot indeed.

Edward Trevellyn leaned on the mantelpiece and smiled fondly at his...future feline. Victoria plumped down on a sofa, the ruffles of her yellow muslin gown floating around her. "I wished to apologize to you.

Both of you. Edward thinks I should. He has made everything clear to me." She and Trevellyn exchanged a doting smile. "He is very wise." Trevellyn basked in her admiration.

"Er, no doubt," said Robert. Not a word he would have chosen to describe the fellow, but he wasn't besotted with him.

Victoria clasped her hands at her bosom. "I see now that what I felt...thought I felt about you was just a silly schoolgirl crush." She was as earnest as a parson. No, not a parson, Robert amended. Randolph was never that complacent. "I mean, it was ridiculous, really. You and me?"

"Just so." Robert barely stopped himself from saying, "Couldn't agree more." Flora's stifled choke of laugher didn't help.

"I require a husband with true depth, not mere surface flash." Victoria gazed at Trevellyn.

"That isn't fair..." began Flora.

Robert silenced her with a sidelong glance. The last thing they wanted was to prolong this conversation.

"You're not angry with me?" Victoria treated them to a melting gaze. She had a real flair for drama, Robert thought. She could have dominated the stage if only she'd been able to memorize lines. "Not at all," he said. "Quite the contrary. I wish you very happy. You too, Trevellyn."

"Good of you." The other man stepped forward, extending a hand.

Robert shook it.

"As do I," said Flora. "I expect you will be happy."

"Oh, we will be." Victoria smiled smugly.

"We'll leave them alone now," said Trevellyn.

Victoria started to object. He smiled and took her hand. She actually subsided and stood up. Perhaps the fellow *was* wise, Robert thought with silent thanks.

Lord Philip Moreton barged through the half-open door. "There you are. Heard your voice. I wanted to speak to you about—"

"Lord Robert is engaged to Miss Jennings," said his sister.

"Oh yes? I wish you very happy. Could you come with me to speak to Phelps? I had this idea about the display tonight. It occurred to me that—"

"No," said Robert.

Philip gave him a reproachful look. Randolph popped through the door exclaiming, "Congratulations!" He checked, clearly bewildered by all the people present. Robert gave him a nod for his vote of confidence.

"Splendid, isn't it?" said Victoria.

"It's just that they listen to you," Philip argued.

"About what?" said Randolph. "Who? Did you ask her?"

"They're engaged," said Philip. "All right? Now can you all just—"

"Oh good." Randolph grinned. "I was thinking the Guy Fawkes fireworks could be like a celebration of the engagement. Between, ah, ourselves, that is." He looked at the others dubiously.

Flora emitted a small gurgle, like a woman who could contain herself no longer. Then she started laughing. Robert wasn't sure if this was a good sign or a bad sign until he met her eyes. Consigning the others to perdition, he took her hand. The way her fingers interlaced with his—naturally, confidingly—buoyed his spirits.

"We won't go anywhere near the mud," Philip explained. "And it won't take long." He jumped. "Hey!"

Plato had set his teeth into the ankle of Philip's boot, Robert noted. It was a rather old boot, and Plato wasn't biting down.

"Come on," said Victoria. She grabbed her brother's coattail and tugged him toward the door. With these reinforcements in place, Plato released him.

"But I haven't finished. Stop that! You'll tear my coat."

She kept pulling. "They want to be alone," she said, glancing pointedly at Randolph.

"Oh, of course," said the latter.

The daughter of the house shoved the three gentlemen ahead of her into the corridor. And then, miraculously, they *were* alone, and Flora walked into Robert's arms. She was still laughing.

"I hope the, ah, unanticipated addition didn't spoil the proper proposal?" he asked.

"It was everything a lady could want," she replied. She smiled up at him. "And so much more."

Robert thought she sounded determined to be happy. Which was not *quite* the same as simply happy. But it was a mistake to overanalyze. He kissed her.

Twenty-one

NOVEMBER FIFTH DAWNED COLD BUT CLEAR, AND
Salbridge Great Hall buzzed with anticipation of the
Guy Fawkes Day observance. Even though all the
arrangements had been in place for some time, people
were continually pacing in and out of rooms and asking
about this or that bit of the schedule. They congratulated
one another over the shorter autumn days, eager for
darkness to fall so that all could begin. Dinner was to be
an informal buffet, for guests to graze as and when they
liked, so that more servants could join the festivities.

The crowd that gathered around the great pile of
wood behind the kitchen garden as the day's light faded
included people from the village as well as the estate. The
promise of fireworks later had drawn the whole countryside. The sound of their chatter rose into the chilly air on
the steam of their breath. Children ran through the press
carrying small homemade effigies and crying, "Penny for
the Guy." Watching them, Flora wished she'd brought a
supply of small coins. Then she saw that the countess had
come prepared and was giving them out.

The earl stepped forward with a flaming torch. "For

the happy deliverance of England from a most traitorous and bloody-intended massacre!" he recited, and shoved the end into the base of the woodpile. It caught at once, leading Flora to suspect that some substance had been hidden among the logs to ensure that. The flames climbed quickly, giving an orange glow to the circle of rapt faces.

A group of young men pulled aside the oilcloth and picked up the straw man dressed as Napoleon. They carried it, tossing it up and down, around the fire several times. Then, to a great cheer, they threw it high and hard into the fire. It went up with a roar.

The flames were intense. Flora backed off a little, putting a few more people between her and the heat. She looked for Robert. He and Randolph had been right there a moment ago. When she felt a hand on her upper arm, she turned, smiling. Until she found it belonged to Lydia Fotheringay.

Flora's heart sank. She'd been avoiding Mrs. Fotheringay and her complaints. Most people were, which made her even more exigent. Now, the older woman jerked at Flora's cloak. Flora pulled away. Mrs. Fotheringay threw an arm around her shoulders and used her weight to pull Flora farther back in the crowd. Flora was too surprised to react at once, and they were soon at the very back, with only darkness behind them. Flora started to struggle.

A far-stronger pair of arms closed around her and dragged her away. When she cried out, a large hand closed over her mouth. She probably wouldn't have been heard anyway, she realized, over the roar of the fire and buzz of talk.

Flora squirmed and kicked. She bit at the hand pressed to her face. With a coarse oath in her ear, it withdrew. She yelled and received a stunning blow to the side of her head. It made her stagger. Her assailant took the opportunity to drag her more quickly, past some trees and shrubbery to the shore of the lake. Flora could see the water and treetops, sporadically illuminated by the towering fire.

The arms let her go. Flora stumbled forward, whirled, and discovered the footman who'd been bribed to help with Durand's card games. Mrs. Fotheringay was gone. "What do you think you're doing?" she demanded.

"I've brought her and that's all," the man said, speaking over her shoulder. "I won't have anything more to do with this." He backed away.

An even more unwelcome voice replied from behind Flora. "You've done your part." As the footman hurried away, Flora turned and faced Anthony Durand. He didn't pause to gloat. He strode over and grasped her upper arms with bruising force. He shook her. "Didn't expect to see me again, did you?"

Flora twisted and kicked him. "Let go of me!" Her head was still ringing from the footman's blow.

He winced and tightened his grip. "You managed to ruin me, but I'll have the satisfaction of doing the same to you before I slink off to France. See how lord almighty Robert Gresham likes that!" He jerked her off balance and tried to push her to the ground. Flora staggered, swayed, and managed to stay upright.

He shook her until her teeth rattled this time. His fingers dug into her arms like metal pincers. He was terribly strong. Flora felt a flash of stark fear. "Help!" she shouted.

Durand spun her around and imprisoned her against his chest with one arm, while the other immobilized her head, covering her mouth. "You will be quiet," he hissed in her ear. "Unless you wish to be seriously hurt."

Flora froze. It felt as if one twist of his hands would snap her neck. The terror of being imprisoned alone in darkness descended on her, muddled with all the stories she'd heard from broken children. They flapped though her mind like a flock of carrion birds. There was no escape from men like this; they took whatever they wanted. He would enjoy hurting her. Flora panted with terror.

And then, through her fear, a fierce inner voice flared up. She was not a captive child, tiny and weak. She was not ignorant or inexperienced. She might, technically, be a damsel in distress, but hadn't she wished, so ardently, to save herself?

Flora stopped squirming and began to calculate. She looked about her, noting every detail she could make out in the dim light cast by the far-off bonfire and the rising moon.

Durand must have thought her cowed, because he lessened his grip a little. He would have to let her go in order to ravish her, Flora thought. He was relying on intimidation and the threat of violence, and he had good reason. She wouldn't have more than one chance.

He shoved her a few feet farther, to a screen of bushes at lakeside. Eyes on the ground, Flora saw that he'd brought a blanket. This bit of foresight chilled and further infuriated her. She waited. When his hands loosened to grope her body, she let herself fall, using her full weight to get free of his grip. As she went down, she used the information she'd gathered through observation, pivoting and pushing hard with her shoulder.

Durand staggered backward, trying to recover his balance. He reeled, recovered, missed his footing, and tumbled over the two-foot drop Flora had seen and into the lake. His gasp when he hit the icy water was very satisfying. It wasn't deep, but he'd gone in flat on his back and was immediately soaked.

Flora ran over and snatched up a broken tree branch she'd spotted on the ground. Durand lurched out of the lake, dripping and furious, his hands outstretched to grab her again. But his lunge was hampered by knee-deep mud. Rather than run away, Flora stepped toward him and swung the branch with all her strength.

It hit him first on the shoulder. He swayed but kept coming. Flora got in another blow to the side of his head. Durand reeled, tried to shake it off like a maddened bull, and then, abruptly, sat down. He pushed at the ground, trying to rise. Flora hit him again. He slumped, blinking and stunned. This time, he didn't try to stand. Breathing hard, as if she'd been running, Flora backed away, branch still in hand.

From close behind her came an incongruous sound. It sounded like—but couldn't be—applause.

Flora whirled. There, in the ruddy light from the distant fire, stood Robert, clapping. "What…what the devil are you doing?" she said.

"Acknowledging your triumph," he answered. "Well done. Very well done indeed."

"Have you been there the whole time?"

"Not far away. I saw Fotheringay accost you and suspected it couldn't be for any good purpose."

"You let them drag me off? Let that vile man assault me?" She pointed at Durand with her branch.

"I let you rescue yourself."

The echo of her own words rang in her ears.

"And a very good job you made of it."

"But what if he'd—"

"Oh, I stood ready to kill him at any time." He sounded perfectly serious. There was rage in his voice. "Refraining from doing so was the most difficult thing I've ever done. I don't think you can imagine how difficult."

There could be no doubting his sincerity. His hands opened and closed with tension. Flora gazed at him. "You did it for me?"

He gave a terse nod. "And now I can't even kick him. Because he's down. It's intolerable. But I've thought very hard about what you said."

"Said when?"

"Ever," he answered.

Flora swallowed. She was trembling again, but not with fear. "I rescued myself."

"And we see, in action, how very strong and capable you are." He gestured at Anthony Durand, still on the ground. The man stirred, clawed at the earth. "You don't think I could kill him? Now that you've proved your point."

A choked laugh shook Flora. "A very tempting offer. And yet, I don't believe I can allow it. I can't have my betrothed taken up by the magistrates." Flora flexed her fingers on the tree branch. She rather felt like hitting Durand again. She turned to look down at him. He was shivering.

"Are you finished with this sickening blather?" Durand asked. He didn't look as assured as his words suggested, however. He put his hands to his head. "My God, you've split my skull."

Flora found she couldn't strike in cold blood. "We'll let the magistrates have him instead," she told Robert.

"Oh, very well." He came closer. "There's one other thing."

"Yes?"

"Never expect me to hang back like that again, as long as you live," he said, his tone steely. "I will not, cannot do it. I must insist on standing with you, beside you. Really insist, Flora."

She took in his set expression. It brooked no argument, and she found she didn't mind. "I don't suppose we'll ever face another such situation. I hope not."

"Whatever we do face," Robert declared.

In firelight and moonlight, she admired the resolve on his handsome face. From now on, they would rescue each other, she realized. Without keeping count of who had done the most. And that was the way it should be. He'd given her the opportunity to see that, no matter how much it had cost him. "Yes," she said. The locks in her mind weren't needed any longer, she realized. The darkness of the world remained, but she didn't face it alone. "Yes."

Anthony Durand groaned. "Send me to Botany Bay. Set me to breaking rocks. Just stop this blithering."

"I'll fetch the earl," said Flora. She handed Robert her tree branch.

He took it. "You're not going to argue with me about who is to stay here?"

"Not this time." Smiling, buoyant, she hurried off toward the bonfire.

Twenty-two

THE FIREWORKS DISPLAY BEGAN AN HOUR LATER. Due to Robert's earlier expedition with Philip, he easily found a spot on the bank of the lake where they could see every flash and yet be alone. They appropriated Anthony Durand's blanket, which oddly seemed to irritate the man more than being led away by some of the earl's men. Cozily settled on the thick wool cloth with their backs against a boulder and Flora's cloak draped over them, they watched bursts of colored light open in the sky, their brightness reflected in the sheet of water before them. The oohs and aahs of the crowd farther down the shore punctuated each display.

Here was the happiness he'd been looking for, Robert thought. With Flora nestled under his arm, her body warm against his, he felt exultation bubble through him. The victory was hard won. When he thought of standing back as Durand grabbed Flora, his brain nearly exploded like one of the rockets the Phelpses were shooting off. Flora would never know how close he'd come to wading in and taking over when she cried for help. Indeed, he was surprised that Durand hadn't seen him. He'd been poised to pounce when Flora dropped to the ground and shoved the blackguard into the lake. The memory of Durand's gasp and sputtering and dripping rise from the mud made Robert smile grimly.

He still wished he could thrash the fellow. Durand hadn't seemed nearly sorry enough for what he'd done. And society decreed that it was a man's place to do such things. What would his father think of the way he'd stood back? His brothers? Robert felt the beginning of a cringe at the questions, and then a word floated up from the depths of his mind. "Restraint," declared Papa's voice in his head, "and knowing when to exercise it, is a far more arduous discipline than unconsidered action." Robert repeated the sentence silently. He couldn't recall when he'd heard it, but the sentiments echoed and unfurled inside him. Perhaps he was something like a duke after all, Robert thought.

He pulled Flora closer against him. Whatever the case, he'd had to cede the satisfaction of beating Durand to her. She'd *needed* to strike the telling blow. He'd merely wanted to. It was a fine but important distinction. And who would have predicted he would ever have a thought such as that.

"What are you laughing about?" asked Flora.

"I'm…bemused," he answered. He looked down at her as a burst of light from a rocket gilded her lovely face. His, she was his, exulted an eager inner voice. "I was thinking about…hierarchies of motive."

Part of him smiled sardonically at the phrase. What

idiot would say such a thing when he had a lovely woman in his arms, fireworks bursting above? One who held Flora Jennings, another part answered.

His incomparable, intellectual love looked interested. "Some being stronger than others, you mean?"

"More exigent," he replied. "More important for the...well-being of the person in question." Flora turned a little more toward him, sending a spike of desire through his frame.

"And so to be given precedence?" she said.

"Exactly." There was no one on Earth quicker or sharper, he thought. Or more delectable.

"So it's a matter of recognizing this hierarchy and... trading, perhaps."

"Well, I don't think one can measure it in terms of trade."

"Too common for your aristocratic sensibilities?" Flora interjected, only half playfully.

Robert shook his head. "Not what I meant. I think it might not be that kind of...exchange. Keeping accounts, you know. Watching for a return." How did one balance the needs of two strong-willed individuals? Perhaps he'd ask his mother about that. Sometime. He suspected she would know the answer. Or one answer, at least.

"But one must consider fairness," Flora objected. "It can't be all on one side. That would cause resentment."

"Not if there was a clear understanding of the stakes."

"I'm not sure you're right."

"Are you ever?" Robert asked with a smile. He adored her tenacity. "So, you would say that I am owed a...concession?"

Flora smiled back. "You said it wasn't a trade."

"And you held that fairness was vital."

Their smiles widened in tandem as they gazed at each other. Colored light washed over their faces as another rocket burst high above.

"Shall we be married in London?" Robert said. "Next week, say."

"That's not much time to prepare."

"*I* am entirely prepared. How much fuss do you require?"

"I care nothing for such things. But our families might like a bit of pomp."

"Mine has had enough weddings to surfeit a regiment of maiden aunts," Robert replied.

"Well, Mama has not. And I am her only child. She will have...views."

"So we do the thing in Russell Square. Invite all your father's old friends. Send out the announcements in cuneiform symbols."

Flora laughed. "I wouldn't go *that* far."

Robert admired the exquisite planes of her face, the line of her neck. "Will we never stop arguing?" he wondered.

"Is that what you want?" She cocked her head at him. "Isn't it rather...stimulating?"

She was right. It was. "There's one area where I hope we will always agree."

"What?"

He bent his head and kissed her—tenderly, passionately, quite thoroughly.

"Oh," Flora said breathlessly when at last he drew back. "That area. Yes, absolutely." She pulled him close and kissed him back with riveting enthusiasm.

Quite a time passed in a delightful demonstration of their concurrence. Garments were loosened. Hands roamed. They slid off the boulder into a recumbent position.

"Shall I stop?" asked Robert when it was clear that matters were reaching a crucial point.

"Under no circumstances," Flora ordered.

He had no argument there.

*Keep reading for a sneak peek of the next book
in the Duke's Sons series*

THE DUKE KNOWS BEST

Lord Randolph Gresham attracted more than one admiring glance as he walked along Grosvenor Square toward Bond Street on a Tuesday morning. And indeed he felt unusually dapper. His dark-blue coat had arrived from the tailor only yesterday. His dove-gray pantaloons outlined a muscular leg. His hat sat at a jaunty angle. He'd often been told that he was the best looking of the six sons of the Duke of Langford—tall, handsome, broad-shouldered men with auburn hair and blue eyes—and today he thought he almost deserved the accolade. He breathed in the early April air, invigorating with a tang of spring, and listened to the birds calling in the trees. For the next four months, in the interval between parishes, he was not a vicar or a model for proper behavior. He had no special position to uphold and no clerical duties. He was free to enjoy the London season, and he fully intended to do so.

A familiar shape caught his eye in passing. He turned, then went quite still. His feet had taken him automatically into Carlos Place. How odd. His body had somehow remembered what his brain had passed over. He would not have come here consciously, although in an earlier season, six years ago, he'd walked this route nearly every day.

Randolph went a bit further and stopped again to gaze up at a narrow brick house. Behind those tall, narrow windows he'd wooed Rosalie Delacourt, asked for her hand, and been delightfully accepted.

A vision of her laughing face assailed him. She'd so often been laughing, her lips curved in the most enticing way. Her hazel eyes had sparkled like sunshine on water. She'd been elfin slender, with chestnut brown hair and a few hated freckles on her nose. She was always trying to eradicate those freckles with one nostrum or another.

From the moment they met, introduced by a friend of his mother's at a concert, he'd thought of no one but Rosalie. The fact that she was eminently suitable—by birth and upbringing and fortune—was pleasant, but irrelevant. He would have married her if she'd been a pauper. She said the same. It had all been decided between them in a matter of weeks. Life had seemed perfect to a young man freshly ordained, with a parish, ready to set off on his chosen path.

Gazing at the unresponsive house, Randolph felt a reminiscent brush of devastation. Why had he come here? His grief was muted by time. He didn't think of Rosalie often now. The Delacourts no longer lived in town. Indeed, he'd heard that they rarely came to London. And who could blame them?

Not for the first time, Randolph was glad that only his mother had known about his engagement to Rosalie. Randolph had enjoyed keeping his courtship private, away from the eyes of the *haut ton*. His brothers had been busy with their own affairs. And so, in the aftermath, he'd been able to stumble quietly off to

Northumberland and what he'd sometimes thought of as exile, though of course it wasn't. He'd found solace in his work and the good he could do, and gradually his pain had eased.

Randolph took a moment to acknowledge the past with a bowed head and then walked on. He wouldn't come this way again.

A few minutes later, Randolph reached his original goal, another place he hadn't been in years, Angelo's Academy on Bond Street, next to Gentleman Jackson's boxing saloon. Entering, he heard the familiar sounds of ringing steel and murmured commentary. Pairs of men fenced with blunted foils, guided and corrected by the famed proprietor and his helpers. Others worked on their stance or observed. Randolph joined the latter until he was noticed, and the owner of the place hurried over. "It's been far too long since we've seen you, Lord Randolph," said Henry, scion of a dynasty of fencing masters.

"And I've probably forgotten most of what you taught me," replied Randolph. "But I thought I'd try a match if it could be arranged." The clash of blades filled him with pleasant nostalgia. He'd spent many a satisfying hour surrounded by that sound. Angelo's was a fashionable gathering place where gentlemen socialized as well as learned the art of swordsmanship.

"Of course. I'd like to see how one of my best pupils has kept up his skills."

"You mustn't be too harsh," replied Randolph with a smile. "I had no opportunities to fence in Northumberland." He had practiced the moves, now and then, but he'd found no partners in the North.

A young man nearby stepped forward. "I'd be happy to oblige."

Henry's smile went slightly stiff. "Unnecessary, Mr. Wrentham," he said. "I'll take on Lord Randolph myself."

"Oh, but I'd like to try my chances against one of your *best pupils*."

The newcomer spoke with a belligerent edge, as if Henry had angered him somehow. Randolph eyed him. A well set-up fellow in his twenties with dark hair and eyes, he looked familiar. "We've met, haven't we?"

"At Salbridge," the younger man agreed. "Charles Wrentham."

"Of course. You acted in the play."

Wrentham grimaced as if he'd criticized him. "So, shall we have at it, then?"

Randolph understood from Henry's stance and expression that he would prefer otherwise. But Wrentham's face told him there was no way to refuse without giving offense. Randolph agreed with a bow.

Donning fencing gear brought back more memories. Randolph relished the feel of the canvas vest and wire mask. He took down a foil and swished it through the air, feeling old reflexes surface. It was said that physical skills learned as a youth stayed with you, and he didn't think he'd lost his touch. He tried a lunge and parry. Fencing had fascinated him from the moment he'd picked up a sword. The combination of concentration, precision, endurance, and strength exactly suited his temperament, and he'd picked it up quickly. Faster than any of his brothers, which added to his enthusiasm, he acknowledged. Here was one area where he outshone them all. Well, except Sebastian, who had a cavalryman's fine slashing style with a saber from horseback. That was quite a different thing, however. No one fought to the death at Angelo's.

Randolph moved to an open space on the floor. Wrentham faced him, raising his foil in a salute. Noting that Henry was hovering, and wondering why, Randolph matched Wrentham's gesture and took his stance. Muscle and mind meshed in the old way. He smiled behind his mask.

Randolph let Wrentham make the first move, to get a sense of his style and skill. The young man came in with a lunge. He overextended, and Randolph parried the thrust. Wrentham pulled back and slashed downward. Randolph blocked the blow. And so it went for some minutes, Wrentham attacking and Randolph easily fending him off. The younger man had some ability, Randolph noted, but he lacked control. And he didn't seem to pay much heed to his opponent. Divining your adversary's next move was half of winning.

Satisfied, Randolph went on the offensive. He knocked Wrentham's blade aside with a ringing clang and scored a hit on the younger man's chest with a clever riposte. Wrentham sprang back, then surged forward again. Randolph feinted left. Wrentham reacted. Randolph struck through the resulting gap in his defenses, scoring another hit.

Wrentham reacted with a flying lunge, a move usually reserved for saber matches, leaping and thrusting all at once in an effort to surprise.

Randolph dropped low, touching the floor with his free hand for balance. Straightening his sword arm, he stabbed upward and scored a third hit to Wrentham's ribs before drawing back under his opponent's blade.

Something seemed to snap in Wrentham at this clever exhibition of superior skill. He went wild, beating the air with his foil like a windmill. Randolph met his slashing blows—above, left, right—with a clang of metal that he felt all the way down his arm. He could hear Henry commanding them to stop, but he couldn't spare an instant's attention. The blunted foil wouldn't stab him, but a great whack to the head or shoulder would nonetheless hurt. He'd seen men knocked silly by flailing like this. Nothing for it but to fight him off. Randolph blocked and parried over and over again, waiting for a chance to end it.

At last, Randolph found an opening and used a move Henry had taught him, twisting and flicking his sword to disarm Wrentham. The younger man's foil went flying across the room, hit, bounced, and skittered over the floorboards to a stop.

With a curse, Wrentham jerked off his wire mask and hurled it against the wall. A flake of plaster came loose and dropped with it. He stalked out, chest pumping, teeth bared.

Silence filled the academy. All the other fencers had stopped to watch this unusual bout. "Well done," called several of them.

Randolph removed his own mask. He was breathing fast but not panting, he was happy to see.

Henry took his foil. "Very well done," he said quietly. "You're as skilled as ever, my lord."

"What the deuce is wrong with Wrentham?" Randolph asked.

"He's an overly dramatic young man," said Henry. "With a tendency to lose his temper at the least obstacle. I've been trying to teach him there's more to fencing than the win."

"Can you teach that?"

Henry shrugged. "Sometimes. Mr. Wrentham was doing much better before he went out of town for the winter."

Randolph unbuckled the straps of his fencing vest and pulled it off. "I can see why you tried to discourage that bout."

Henry bowed. "Discernment was always one of your greatest strengths, my lord."

This remark came back to Randolph later that day, as he sat in his room at Langford House. He was in London, in fact, to acquire a wife. A churchman was expected to have a partner in his parish work, and it was past time for him to find one. He'd waited long enough for another love. He was reconciled to the idea that he'd had his chance with Rosalie and lost it. There would be no other grand passion for him.

This was no huge hardship, Randolph told himself not for the first time. Or the twentieth. He would find a young lady who shared his values, and they would come to an agreement. During a London season, he'd be surrounded by eligible girls eager to find husbands, a plethora of choice. What more could a man ask?

Randolph rose and went over to the cheval glass. He gave himself an encouraging nod. He'd been invited to an informal evening party, a mere nothing before the season truly began, the hostess had claimed. It sounded like an ideal opportunity to ease his way into the *haut ton*.

❧

Verity Sinclair looked around the opulent drawing room, drinking in every detail of the decor and the fashionable crowd. She had to resist an urge to pinch herself to prove she was actually there, and not dreaming. It had taken her five endless years to convince her parents that she should have a London season. They hadn't been able to see the point of it, no matter what advantages she brought forward. Papa and Mama were quietly happy living in a cathedral and being held up as models of decorum for the whole bishopric. Verity, on the other hand, often thought she'd go mad within those staid confines.

Verity sighed. She loved her parents dearly, but for most of her life she'd felt like a grasshopper reared by ants. Indeed, at age eight, she'd shocked her parents by asking if she was adopted. She hadn't meant to hurt their feelings, or to imply any lack of affection. Their differences had just seemed so marked. Mama and Papa relished routine; she yearned for adventure. They read scholarly tomes; she pored over *Robinson Crusoe* and the voyages of Captain Cook. They preferred solitude or the company of a few friends; she liked a large, lively company. They took sedate strolls; she tried to teach herself knife throwing, which would come in very handy if—when—she required food in the wilderness.

Her mother was watching her with the expression

that gently suggested skepticism. Verity smiled at her and turned toward the chattering crowd. She was in the capitol at last, in position to carry out her plan. Surely this room was full of men who were *not* clergymen—who were, or were acquainted with, far more intrepid types. Indeed, from some news she'd picked up recently, it appeared that 1819 might be the perfect year for her purposes, even if it meant she was twenty-four and seen by some as practically on the shelf. She *would* succeed, despite the misfortune of possessing hair the color of a beetroot and milky skin that freckled at the least touch of sun. Despite the fact that nature had chosen to endow her with a bosom that seemed to positively drag men's eyes from her face and her arguments. Which was not her fault, as her father sometimes seemed to think. It was a reasonably pretty face, she thought. Her features were regular; she'd been told her blue-green eyes were striking.

"Miss Sinclair."

Verity turned to find her hostess beside her, along with a tall, exceedingly handsome man. He had wonderful shoulders and intense blue eyes. Compared to the fellows she knew, he looked polished and sophisticated. More than that, he met her gaze, with only the briefest straying to other regions of her anatomy. Verity smiled. This was promising.

"May I present Lord Randolph Gresham," the woman continued. "Lord Randolph, Miss Verity Sinclair."

A lord, Verity thought. Not a requirement from her list, but nothing to sneeze at either.

"I think you will have much in common," their

hostess added. Addressing each of them in turn, she said, "Lord Randolph is vicar of a parish in Northumberland. Miss Sinclair is the daughter of the Dean of Chester Cathedral."

As the woman left them together, Verity's budding elation collapsed. It could not be that the first man she met in London—and such an attractive man—was a clergyman. Were there so many in the world that she couldn't be spared another? Possessed by an oddly urgent sense of danger, Verity blurted, "I could never abide life in a country parish."

He blinked, clearly startled.

"I would find the limited society unendurable." It came out sounding like an accusation. Verity bit her lower lip. There was no reason to be *this* keenly disappointed. What was the matter with her?

"I don't recall asking for your opinion," he said.

"The isolation makes people narrow-minded."

"I beg your pardon?"

He looked offended. Verity couldn't blame him. She was right, of course; she'd observed the tendency often enough, but there was no need to say it aloud. Or to continue this conversation. She should move away, find a more promising prospect. Instead, she said, "And quite behind the times. Antiquated, even."

"Indeed?"

His blue eyes had gone cool. What had come over her? She was never rude. She ought to apologize.

"If you will excuse me, I see that some friends have arrived."

Lord Randolph gave her a small bow and walked away. Which didn't matter, Verity thought. She'd meant to stop talking to him. And yet a pang of regret shook her. Stop it at once, she told herself. That was not the sort of man who searched for the wellsprings of the Blue Nile or discovered unknown species or peoples. Silently, she repeated her talisman phrase—Twelve Waterloo Place—and turned to find other town dwellers to meet.

Randolph crossed the room to join his brother Sebastian's party. They'd come in at just the right moment to cover his escape from the opinionated young lady. Who had asked what she thought? Who did she think she was? "I've just met the most fearsome girl," he said.

"Really?" His military brother looked sleepily formidable, as usual.

"Which one?" asked Sebastian's lovely blond wife, Georgina, resplendent in pale-green silk. Her sister Emma stood just behind her, a younger, less self-assured version of Stane beauty.

"The one over there, with the extremely vivid hair."

"And the generous…endowment?" Sebastian said. When Georgina elbowed him, he added, "I was only making an observation. It's nothing to me."

The pair exchanged a lazy smile that told anyone with eyes of their marital bliss. Randolph envied both the fact and the ease of it. "That's the one. Miss Verity Sinclair. Daughter of the Dean of Chester Cathedral, if you please." Which had seemed promising. Until it turned out that it wasn't.

"Cathedral? I would have thought that was right up your alley," his brother replied. "What's so fearsome about her? She looks harmless enough."

"She imagines that I am narrow-minded. And antiquated."

"What? Why would she do that?" Sebastian frowned.

"Whatever did you say to her?" Georgina wondered.

"I had no opportunity to say anything. She…graced me with her opinions all unasked."

"Will there be any dancing?" Emma asked.

Georgina turned to her sister, shaking her head. "Not tonight. This is a small party, a chance for you to make some acquaintances before the big squeezes later in the season."

Emma scanned the crowd. "Everyone looks old."

"Not everyone. You'll meet plenty of young people."

"Georgina's been studying up," said Sebastian proudly. "She means to give Emma a bang-up launch into society."

"You make me sound like some sort of ship," Emma replied. But she smiled.

Scanning the crowd, Georgina did look rather like a canny navigator plotting a course. "Come along," she said to Emma, ready to plunge in. Then she paused. "Sinclair," Georgina said. "Wouldn't she be a connection of the Archbishop of Canterbury?"

"Would she?" It needed only that, Randolph thought. Given his unfortunate…incident with the archbishop, the chit was a walking recipe for disaster. It was fortunate that she'd put him off. Who knew what trouble he might have fallen into otherwise? Now he could make a point of avoiding her.

The ladies went off to begin Emma's introduction

into the *ton*. The Gresham brothers snagged glasses of wine and stood back to observe.

"Did you meet Georgina at an evening like this?" Randolph asked after a while.

"At a ball," replied Sebastian.

"Dancing is a good way to become acquainted."

"I had to fight my way through a crowd of fellows to snag one." Watching his wife, Sebastian smiled. "Say, Georgina could give you a few pointers." He offered Randolph a sly grin. "Bring you out along with Emma."

"I'm no bashful eighteen-year-old," replied Randolph, revolted.

"Or you could marry Emma. Two birds with one stone and all that."

"No!" The word escaped Randolph without thought. "I mean, she's a nice enough girl, but—"

"Only joking," Sebastian assured him. "You'll want a serious, brainy female. Likes poetry and that sort of thing. Emma's more along my line, a bit dim."

"You aren't dim," said Randolph. Unwillingly, he found his gaze straying back to Verity Sinclair. At first glance, she'd seemed so beguiling, her eyes brimming with interest and…a crackle of spirit.

She turned, and he looked away before he could be caught staring at the archbishop's relative, for goodness sake. It was a sign, he concluded, a warning to be careful on his hunt. One spent one's whole life with a wife. A mistaken choice would be disastrous. He turned his attention back to his brother.

Toward the end of the evening, Verity found herself briefly alone. Even though this had been called as a small party, her mind whirled with names. It seemed as if she'd been introduced to scores of people, more than she met in a month at home. The buzz of conversation was positively thrilling.

Verity ran her eyes over the crowd. She noted the whirl of colors in the clothes, particularly the ladies' dresses, the sparkle of jewels and candlelight. She breathed in the mingled scents of perfumes and pomades and hot wax. She absorbed the oceanic rhythm of talk. The taste of lemonade lingered on her lips. She gathered all these details into one impression and fixed it in her mind with a mental *click*. Then she added this Moment to a string of such memories stored in a special place in her mind—a string of vivid scenes that punctuated her life. She'd been creating Moments since she was quite young. She could move down the string and revisit each epoch of her life. And before long, she'd be adding far more dramatic, exotic Moments to her collection. She was absolutely resolved on that.

Verity looked about her. The blond girl nearby was Lady Emma Stane. Verity remembered her not only because she was one of the few here near her own age, but also because she was part of the group Lord Randolph had joined when he abandoned her. Not abandoned, Verity thought. What a poor choice of words. She'd wanted him to go away. Indeed, she'd repelled him. On purpose. A country clergyman! Still, she drifted toward Emma. They'd been introduced as cohorts, both at their first *ton* party. Emma was obviously younger, but Verity had as little experience of high society. "Have you enjoyed the evening?" she asked.

"Oh, yes," Emma replied. "I've waited so long to be in London!"

"I too. I had such a time convincing my parents to give me a season."

"Mine just refuse to come to town," said Emma with an incredulous smile. "They are absolutely fixed in Herefordshire."

"And so you are here with——?"

"My sister Georgina." Emma indicated the beautiful blond woman Verity had noticed earlier. "She married Lord Sebastian last summer."

Following her gesture, Verity eyed the two handsome men in the corner of the room. Lord Sebastian and Lord Randolph, then. They were clearly brothers.

"And now she's brought me to London just as she promised. I intend to have a *splendid* time. The duchess has promised me an invitation to her ball."

"Duchess?"

"Lord Sebastian's mother. She's positively the height of fashion."

The man was a duke's son? As well as handsome and obviously self-assured? Why bury himself in a country parish? Not that she cared. It had nothing to do with her. Verity turned her back on the impossible Lord Randolph. Her mother was beckoning. It was already time to go.

About the Author

Jane Ashford discovered Georgette Heyer in junior high school and was captivated by the glittering world and witty language of Regency England. That delight was part of what led her to study English literature and travel widely in Britain and Europe. She has written historical and contemporary romances, and her books have been published in Sweden, Italy, England, Denmark, France, Russia, Latvia, the Czech Republic, Slovakia, and Spain, as well as the United States. Jane has been nominated for a Career Achievement Award by *RT Book Reviews*. Born in Ohio, she is now somewhat nomadic. Find her on the web at www.janeashford.com and on Facebook. If you're interested in receiving her monthly newsletter, you can subscribe at www.eepurl.com/cd-O7r.